A TIMESHARE IN FRANCE

by

J. D. MALLINSON

1

WAXWING BOOKS,

NEW HAMPSHIRE

Inspector Mason novels:-

Danube Stations
The File on John Ormond
The Italy Conspiracy
The Swiss Connection
Quote for a Killer
Death by Dinosaur
The Chinese Zodiac Mystery

CHAPTER 1

It was a rather cloudy morning around the middle of June, 1991, when Brother Aelred drove his new Audi through the hardscrabble industrial townships north of Manchester into open country. He breathed a sigh of relief. His current role in the Aurelian Brothers involved a fair amount of motoring and he was always glad to put the congested traffic of northern English cities behind him, in favor of open fields and copses. In the background were the rolling Pennines, ancient limestone hills worn down over the centuries to moorland ideal for grazing sheep. As he eased his car over the narrow bridge across the River Calder on his way to the village of Dovestones, he felt his customary sense of pleasure at re-entering this little-known and, to his mind, most beautiful part of England, off the beaten tourist track. He checked his watch. He should reach his destination within the hour.

Aelred was a lean, ascetic man in his mid-fifties. Born in County Mayo, in south-west Ireland, he had joined the Aurelian Brothers, an order of educators specializing in boarding schools for boys, at the age of eighteen. He had spent most of his teaching career in England, rising up through the ranks to become principal of their school in Sussex, before his appointment as Brother Visitor. This new role, which he had stepped into only last year, involved general oversight of the order's several schools and their teaching staffs, consultations on fabric repairs, property extensions and a host of related matters. He paid a routine visit to each establishment in turn, during the course of the year, to ensure its smooth operation and to address any problems, including disciplinary matters, that from time to time arose. On this rather overcast June day, his objective was St. Dunstan's School, just beyond the Pennine village of Dovestones.

On arrival, the principal, Brother Austin, strode out to greet him, the moment he heard the scrunch of tires on the loose gravel of the forecourt. A short, stocky man, somewhat in the mold of a Friar Tuck, his attitude towards his guest was deferential. The Visitor was the most important individual in the English province, answerable only to the order's Superior General in Rome

"Had a good trip out?" he enquired.

"You know what it is like," Aelred

ironically replied, alighting with his leather briefcase, "negotiating the congested traffic north of Manchester. It's fine, once you gain the open country."

"The Calder was in flood in the spring," Austin said, leading the way into his office, "after a series of heavy storms which unfortunately caused some damage to the roof of the dormitory block."

"Use the general fund for the repair," Aelred advised, "and put the matter in hand as soon as possible."

"I have already contacted a local builder," the school principal said. "He can make a start early next week."

"Excellent," the Visitor replied, occupying the straight-backed wooden chair facing the principal's desk. "Now, apart from that, what other little problems have surfaced at St. Dunstan's?"

There was a mischievous twinkle in his eye as he spoke those words, a way of understating beforehand what both men knew could be serious matters in the day-to-day relationships between staff and pupils, as also among the pupils themselves. Brother Austin's steady return gaze reassured him. There would be no repeat of last year's rather delicate situation involving a romantic liaison between the young female teacher of drama and one of the senior boys. It had been Brother Aelred's first major concern on his new appointment. As a professional celibate, he had not relished involvement in affairs of the heart and he was pleased that the drama teacher had resigned of her own accord, avoiding any hint of a scandal that might have deterred prospective parents and benefactors.

"Our secretary and bursar, Jean Wildgoose, is leaving us at the end of the school year to get married," Brother Austin announced. "We shall have to find a replacement. A pity, really. She has been with us quite a while and had developed a knack of divining the boys' personal needs far better than any of the teaching staff. She will be difficult to replace."

"You have the rest of the summer to attend to it," Brother Aelred advised, as the office door opened to admit a much younger brother bearing a tray of light refreshments. The newcomer, of rather delicate Oriental features, placed a tea service and a plate of plain arrowroot biscuits on the table between the two senior men, before discreetly withdrawing.

"Brother Paulus, from Manila, is over here to improve his English," Austin explained, in answer to Aelred's unspoken question.

"And he is fitting in all right?" the Visitor was keen to know. "Getting the hang of things?"

"He assists Brother Camillus in the kitchens, mainly," Austin explained. "And

Brother Henry in the school grounds and nurseries. They are both very talkative individuals who give him lots of conversation practice. He would also like to do a small amount of teaching as his English improves - botany is his preferred subject - so I have penciled in a few hours each week on the General Science program for the junior boys next term. Botany and biology are minor options."

He broke off to pour tea for them both.

"Milk, but no sugar," Aelred requested, leaning forward eagerly to grasp the welcome refreshment after his taxing drive. "Now, about Jean Wildgoose's replacement?"

"I thought of placing an advertisement in the Situations Vacant column of *Lancashire Evening Post*," the principal explained. "The broadsheet is widely read throughout the northwest."

"It will not be very easy getting a young woman to live out here in this remote spot," the Visitor advised, "away from city life with its shopping malls, restaurants, night life and such-like."

"It does not necessarily have to be a young woman," Brother Austin countered. "It could equally be someone more mature, a widow perhaps, or a divorcee, who might enjoy a quiet life in the country."

"Perish the thought!" Brother Aelred said, in mock horror at the thought of a divorced person at St. Dunstan's. "But I do see what you are driving at, Austin. Some older women, in certain circumstances, would be more likely than a young single person to accept a residential position. Free board and lodging also have their appeal, especially to someone in straitened circumstances, such as, as you suggest, a recent widow. You should place the same advertisement in, for example, *The Lady*, as well as in the evening newspaper, to see what sort of response you get. Be careful to vet references thoroughly before hiring, since in her capacity as bursar the new hire will have authority to sign checks."

"I shall draw up a short-list," Austin promised. "I shall also obtain references as to character and professional competence. You can then assist me in making the final choice."

"Gladly," the other agreed. "But you will need to fax me the material. My heavy schedule won't permit another visit to Dovestones for at least twelve months."

They quickly drained their cups and rose to their feet, Austin looking expectantly at his senior colleague.

"Well now," Brother Aelred continued, checking his watch, "there should be just sufficient time before lunch to look over the school premises and grounds, to check that everything is running smoothly. In particular, I wish to inspect the site of the proposed new dormitory block. If I can get the go-ahead from Rome this summer, construction can begin around the middle of the autumn term and should be completed by Easter. The bishop is very keen for us to increase our pupil intake from this diocese."

"Pressure from parents in the local parishes, I expect," the principal observed.

"It is the same across the board," the Visitor explained. "Anglican and Jewish schools are facing similar pressures. Discerning parents often feel that church-run schools offer the best academic standards and character formation in these permissive times."

"Who can blame them for that?" his confrere commented.

"This afternoon," Aelred continued, taking the last question as rhetorical, "I should like to visit the classrooms, listen in briefly on the lessons and introduce myself to the boys."

"We at St. Dunstan's are very gratified and honored by your visit," Austin said, a trifle obsequiously. "Everything shall be done to meet with your requests, so that you get the fullest picture possible."

"No skeletons in the cupboard...eh, Brother Austin?" Aelred responded, with a twinkle in his eye, giving his shorter colleague an encouraging pat on the back.

They then made their way out of the rather cramped office and along a narrow corridor flanked by wood-and-glass partitions screening off the classrooms. The hum of young voices conjugating Latin verbs in unison was distinctly audible.

*

One month later, around the middle of July, Brother Aelred was again on his travels. The London-Paris Eurostar express he had boarded at Ashford, Kent had just emerged from the Channel Tunnel and was racing at top speed through the flat, open countryside of Picardy towards Amiens, the last stop before reaching the French capital. Opposite him sat a smartly-dressed woman so fully engrossed in her magazine that he did not once notice her glance up at him, or even out the window at the unfolding scenery. She was in her mid-forties, he estimated, with shoulder-length blond hair that he took to be - although no expert in such matters - her natural color. As the train slowed down on the outskirts of Amiens, she finally glanced up from her reading, seeming to notice for the first time the gentleman in clerical garb sitting opposite. Instinctively adjusting her skirt to cover her knees, she gave him a fleeting smile and averted her gaze.

"I see you are reading *The Lady*," he observed, taking her quick smile as an opening.

"You are familiar with it?" she asked, in some surprise.

"Not, I am afraid," he replied, "in the sense that I have ever read the contents. I do not have much time for light reading."

"Nor do I very much. Except on long train journeys."

"It is just that my organization is running an advertisement in it," Aelred explained. "It could be in this month's edition, if we made the deadline. Or possibly in the August issue. It will also appear in *Lancashire Evening Post*."

"Would you like me to check?" the woman obligingly offered, flicking quickly through to the classified section.

"If you would be so kind," the cleric said, leaning forward in anticipation. "It is for the position of bursar at one of our boarding schools in Lancashire. The current incumbent is leaving to get married."

"Would this be it?" she asked, indicating an item with her thumb as she passed the text across to him.

A smile of satisfaction spread across Aelred's ascetic features, as he carefully perused Brother Austin's concise wording before handing the magazine back. The train came to a smooth halt at Amiens station.

"Sounds interesting," the woman said, objectively.

"Your line of country, by any chance?" Aelred asked.

The woman straightened her posture and adjusted her skirt, which had again ridden up above the knee. Glancing wistfully through the carriage window as the train accelerated out of the station, her mind seemed a long way away, as if his query had not registered. After several moments, however, she suddenly surprised him.

"I have, in fact, already seen your advertisement. I read it at St. Pancras Station, just after boarding this train."

"You mean that you are actively seeking employment?" he asked, encouragingly.

"My current contract," she explained, "expires at the end of this month. But I intend to take a vacation in Provence before resuming work. Besides, I have always in the past obtained my positions through an employment agency."

"What, precisely, is your line of work, may I ask, Miss…?"

"Maxine Walford," the woman emphasized.

"Brother Aelred, of the Aurelian Brothers," he said, extending his hand.

"School administration is, in fact, my line of country," she continued. "Until July 31st at any rate, I am deputy office manager at a large private girls' school in the Paris suburb of Clichy."

Brother Aelred leaned forward, more attentively.

"And you will be seeking fresh

employment by, let us say, the end of August?" he suggested.

Maxine Walford nodded and re-read the advertisement, a slow smile spreading across her intelligent features.

"Your reason for leaving?" he asked.

"It was a two-year contract, in the first instance," she explained, "with the option to renew. But, quite frankly, I find Paris a very expensive place to live. Over a third of my salary goes on rent and utilities."

"The position at St. Dunstan's is residential," Aelred said. "An apartment is provided in the main building, directly above the principal's office. It has limited kitchen facilities, since main meals are taken with the student body in the school refectory."

Maxine Walford looked intently towards him, then out of the carriage window, as if her mind was far from the subject under discussion. The Eurostar was now speeding through the dormitory towns just north of Paris.

"Are you making me an offer?" she suddenly asked, with a quizzical smile.

Brother Visitor was a man of some experience in the ways of the world. He also considered himself a good judge of character, from his dealings with a wide variety of individuals, both within and beyond the narrow clerical and academic fields he normally frequented. This smartly-dressed, professional-looking woman sitting opposite him might just, he considered, fit the bill and save Brother Austin the time-consuming task of sifting applications and taking up references. It would also save himself the task of vetting the principal's short-list. Any time saved, in his full schedule of duties, was a blessing.

"Would you be interested, if I were to offer it?" he tentatively enquired.

"I may wish to consider it," came the non-committal reply. "Your advertisement mentions the village of Dovestones. That is a far cry from the bright city lights, but if accommodation and meals are included that would help me save towards the cost of a cottage in the Lake District, where I plan to retire… eventually, of course."

The cleric nodded, understandingly.

"You could save a tidy sum over the next two or three years, or even longer," he proposed. "St. Dunstan's is a very friendly school, with lots going on during the course of the year. It includes chamber concerts and plays, performed by the boys. Saints' days are celebrated with a holiday and special fare. You would also be invited along on day-trips to the Lancashire coast, to help out with the younger boys and assist the school nurse, where applicable. Dovestones is in unspoiled countryside, not very far south of Windermere, in the Lake District."

"It all sounds rather appealing, Brother

Aelred," Maxine said, as if warming to the idea.

"If you do decide to make formal application for the position," the cleric said, "I advise you to do so by the end of this month. Mail a brief cover letter, together with a curriculum vitae and the names of two character references, to Reverend Brother Austin, St. Dunstan's School, Dovestones."

Maxine Walford noted the address in neat ballpoint in a small note-pad she withdrew from her handbag.

"The new term starts...? she enquired.

"On September 5th," he replied. "I shall tell Brother Austin to look out for your letter. And would you have any objection, since I shall be in Paris a few days before moving on to Rome, to my contacting your current employer?"

"Not at all," she said, tearing a leaf from her pad and jotting down the address and telephone number of Ecole Madeleine, Rue de Verdun, Clichy. "The principal's name is Madame Clementine Arnaud."

"Seems we have reached our destination already," Aelred said, as the slate roofs of the Paris tenements began to fill the skyline and the Eurostar suddenly decelerated to less than half its normal speed, before coming to a smooth halt at Gare du Nord. On gaining the platform, they took cordial leave of each other and went their separate ways, the cleric heading to Notre Dame Cathedral for a memorial service for a senior French colleague who had recently passed away.

CHAPTER 2

About a month later, around the middle of August, Maxine Walford was strolling beneath the palm trees on the English Promenade at Nice, on her way to the Vieux Port, the ancient harbor of this Mediterranean city, noted for its colorful fishing smacks, accordion players, quayside restaurants and gourmet seafood. She was feeling quite pleased with herself, having that very day received a positive reply from Brother Austin in response to her letter of application for the post of bursar at St. Dunstan's School. The job was hers, if she chose to accept it. As she covered the fair distance between her timeshare apartment at the far end of the promenade and her evening destination, her thoughts returned to a certain train journey from London to Paris, and to the ascetic-looking gentleman in clerical garb who had first mooted the idea of working at a boarding school for boys in rural Lancashire. She was a little surprised, in fact, that he had found her background acceptable. She was not a member of Brother Aelred's faith; but she had evidently made a good personal impression, and Madame Arnaud had given her a good reference. Teenage boys would be a challenging contrast, she considered, to the feminine milieu she was more familiar with at Clichy.

She had been at the timeshare, Les Palmiers, since the beginning of the month, realizing her dream of spending at least part of each summer on the French Riviera. This was only her third visit to Nice, but she was already quite familiar with the environment, paying a customary visit to Grasse, a noted center of the perfume industry, as well as to St. Tropez to watch yachting events on Ligurian Bay. If her hope was to meet an unattached male, preferably an Englishman, aged fifty at most, she rarely gave expression to it. It would happen quite by chance, if it were going to happen at all. She was pleased, at least, to have made a friend of her own sex and approximately her own age. It was someone she had met at the English Tea-Room on Rue Alphonse Daudet a few days ago, and who had suggested meeting for dinner at Vieux Port.

Roslinda Kramer was already seated at a table with a red-and-white checkered cloth, beneath an umbrella shade. A single red carnation in a glass vase caught Maxine

Walford's eye as she approached. Her new friend was drinking an aperitif and gazing down at the crowded harbor, watching the crews of the fishing boats prepare for the evening sail, pretending not to be aware of their flirtatious glances in her direction, nor of their occasional wolf-whistles. In her mid-forties, she had the sex appeal of the maturer woman, well-groomed yet not over-sophisticated, with a shock of dark hair and strong, quite pronounced features, including a rather square jaw.

"Here you are at last," she said, turning at the sound of approaching footsteps to greet her dinner companion.

"It was a longer walk than I anticipated," Maxine said, apologetically.

"It is only just turned seven," Roslinda said. "Do sit down and let us order at once. I for one am starving, after an afternoon swimming off the beach."

Maxine sat down and took up the elaborate menu, hand-written in French with no concessions to guests unfamiliar with the language.

"I was hoping you could translate it for me," Roslinda said. "It is double-Dutch to me. Would you care to join me in an aperitif?"

"I think a bottle of wine with the meal will suffice," Maxine replied, after a brief interval. "A white wine perhaps, since the entire menu consists of seafood, except for the escargots."

"Your French must be really good," the other said, with a touch of envy, "to scan all those items so quickly. There must be over a dozen options there."

"The chef's specialty is bouillabaisse," Maxine explained, "*and* rather expensive."

"I know what that is," her companion promptly remarked. "It is a kind of elaborate fish stew, with everything they can dredge up from the ocean thrown in for good measure. Considering how polluted the Med is, I think I shall pass on that."

Maxine swallowed hard, but did not rise to the remark. Was Roslinda Kramer, she wondered, one of those tourists highly suspicious of foreign food? She herself had ordered bouillabaisse several times in the past, finding it a most appetizing dish. But since the minimum serving was for two, she made a different suggestion.

"How about *Morue Atlantique*?" she proposed. "That's Atlantic cod, sautéed with red onions, vine tomatoes and mushrooms. A chilled Muscadet from the Loire Valley would go well with it."

Roslinda beamed approval.

"That is fine with me," she said. "You evidently know your way around. Where did you pick up so much French?"

"In Paris," the other rather diffidently replied, as the waiter took their order and reappeared almost immediately with the wine. He uncorked it with aplomb, poured two measures and placed the bottle in a cooler next to the table.

The sun was beginning to dip towards the horizon, casting the still water of the harbor and its motley assortment of boats, everything from ocean-going trawlers to recreational yachts, in a reddish glow, enhancing the quayside ambience while softening Roslinda's rather masculine features.

"Let us drink to my new job offer," Maxine said, raising her glass.

"Indeed?" rejoined Roslinda. "And what might that be?"

"I am planning to accept the post of bursar at St Dunstan's School, starting September 5th."

"And where exactly is that?" her companion asked, with keen interest.

"It is a boys' boarding school near the village of Dovestones, in up-country Lancashire. It was practically offered to me in the course of a train journey from London to Paris a month ago, by a clerical gentleman sitting opposite me. I received a formal offer from the principal only this morning."

"Good for you!" Roslinda exclaimed. "I shall drink to that."

They touched glasses and sampled the dry, crisp wine, finding it much to their taste on the warm summer evening.

"School bursar, eh?" Roslinda continued. "That is a form of accountancy, isn't it?"

"Well, sort of," Maxine agreed, "in that it involves book-keeping, fee records and the entire budget for administering the establishment. Staff salaries, catering costs, fabric repairs and so on. It is a very responsible position."

"Sounds like it," Roslinda agreed. "I expect I too could handle a job like that."

"You mean," Maxine asked, doubtfully, "that you have the right qualifications and experience?"

"Formal qualifications, no," the other replied, "if by that you mean a college degree. But I have done secretarial work and double-entry book-keeping."

"Then you should try your luck," Maxine suggested, while inwardly harboring some doubts as to her new friend's suitability. "St. Dunstan's advertised in *The Lady*, but Brother Aelred - he's the person I met on the train - told me they also ran the advertisement in *Lancashire Evening Post*."

At that point, their meal arrived, served on a large platter from which they helped themselves to generous portions, accompanied by jacket potatoes and an endive-and-tomato salad. The serious business of eating absorbed their attention, as the sun sank lower into the Mediterranean and the fishing smacks began to head silently out to sea, leaving the quay and its gourmet restaurants to late diners. At an adjacent table, Maxine noted with interest, an American couple were about to tackle the bouillabaisse. She caught sight of mussels and crabs floating atop the dark broth.

"I expect you shall have everything thrown in," Roslinda eventually observed. "Accommodation, meals, laundry, et cetera."

"Quite so," Maxine replied, with satisfaction. "I shall have a self-contained apartment in the main building and my meals in the refectory, with the teaching staff and the pupils."

"Sounds idyllic," the other said, approvingly. "Perhaps I should buy a copy of that magazine, *The Lady*, when I get back to England."

"This dish is quite excellent," Maxine said, promptly changing the subject.

"You could not have made a better choice, Maxine," Roslinda agreed. "I cannot remember when I had such delicious food."

An accordion player, perched on a stool at one end of the quay, began playing a medley of French tunes popularized by Edith Piaf. Conversation at nearby tables lulled as the diners gave him their full attention. To Maxine and Roslinda, it was the perfect way to fill out a southern evening. Their bottle of Muscadet already downed, they ordered coffee and liqueurs, remaining at table until the dark-red globe of the sun finally sank below the horizon, casting the picturesque harbor in deep shadow. The restaurant staffs then lit quayside lanterns.

"We should repeat the experience soon," Roslinda proposed, as they settled their bill and commenced strolling back along the English Promenade.

"Amen to that," Maxine Walford replied, pleased that the evening had gone so well.

*

Three weeks later, in early September, Brother Austin climbed into the new Citroen sedan the school had acquired during the summer and drove down to Dovestones village to meet the new bursar Brother Aelred had strongly recommended to him. He relied heavily on the Visitor's judgement, and on the satisfactory reference he had obtained in person from Madame Clementine Arnaud in Paris. He parked his car on the station forecourt just as the afternoon train from Manchester to Penrith was pulling in. A handful of passengers alighted, among whom he espied a brunette clad in a modish gray two-piece suit and gripping a large suitcase.

"You must be Maxine Walford," he said, immediately approaching her. "Let me introduce myself. Brother Austin, principal of St. Dunstan's. Let me take your case. My car is parked just outside."

"That is very kind of you," the woman said, as he led the way out through the ticket barrier, approached his car and raised the trunk. With some effort, he heaved the heavy suitcase aboard.

"Had a good trip?" he enquired, as they covered the short, tree-lined distance to the northern edge of the village. "Brother Aelred, whom you met on the Eurostar, tells me you have been in the South of France for the summer."

"It was marvelous," the other replied, recalling to mind, among other highlights, a certain idyllic evening at a restaurant in the Vieux Port.

"You may find Dovestones quite a big change," the principal said. "Especially the weather. We had just about the highest rainfall of anywhere in the country last month. But see how green everything is, as a result."

"I like the English countryside for that very reason," she remarked. "The French Riviera can get dry and rather arid in places."

"Then you shall enjoy being with us, I am sure," Austin encouragingly remarked, bringing the sedan to a halt outside the school main entrance, where a small group of senior boys were engaged in conversation.

"Wilson," he said to one of them, hopping out to open the trunk. "Grab this suitcase, would you, and take it up to the bursar's apartment on the second floor. We shall be up directly."

He then opened the passenger door to allow the new arrival to alight. She stood for a moment smoothing the wrinkles from her skirt, while gazing at the ivy-covered building in a kind of awe.

"1640 A.D.," Brother Austin said, with evident pride, noting her interest. "Built originally as the main residence of the 5th Duke of Skipton. The Aurelian Brothers acquired it in 1935, to open a boarding school for boys. Now, over half a century later, we are planning our first major extension."

"Oh? And what might that be?" the newcomer asked, keen to show an interest.

"A new dormitory block so that we can increase our intake. The bishop has been pressing us to do so for some years now. We have finally got round to it. The ground will be broken during the coming term. But enough of our concerns. I expect you shall want to rest and freshen up after your journey. I'll show you to your private quarters and leave you to yourself until dinner. That will be in the school refectory, at 6.00 p.m. sharp."

Suddenly noticing that he seemed to be staring at her, she said:

"Is there something the matter, Reverend?"

"Pardon me," Austin profusely apologized. "It is just that Brother Aelred happened to mention that you were blond."

"Oh!' she replied, laughingly. "That is just the way I wear it in the summer. Brown is my natural color."

"Forgive me," he said, with an ironic smile. "We monks are hardly experts in such matters."

She chuckled again, following him through the arched portal into the rather dim interior of the building and up a creaking wooden staircase to the second floor. Opening the first door on the right, without entering, he said:

"Please make yourself at home, Miss Walford. "We shall expect you at dinner, after which there will be a brief reception in the school hall, to introduce the new teaching and administrative staff, including your good self."

As the principal turned on his heels, she gripped the suitcase the boy named Wilson had left just outside and entered what was to become her private world. She found a large bed-sitting room, plainly but adequately furnished, with a small en suite bathroom and minimal kitchen. Crossing to the window, she found that it overlooked a belt of open moorland with some higher peaks, possibly the Cumbrian Mountains, etched on the distant skyline. Opening the casement, she took a deep breath, finding the air good and slightly scented, as of apple orchards in the vicinity. She then tested the bed, finding the mattress a little too firm for her liking. Typical boarding-school Spartan, was her reaction. Leisurely completing the task of unpacking and putting her effects neatly away in the drawers and closets, she decided to test the shower. The water was barely warm and the flow hesitant. She would need to make do, the best she could.

After bathing, she lay full-stretch on the firm bed and switched on her portable radio to catch the early-evening news. Just before six o'clock, she dressed for dinner and went downstairs, soon drawn in the direction of the refectory, which adjoined the far end of the entrance hall, by the noise of boys talking animatedly and the clatter of plates and cutlery. Standing uncertainly in the doorway, she was soon spotted by Brother Austin and shown to what was to be her regular place towards the end of the high table, at whose center sat the principal, flanked on either side by black-robed Brothers. On her right sat the only other female presence in the shape of the school nurse, who introduced herself as Eileen O' Connor.

When everyone was in place, Brother Austin rang a small hand-bell. Talking ceased at once and the assembly stood to say grace. Conversations then resumed with vigor as the monitors for each long table repaired to the serving hatches to collect the large tureens and platters holding the food. These were placed at strategic intervals along each table, so that the pupils could serve themselves. Almost directly in front of the new bursar were placed a tureen of mashed potatoes, a platter of lean grilled ham slices and another of poached eggs. Large metal pots of tea, with the milk already added, soon followed; many had twisted spouts and dents in the side, indicative of long service. A far cry from the gourmet restaurants in the Vieux Port at Nice, she mused as, prompted by the school nurse, she helped herself to moderate portions of the wholesome fare. A glass or two of Merlot might help it down, she considered, wondering if the Brothers were tea-total.

*

The following morning, after sleeping soundly in the country air coming through the part-open casement and skipping breakfast, she arrived at the school office promptly at nine o'clock. Brother Austin and the assistant principal, a person introduced to her at the previous evening's reception as Brother Clement, were waiting to greet her.

"We trust you enjoyed your introduction to the school refectory," Austin genially remarked, as the smiling Clement looked on. "The fare is rather plain, I am afraid, but wholesome enough. And we have fish twice a week, freshly shipped in from Morecambe Bay."

"I shall look forward to it," she replied truthfully, relieved that the clerics were not, after all, tea-total. Vintage port and sherry had both been served at the after-dinner reception, with finger snacks.

"This will be your post, Miss Walford," the principal said, indicating a large oaken desk, mounted by an IBM computer. Before it stood a heavy swivel-chair. The new bursar was pleased to note that she would have the small office to herself.

"I shall be in the adjoining room," he went on, indicating a glass-paneled door to his left, "in case you have any queries or concerns. Just knock and enter. Your first task this morning will be to make a computerized record of fees paid. Reminder notices should then be sent out on the school letterhead, pointing out that interest will be charged at an annualized rate of six per cent on outstanding balances. That usually encourages prompt replies."

He exchanged knowing looks with Brother Clement at this remark, as the assistant principal picked up a Latin primer from the desk and hurried to his first class.

"Letterheads?" the newcomer enquired.

"In the top drawer of the desk," Austin

briskly replied. "Just before you go for lunch - you will hear the school bell ring at noon - bring the reminder notices to me for signing. Checks already received are in a buff-colored folder in the second drawer. Once recorded, you could walk down to Pennine Bank in Dovestones, deposit them in the school account and mail the reminder notices at the same time from the post office. That will give you an opportunity to look over the village, ahead of personal shopping you will need to do from time to time."

The newcomer had barely thanked him when the telephone summoned him to his private office. He closed the communicating door softly behind him, leaving her to her own devices.

As she sat down, she caught the sound of footfalls in the corridor outside, as the boys came in from the playground and filed into class. It seemed to go on interminably, but within a few minutes complete silence reigned, as the rigors of academia asserted themselves. She took out the appropriate folder and commenced recording the fees paid, with a distinct feeling that Brother Austin was optimistic if he expected this task to be completed by midday. There must be close to two hundred items here, not to mention the reminder notices that would need to be written.

Half-way through the morning, one of the

kitchen staff knocked and entered with a tray of coffee and digestive biscuits, at which point Eileen O' Connor, the school nurse, popped in for a brief chat.

"Are you settling in all right?" she asked.

"Just getting my head round this pile of stuff," the newcomer replied. "How many pupils *are* there at St Dunstan's?"

"About two hundred-and-fifty," the nurse replied. "They keep me pretty busy, I can tell you, with their little ailments and their cuts and bruises. Just wait until the flu season starts. I shall be working round the clock."

"Rather you than me," the other remarked.

"You will have a lot on your hands too," Eileen said. "Especially when they make a start on the new dormitory block. Dealing with the builders, settling accounts and so on."

"I expect it will be quite a hectic time."

"You should be able to handle it all right," Eileen said. "You look the capable type."

The newcomer returned an ironic smile, as the nurse left to attend to her own business, pouring the fresh coffee and allowing herself two digestive biscuits and a ten-minute break. As the hands of the wall clock eventually moved towards noon, Brother Austin put his head round the door.

"Reminder notices?" he enquired.

"I am only part-way through recording the fees paid," the new bursar explained. "But I shall gladly work through the lunch hour if it is that urgent."

The principal looked a little put out, but soon recovered his customary poise.

"Oh, there will be no need for that, Miss Walford," he said, stepping momentarily into her office. "Of course, it will take you some time to familiarize yourself with the routine tasks that your predecessor, Jean Wildgoose, had off pat. What I suggest is that, when the bell rings, you come down to the refectory and have a good warm meal. If you have finished recording the fees paid by mid-afternoon, you will still have time to walk down to the village before the bank closes at four. The reminders can just as well go out tomorrow. One day won't make very much difference."

She breathed a sigh of relief as the principal withdrew, feeling pleased to get an early opportunity to look round Dovestones, which seemed a most attractive village, where she could attend to personal needs. She continued at her desk until shortly after the school bell rang, arriving at her place in the refectory after grace had been said and the meal was being served. Some kind of casserole, she decided without much enthusiasm, whose main ingredient seemed to be shell pasta. One of senior boys mounted the lectern and began reading aloud to the attentive assembly from G.K. Chesterton's *Father Brown* series. Her neighbor Eileen O'Connor served herself a large portion of the dish, while she herself took little, thinking she would stock up on fresh fruit in the village. After several minutes, Brother Austin rang his hand-bell to indicate a change of reader, and so the meal continued without conversation and with a succession of boys mounting the lectern, receiving admonitions from the high table if they did not read loudly or clearly enough. To the new bursar, it was a novel experience to be read to while eating. It was a custom which she found quite agreeable, especially since she had never read Chesterton's novels, while also wondering if the school limited its literary fare to authors of the Catholic faith.

When the meal finally finished, following a sponge cake-with-custard dessert, and the boys silently filed out into the playground, she returned to her office and set to work with a will to finish her task. Just before three o'clock, she breathed a sigh of relief as she gathered up the large bundle of checks and placed them securely in her shoulder bag. Slipping on her anorak, since there was a fresh breeze blowing in from the Irish Sea, she left the premises and soon covered the short distance to the village. It consisted largely of stone buildings fronting a central square, behind which was a small park with children's swings, bordered on the far side by a shallow river that soon disappeared under the railway bridge. There were few enough people about, mainly women calling at the food shops or the pharmacy, plus a small group of men drinking pints and smoking cigars or pipes outside the village pub, The Dovestones Arms.

She soon espied Pennine Bank on the far edge of the square, just beyond the pub. Entering it, she deposited the fee checks in the school account, obtained her receipt and debated whether to open an account in her own name. It was a small branch with just two tellers, efficient-looking older women with an air of long tenure. A closed door to the right was marked MANAGER, the sound of voices audible within. Deciding that it might be better to use a different bank for her personal affairs, she bade the teller good day and crossed the square to a branch of Ribblesdale Bank, situated between the doctor's surgery and the bakery, with its aroma of freshly-baked bread and muffins. Here, there was just a single teller, a young man in a dark suit who attended to her requirements with speed, efficiency and few words. That suited her purposes better than dealing with members of her own sex, who might wish to draw her into conversation and delve into her personal affairs. She quickly completed the formalities, opening her account with a ten-pound note from her purse, and left the bank. She checked her watch as she stood outside in the afternoon sunshine noting the location of other amenities she might need from time to time. It was almost four o'clock. Time enough before dinner to call at The Open Book, situated down a short side-street from the bank, to buy a good paperback for quiet, solitary evenings, and to take some light refreshment at the quaint little tea-room with dimpled-glass windows she had spotted at the edge of the park.

Within half an hour, she was comfortably seated at a window table, pouring herself a cup of orange pekoe from a china tea-pot. The tea-room was quiet at this hour, only two other tables being occupied by small groups of women meeting up after shopping. Adding milk and sugar before taking her first sip, she took out the novel she had just purchased and scanned the blurb on the back cover. *A Murder of Quality* by John le Carre was exactly the sort of thing she was looking for. She had always enjoyed British spy novels, particularly those by Carre who, she was aware, had once worked in intelligence at the British Embassy in Germany, giving his work an aura of authenticity. Satisfied that she had made a good choice, she replaced it in its wrapper and put it back in her bag, to read later. As she sipped her tea, she registered a degree of satisfaction at her present situation. St Dunstan's had indeed a friendly atmosphere and the work so far did not seem too onerous. The surroundings were pleasant and she could escape to the village as often as she chose, perhaps even spend an occasional evening at The Dovestones Arms. She would bide her time and take full advantage of whatever opportunities presented themselves.

CHAPTER 3

It was a rather misty morning in mid-October when Inspector George Mason emerged from the Circle Line tube at Westminster and strolled past the Houses of Parliament to the offices of Scotland Yard on Broadway. It being Friday, he was looking forward to nothing more demanding after a busy week than a visit to his aged mother, a long-term resident of a care home run by the Church of England in the Yorkshire market town of Skipton. These autumn mists should clear by noon, he speculated, with the promise of better weather for the weekend. And if the BBC forecast was accurate, that should hold good for the whole country, including the more variable north.

Chief Inspector Harrington was barking at someone on the telephone in his usual gruff manner, as Mason entered his office on the third floor. He remained on his feet until the terse conversation was concluded.

"Have a seat, Inspector," the senior officer said, affecting a degree of bonhomie.

"Any firm plans for the weekend?"

George Mason quailed inwardly, unsure if his chief was not about to invite him down to Surrey for a few rounds of golf, or to help crew the small yacht he had recently moored at Worthing marina.

"As a matter of fact," he replied, as evenly as he could, "I was planning on going up to Yorkshire later today to visit my mother. Adele has been invited over to Berkshire to stay with an old school friend. It seemed like a good opportunity..."

"Just the ticket!" Bill Harrington boomed, cutting him short and striking the desk so hard with the palm of his hand that his china coffee cup rattled in its saucer. "You can kill two birds with one stone. Metaphorically speaking, of course."

"I don't quite follow," Mason guardedly remarked.

"Did you not once tell me that your mother resided at Skipton?"

George Mason nodded.

"Then this little matter that has cropped up will be practically on your doorstep."

"What little matter might that be?" his colleague enquired, with the creeping feeling that his free weekend was slipping away from him.

"I had a call just now from the Yorkshire Constabulary. It seems that some skullduggery has taken place at a boys' boarding school at Dovestones."

"What exactly do you mean by skullduggery?" Mason asked, leaning forward attentively.

"The school bursar has done a runner," the chief inspector explained. "Apparently with quite a large sum of money. The Yorkshire police feel that it has passed beyond their bailiwick and they want Scotland Yard to put out a national alert. It should not take more than a couple of hours out of your weekend. While you are in the area, go and see what it is all about and get what information you can for a police profile. The bursar's name, by the way, is Maxine Walford, a single woman in her mid-forties. More than that I cannot tell you."

"You could perhaps tell me the name of the school," Mason pointedly remarked.

"Did I not mention it already?" Harrington retorted, sipping his Italian roast. "St. Dunstan's, a church school run by the Aurelian Brothers, a teaching order of monks with headquarters in Rome. The principal is Brother Austin. He would be the man to deal with."

George Mason jotted these few relevant facts on a piece of his senior's notepad and placed it in his pocket, before rising to his feet.

"I want you to report to me first thing Monday morning," Harrington said. "In fact, you might as well take the afternoon off and get up to Yorkshire straight after lunch. That is, if you can get any outstanding deskwork finished in time."

Mason smiled to himself as he retreated to his own office. An early start would suit him just fine. He would ring Adele to wish her an enjoyable weekend and tell her that he planned to go directly from Westminster to King's Cross Station to catch the 2.08 p.m. express to Leeds. From there, he would take the local connection to Skipton, reaching his destination well before dinner. He would book into one of his favorite inns, The Dalesman, for a two-night stay. They did a first-rate roast beef and Yorkshire pudding, he recalled from previous visits.

*

On the Saturday morning, after a good dinner and an early night, George Mason took the Pennine Rail service to Dovestones. On arrival, after asking directions of the station master, he set off on foot to St. Dunstan's School. Striding along the tree-lined road, with moorland views on either hand, he remarked what an ideal location it was for a boarding school, contrasting it with his own schooldays in a more urban environment. On reaching the premises at just turned eleven o'clock, he rang the doorbell and was immediately admitted to the principal's office, where an air of sadness and disbelief reigned.

"Inspector George Mason, of Scotland Yard," he said, introducing himself to two black-robed monks, who registered surprise at his sudden, unannounced arrival.

"Brother Austin," the shorter of the two monks said, stepping forward to greet him. "I am the school principal. And this is Brother Clement, my assistant. We were not informed that Scotland Yard would be involved."

"The Yorkshire Constabulary have requested our assistance," the detective explained. "I was assuming they would have informed you in advance. But perhaps they were not expecting anybody up from London before Monday, it being weekend and all."

"That is very likely the explanation," Austin said. "Please have a seat, Inspector. We hope this matter has not put you to any inconvenience?"

"On the contrary," George Mason replied, sitting round the scrupulously tidy desk with the two clerics. "I was already up here on a social visit, as a matter of fact. You see, I am from the northcountry myself. My mother lives at Skipton."

The Brothers' cautious smiles expressed satisfaction. This was a local man, not a southerner. Their worried aspect slowly gave way to one of muted optimism.

"Now, about your bursar, Maxine

Walford," the detective began.

"She has been missing since Wednesday," the principal explained. "And a large sum of money from the school building fund has disappeared along with her."

"How large a sum?" the visitor immediately asked.

Brother Austin's eyes narrowed and his lips tautened as he hissed, half-aloud:

"Fifty thousand pounds."

George Mason's features registered due concern.

"Can you explain the circumstances?" he enquired.

"As school bursar," the principal went on, in more even tones, "Miss Walford had authority to write checks. On Monday last, she was instructed to make a down payment to Boyce Contractors Ltd, a family building firm at Skipton."

"We are planning a new dormitory block," Brother Clement explained, "so that we can increase our pupil intake as of next Easter, or next September at the very latest. Work on it was due to commence later this term."

"Now it may have to be put back indefinitely," Brother Austin said, with heavy regret.

"The principal and I were away until Thursday," Clement explained, "at a residential conference in York on Information Technology and its relevance to modern education. Late Thursday afternoon, since Maxine Walford unaccountably was not here on our return, I called the contractors to check that they had received the money."

"Which they had not?" Mason prompted, quickly getting the picture.

Brother Austin gravely nodded his head.

"I then contacted Pennine Bank, Dovestones," he said. "The funds cleared the school account on Tuesday. The manager said that he had demurred at first, but the bursar explained that Boyce had requested a cash deposit, to facilitate payment of wages."

"It seems that the woman really put one over on you," the visitor said. "Had she been with you very long?"

"For a little over a month," Austin explained. "She was recommended to us by our Visitor, Brother Aelred, who is normally a shrewd judge of character. He met her on the Eurostar from London to Paris in July. Miss Walford until that time had held a responsible position at a prominent girls' school in the Paris suburb of Clichy. Brother Aelred personally obtained first-class references from the school principal, Madame Clementine Arnaud, while he was visiting the city. Everything seemed ship-shape and Bristol fashion. Walford settled in slowly, but quite adequately, to the school and office routine and seemed to fit in well enough, though I must admit she often skipped school meals. And now this…unbelievable…quite extraordinary. The saints preserve us!"

Rising from his seat, he began pacing the room agitatedly. He was stopped in his tracks by a sudden knock on the office door and crossed to open it. A young blonde woman, with a concerned expression across her delicate features, was standing there.

"Brother Austin?" she enquired. "I hope I am not intruding?"

"By no means," the surprised principal said. "Please step inside."

There was an awkward silence, as the newcomer and the assembled males appraised each other.

"Faye Walford," the woman said, quickly introducing herself. "I am Maxine's half-sister."

"You could not have come at a more opportune moment," Austin remarked. "Maxine has gone missing. Do you have any idea of her present whereabouts?"

"That is what I came here to discover," a perplexed Faye Walford replied, visibly taken aback at his revelation. "I have not heard from her in over a month. Not since she took up the position of bursar here at the beginning of September. And now you say she is *missing*?"

"Since last Wednesday, in fact," Brother Clement informed her. "And I am afraid a considerable sum of money from our school building fund has disappeared with her."

Faye Walford looked aghast, struggling to absorb this totally unexpected development.

"When did you last hear from your half-sister?" George Mason pointedly enquired.

"I received a postcard from Nice towards the end of August," Faye explained. "She was accustomed to going there in the summer, to make use of a timeshare she owned called Les Palmiers. She mentioned her new post here at St. Dunstan's, saying she would write me as soon as she had settled in. That is over a month ago and I grew concerned at not hearing from her. I came up from Knutsford by the morning train, expressly to meet her here."

"As you can see," Brother Austin said, with heavy regret, "she is no longer with us."

"We trusted her implicitly," Clement said, "and she has let us down badly."

The newcomer, with a look of bewilderment, sank into the nearest chair and bowed her head, on the verge of tears.

"Go to the refectory, Brother Clement," Austin said, "and ask them to serve tea and biscuits for four in my office."

As the assistant principal left on his brief errand, George Mason said:

"You have no idea where she might have gone, Miss Walford?"

The newcomer raised her head and said,

with a touch of defiance:

"None whatsoever. I simply cannot believe that Maxine would pull a stunt like this. It is completely out of character. She had substantial means from a family inheritance and steady employment. She would have no incentive to steal money."

An idea suddenly occurred to Brother Austin, from something Brother Visitor Aelred had said.

"You do not look much like your half-sister," he remarked. "Tell me, is she a natural blonde?"

"Very much so," Faye replied. "Hers is a rich strawberry blonde, with reddish tints. And we do, in fact, resemble each other to some extent. Maxine's mother died young and our father remarried. But we both have more of our father's looks."

"That is rather odd," the principal said. "Aelred described Maxine Walford to me as blonde. Yet she had dark hair when she arrived here. I asked her about it, in point of fact, and she told me she usually dyed it lighter for the summer."

Faye Walford rose to her feet and confronted him.

"Then the Maxine Walford you know and the half-sister I know can hardly be the same person," she stressed. "Maxine has never in her life used any kind of hair coloring, not even to disguise the odd strand of gray."

Brother Clement reappeared at that

moment with the tray of refreshments, placed it on the desk and invited those present to join him as he commenced pouring cups of English Breakfast tea, much to George Mason's satisfaction.

"It seems possible," the detective said to Brother Austin, "that you could have hired an imposter."

"That is what I am beginning to think, too," the young woman said, with growing alarm.

The principal added measured amounts of milk and sugar to his tea and sipped it thoughtfully, while nibbling on an arrowroot biscuit.

"I do not see how that could be possible," he said, eventually. "Everything seemed to be well above board, but we did rely heavily on Brother Aelred's recommendation."

"Who met her only once, on a train?" a bemused George Mason queried.

"Aelred went in person to the school at Clichy, to obtain a reference from the principal. He also formed a very good impression of Maxine Walford on the Eurostar. It seemed a way of saving costs on newspaper advertisements, and of sparing time interviewing applicants, so we wrote her offering the job."

"Hold on a minute," Brother Clement said, suddenly rising to his feet. "I think I may be able to settle at least one issue."

The remaining three, not knowing quite

what to expect, glanced at each other in anticipation as the assistant principal strode from the room. A few moments later, he returned with a large Manila envelope. He placed it on the desk and withdrew from it several 9in x 6in color photographs.

"A professional photographer took these views of the main building at the beginning of term," he explained, "to be used for promotional materials when we increase our pupil intake next year. The principal and I have yet to decide which of the four examples we shall use."

He then selected one of them and handed it across the desk for Faye Walford to peruse.

"This shows a woman looking out of one of the front windows," she remarked.

"She peered out quite by chance as the photographer was taking the picture," Clement explained. "I thought we might use it, for the extra human interest, but Austin does not agree."

"And who might this woman be?" George Mason enquired, when the print was in turn passed to him.

"Why, it is Maxine Walford, of course," Clement replied, "peering out from the ground-floor bursar's office. It cannot possibly be anyone else."

"That is not Maxine," Faye adamantly declared.

"Then who could it possibly be?" the

agitated principal asked, wringing his hands.

Those present, in a sense of bewilderment, sipped their tea while glancing at each other for answers. None was forthcoming. Eventually, the Scotland Yard agent said:

"That is something we shall now need to establish, evidently. First of all, I should like to see the bursar's private quarters."

"She occupied an apartment directly above this office," Brother Clement informed him, "but I doubt you will find anything useful there. It is completely bare, apart from simple furnishings."

"Just a matter of routine," the canny detective remarked.

Brother Austin led the way up the creaking staircase, his assistant bringing up the rear. George Mason glanced over the bed sitting-room, briefly noting the titles of the few volumes, including a Douai bible, on the bookshelf over the bed, before entering the small bathroom.

"There is a distinct whiff of perfume here," he said. "The occupant, whoever she may be, probably spilled a little while applying it in haste."

"I believe she did use liberal amounts of perfume," the principal remarked. "I always caught a fairly strong whiff myself on entering the bursar's office. In contrast to the school nurse, Eileen O'Connor, the only other female employee at St. Dunstan's, who generally smelled of lavender, probably from her toilet soap."

"Chanel No.5," I should say," Mason added, turning to Faye Walford. "My wife Adele sometimes uses it while dressing for official dinners."

Faye returned a wan smile.

"Maxine rarely wore perfume," she declared. "And never anything pricier than Estee Lauder."

The two monks looked rather bemused by the turn of conversation. Brother Clement crossed to open the window to air the room, before they trooped down again to the principal's office.

"Did the bursar have her own transport?" the detective enquired.

Brother Austin shook his head.

"I drove down to Dovestones station to pick her up on arrival," he said. "She brought one large suitcase."

"In that case," Mason said, "if she had luggage, she would have needed a taxi back to the village. Did nobody see her leave?"

"Apparently not," Clement replied. "She probably called the local taxi firm during the lunch sitting, when staff and boys would be in the refectory. Her absence from dinner later was noted by the nurse, who thought little of it, since the woman sometimes skipped meals here in favor of the village pub, which does a good table."

"Ring the taxi people now, Reverend

Brother," his visitor continued, "so that we can get precise information."

Austin picked up the phone, dialed the number and spoke briefly with the booking clerk.

"The Village Ride picked her up at 12.15 p.m. on Wednesday," the principal announced. "The Penrith-Manchester train was due at 12.30 p.m."

"So we can assume that this personage, your sometime bursar, was heading south," Mason concluded. "May I take this photograph of her peering through the office window? We could use a blow-up of it to circularize local constabularies throughout Britain."

"By all means, take it," Clement said, handing it to him. "We can hardly now use it for promotional purposes."

"While you are on the trail of a thief, Inspector," Faye Waldron ruefully remarked, "will you also be attempting to locate my half-sister? I have a very uneasy feeling about her."

"We shall do our level best to find Maxine," George Mason assured her. "And I shall keep you informed of any developments."

At that, Faye passed him her card and departed, politely refusing Brother Austin's invitation to stay for lunch. Mason, however, gladly accepted, accompanying the two senior clerics to the refectory, where he listened with much interest to the boys reading from the lectern, while sharing what he took to be standard boarding school fare of meat-and-potato pie with pickled red cabbage and mushy peas. It was followed by slightly-overcooked rice pudding. As the boys were permitted to talk during dessert, the detective engaged Brother Austin in brief conversation.

"Is there anything else you can recall about your bolted bursar?" he enquired.

The principal thought for a few moments, before saying:

"One thing that struck me, Inspector," he replied, "was the way she wrote number 7, when giving me up-dates on fees paid."

"Indeed?" an intrigued George Mason remarked.

"She wrote it with a short horizontal bar across the stem. It may just have been a mannerism, or an affectation of some kind. I had never seen it written that way before, so it caught my attention."

Mason drummed the fingers of his left hand on the faded plastic tablecloth, as large metal tea-pots were placed before them. Clement did the honors for the three of them, pouring cups of tepid, milky tea.

"An interesting point, Reverend Brother," he said. "It could well have been a mannerism on her part. On the other hand, I believe that Europeans often write number 7 in the way you have described."

Austin returned a quizzical look.

"You don't mean to say…?"

"…that she was of European extraction?" Mason completed for him. "Certainly a possibility."

"But she spoke perfect English," the cleric said. "No trace of an accent. But now I come to think of it, she did seem puzzled by some of our northern English expressions. I sometimes had to re-phrase things for her."

"Interesting again," Mason remarked. "But that could be explained if she came from the south of England, where language usage sometimes differs markedly from our own."

"True enough, Inspector Mason," Austin said, as the meal concluded.

The assembly then stood to say grace, before the boys filed out into the playground. George Mason thereupon thanked the brothers for their hospitality and took his leave, promising to keep them posted on the progress of his enquiries.

CHAPTER 4

On Monday morning, George Mason arrived at his desk at Scotland Yard to write up his report on the weekend events in rural Lancashire, recalling with satisfaction that at least he had been able to spend the whole of Sunday with his mother, treating her to a roast beef luncheon with all the trimmings at The Dalesman. English composition not being one of his strongest suits, he took his time and chose his words carefully, checking spellings in his Oxford Dictionary, before printing it out on the word processor. Chief Inspector Harrington was in conference with the Superintendent; it was mid-morning before he returned to his own office, quickly scanning the report Mason had produced.

"Seems like a straightforward case of embezzlement," he remarked, pouring himself a tot of Glenfiddich to chase his mid-morning coffee, which a rookie constable had just brought in.

"There is a useful photograph, too," his colleague said, passing him the publicity material Brother Clement had given him.

"Quite attractive," Harrington observed, with an appreciative eye for the fairer sex. "Not that you can judge a person by her looks. Take it down to the print department and have them mock up a Wanted poster for general circulation. Maxine Walford should be in police custody in no time at all, unless she has skipped the country."

George Mason wondered at that point how carefully his chief, perhaps with weightier concerns on his mind from his meeting with the Superintendent, had read the document placed on his desk.

"Actually, no," he replied. "Miss Walford's half-sister Faye turned up in some agitation at St. Dunstan's while I was in session with the principal and his second-in-command. She was quite adamant that this photograph is not of Maxine, whom she has not heard from in well over a month."

"Then who might it be, Inspector?" the other testily enquired.

"Someone who was able to impersonate Maxine, to the extent of assuming her identity as school bursar. Quite convincingly, too, by all accounts."

"So we now have two missing persons on our hands, as well as the purloined funds," Harrington grumpily remarked. "It looks like you are going to have your hands full for the immediate future."

George Mason smiled ironically to himself. It was much as he had expected, even if it meant postponing his autumn trip to the Lake District with Adele.

"Any clues as to Maxine's last-known whereabouts?" his senior then asked.

"According to her half-sister, she was staying during most of August at a timeshare on the Riviera."

Bill Harrington downed his whiskey, rose from his desk and crossed to the window, drawn by noise from the street below, outside the Houses of Parliament.

"An animal rights group, by the look of it," he remarked, with a hint of cynicism. "I hope they don't snarl up the traffic. I have to be at Blackheath, south of the Thames, by midday."

"I expect the police will disperse them long before then," Mason said.

"I would not count on it," Harrington replied, as Big Ben struck the hour of eleven. "These people know their rights under English law, including the right of orderly assembly, if you can call it that."

"Many people support animal welfare, Chief Inspector," Mason remarked.

"And I suppose you are one of them?" the other quickly retorted.

"I am certainly not opposed to it," his colleague rejoined, waiting patiently for his superior to resume his seat.

"The French Riviera covers quite a long stretch of coast," Harrington then said. "Can you be more precise?"

"Faye Walford mentioned something about Nice," George Mason said. "She may even have told me the name of the timeshare, but it has slipped my mind."

"Where does she live, this half-sister?"

"At Knutsford, Cheshire."

"Then get hold of her and find out all you can. I suggest you start this enquiry at source."

"You mean I should go down to the Riviera?" Mason asked, intrigued at the prospect.

"That is precisely what I mean," Harrington emphatically replied. "And, if possible, get this Faye Walford to go with you. She could be very useful to you. Meanwhile, we shall circulate a Wanted poster this side of the English Channel and hope for speedy results."

"When do you propose I should leave?" Mason asked.

"As soon as you have cleared any backlog and can make the necessary arrangements. Go easy with expenses, by the way. No three-star restaurants for dinner, understood?"

Mason smiled to himself at that last remark, as he regained his own office. He had never come across a bad restaurant, with or without stars, anywhere in France. He certainly would not be consulting the storied Michelin guide, the Egon Ronay or any other

*

Three days later, he was on his way to Heathrow to meet Faye Walford for the afternoon flight to Nice. She had accepted his invitation very readily and had applied for leave of absence from her job as a dental hygienist, to allow two full days in the South of France. She would board the Manchester-London express at Wilmslow, the nearest train station to her Knutsford home, and take the Underground from London Euston to the airport, arriving shortly after midday. The detective, having parked his car in the long-stay facility, was waiting for her at the Air France terminal. Formalities completed, they were soon winging their way over the South Downs, approaching the English Channel.

"Glad you were able to make it at such short notice," he remarked, as they settled into their flight.

"It took some doing, I can assure you," Faye replied, with feeling. "But fortunately my employer, Rick Hargreaves, has a fairly light schedule for the remainder of this week. He was thinking of taking Friday off himself, in fact, to go fly-fishing on the River Lune before the weather turns."

"We should arrive in Nice later this afternoon," George Mason said. "I have booked rooms at Hotel Ronsard fronting the English Promenade. We shall check in and do a spot of orientation - I believe the Vieux Port is well worth a visit - have dinner and an early night, so that we can report to the local gendarmerie first thing tomorrow morning. Capitaine Jules Lemaitre will be expecting us."

"You seem to have everything well in hand," Faye said, impressed. "I have never been to the South of France, but Maxine always loved it. She has been back every year since she bought the timeshare."

"Which she was due to leave at the end of August?" the detective asked.

Faye Walford nodded.

"It already seems quite some time ago," she said, wistfully. "I do hope nothing has gone amiss."

"What do you really think, to be honest with yourself?" Mason delicately put it.

"It did occur to me that Maxine might have been taken ill, and that we might find her at a hospital in the area."

"Wouldn't you in that case have received some sort of communication from the medical authorities?" he said.

The young woman fell silent, aware that her companion had made a valid point. In her heart of hearts she was fearing the worst, but she was loath to admit that to herself. The presence of a Scotland Yard agent on the case had somehow shored up her confidence that she would find her half-sister alive and well.

"We must be somewhere over Paris by now," Mason said, to break a silence.

"I visited there last year," Faye said, "when Maxine was still living at Clichy. She held a good job at a private girls' school there, but found the cost of living too steep."

"So she applied for the position at St. Dunstan's?"

The young woman nodded.

"It was virtually offered to her in the course of a rail journey from London to Paris, oddly enough," she said.

"How curious," the detective observed, recalling that he had heard that line before, in Brother Austin's office.

"Wasn't it so?" Faye said. "All this while, I had been assuming that she was settling in at Dovestones with a busy schedule at the start of the school term and simply did not have time to write or call. Just who are these people who offered her the position?"

"The Aurelian Brothers?" George Mason mused aloud. "An order of educators, with schools in various European countries and perhaps even farther afield, for all I know. They live much as monks, under vows of poverty, chastity and obedience, but have an active, as opposed to a contemplative, ministry."

"They certainly have an unusual way of hiring staff," came the ironic comment.

"Oh, I expect they made thorough checks on Maxine's background and qualifications," the detective remarked. "One has to be very careful these days in any environment involving minors."

"That is very true," the dental hygienist agreed.

Light refreshments were then served. They occupied themselves with the contents of plastic containers holding snacks and red wine. Fifty minutes later, as the stewards were clearing their trays, the pilot announced their imminent approach to Nice airport, requesting that seat belts be fastened. The aircraft descended through a bank of low cloud, before landing smoothly on the runway. On clearing customs, Inspector George Mason and his young companion took the airport bus to the city center, where they soon located Hotel Ronsard. After registering, they repaired to their respective rooms to freshen up, with an agreement to meet up again in the foyer at six o'clock. The detective was down early, keen to get some sea air into his lungs. He was already seated in the foyer after a brisk walk along the seafront, when Faye Walford descended the staircase clad in a pale-beige trouser-suit.

"Let us try the Vieux Port, which is noted for its fresh seafood," Mason suggested, leading the way across the busy main thoroughfare.

"Fine with me," his young companion concurred, with the feeling almost of being on vacation.

They strolled the length of the promenade towards the old harbor. A strong breeze had sprung up, swaying the fronds of the palm trees and lifting the yachts out on the bay, so that they looked about to keel over. Within twenty minutes, they found themselves outside Chez Antoine, a restaurant with checkered tablecloths flapping in the breeze and the vase holding a single carnation lying on its side. It was still fairly mild at this time of year, but with the early sunset Mason thought it might get chilly later on.

"Would you rather sit inside?" he asked.

"By no means," Faye responded at once. "We would miss all the atmosphere along the quay, watching fishing boats prepare for the evening tide. Maxine often described it to me."

"Not many tourists about," Mason observed, as he held a chair for her to sit close to the water.

"It is late season," she said. "Children will be back in school, parents back at work. Tourists hereabouts seem to be mainly retirees."

They took time to scan the menu.

"Would you care to share a bouillabaisse?" George Mason at length enquired. "The dish is meant for two people sharing."

"A kind of fish soup, isn't it," Faye warily replied, "with lots of things floating around in it?"

"Something along those lines," he replied, amused at her turn of phrase. "It is supposedly a gourmet dish, originating here in Provence."

"I am game to try it, if you are," she said, putting down the elaborate menu and peering wistfully out to sea. The sun had begun to dip towards the horizon somewhere over Spain, casting a pinkish glow over the water. It would be dusk within the hour, time to light the hanging lanterns lining the quay.

At that point, the waiter appeared.

"*Vous etes revenue!*" he exclaimed, cordially addressing the young woman.

Faye Walford and George Mason exchanged puzzled looks. The waiter quickly realized his mistake, as the hygienist looked to her companion for an explanation.

"I do not understand French," she said, as the waiter hovered.

"He evidently mistook you for your half-sister," George Mason explained.

"Did he indeed?" Faye Waldron remarked. "Interesting that he remembered her."

"*Votre preference?*" the waiter then enquired.

"*La bouillabaisse,*" the detective promptly replied.

"*Et pour boire, Monsieur?*"

"*Une demi-carafe de Muscadet.*"

"What have you let us in for, Inspector?" Faye genially enquired, as the waiter withdrew.

"The fish soup, with a white wine from the Loire Valley," he informed her, with aplomb.

"I trust your judgement," she remarked. "I expect it will be a very enjoyable meal and a first for me. Curious, though, that the waiter thought he recognized Maxine. She must have eaten at this very restaurant, perhaps more than once, over the summer."

"We shall tackle him about that later," Mason said.

As their dish was being prepared, they observed the increasing activity on the quay. Two of the fishing smacks were casting off and tourists who had opted to dine indoors drifted outside to watch them depart. Returning yachts slipped past the harbor mouth, heading for the large marina farther along the coast. The sun dipped closer to the water, changing its hue from pink to deep-red.

"I could certainly spend time in Nice," George Mason remarked, with feeling.

"You like it here, don't you?" his companion said. "I can tell that from your demeanor."

"Is it so obvious?" he asked, with a smile. "But you are right, of course. I have always enjoyed coastal resorts, especially those with fishing harbors. Not that many of them left, nowadays, in Britain."

"This place puts me in mind of Padstow, Cornwall," Faye said. "The same old-world atmosphere, the pervasive odor of fish, the salt-sea air."

"But no palm trees," he remarked.

The waiter returned. With much ceremony, he placed a large porcelain bowl on the table between them. The two diners peered at it curiously and with a degree of apprehension, as if trying to figure out precisely what was floating in the thick broth with a pungent aroma. The waiter quickly reappeared with the wine and half filled their glasses. He was on the point of withdrawing, saying *Bon appetit*, when the detective checked him.

"By the way, monsieur," he said, "did the person you mistook this young lady for dine here alone in the summer, or did she have company?"

The waiter thought hard for a moment.

"I seem to recall," he said, "though it is some time ago now, that she was in the company of another woman."

"Could you describe her to me?"

"Someone of similar age," came the considered reply, "but with darker hair and a heavier build."

"Can you remember more exactly when it was that they dined at Chez Antoine?" Mason then asked.

"A little over a month ago, I should say.

Towards the end of August."

"And they left together, or separately?"

"That is something I could not say with certainty," the waiter said. "I was very busy all evening. August is our peak month for visitors."

"Did the darker-haired woman return to this restaurant any time afterwards?" the detective asked.

The waiter emphatically shook his head.

"I have not seen her here either before or since that night," he replied, moving away to the next table.

Left to themselves, the visitors turned their attention to the food, which had cooled a little in the meantime.

"You go first," Faye prompted, warily.

George Mason ladled a healthy portion into his dish and began sampling it, tentatively.

"Very tasty," he remarked, with approval. "Mainly mussels, crab and red snapper, I should say. As to the other contents, your guess is as good as mine."

"The broth is quite delicious," his companion said, in her turn. "And I think I also detect bits of squid, shrimp and scallop."

"It's like a lucky dip," Mason said, "from the bottom of a dredger's net."

Faye Walford smiled at that remark.

"You have quite a sense of humor," she said, "for a…"

"…policeman?" he enquired, ironically.

"No offence meant," she said, coloring a little.

"None taken," he gallantly replied.

"Don't you think it is a remarkable coincidence that Maxine also dined here at this very restaurant?"

"With a woman of roughly her own age," George Mason replied, recalling the photograph Brother Clement had shown him of the vanishing bursar. That the subject had dark hair did not of itself mean a lot. The world was full of brunettes.

On eventually finishing their interesting meal, they skipped dessert and settled for coffee and cognac, as dusk settled over the old harbor, now softly lit by the quayside lanterns. Diners emerged from restaurant interiors into the balmy evening air, and began strolling back towards the city center.

"You think something awful has happened to Maxine, don't you?" Faye suddenly remarked, in a sudden change of mood.

George Mason felt taken aback, her unexpected remark wresting him from a sense of contentment over a gourmet meal. He had wanted to break gently to her, perhaps on the way to the gendarmerie in the morning, his deep misgivings about the likely fate of her half-sister, so that she could enjoy their first evening in relative peace of mind.

"We must take things as we find them," he guardedly replied, as they settled the bill and made to leave the now-deserted waterfront. "There are, in a situation like this, several possible scenarios. Let us wait until tomorrow morning and our meeting with the local police, before jumping to conclusions."

"You are quite right, of course," she said, keeping close to him for moral support as they regained the English Promenade and strolled back to Hotel Ronsard. "It was a wonderful meal, thank you, Inspector. I shall sleep like a top after all that liquor."

"My pleasure," he replied, glad that his young companion had recovered a fairly buoyant frame of mind. He would place a call to Adele from his room, to let her know how the evening had gone, and to assure her that his hotel accommodation was satisfactory.

*

The next day, after a light breakfast, they made their way to the gendarmerie in the old quarter of the city, not far from the train station. Capitaine Jules Lemaitre, a youngish, athletic-looking officer with a buzz cut, was expecting them.

"*Bonjour, Inspecteur*," he said affably, ushering them both into his office and inviting them to sit, "Welcome to Nice. Did you have a good trip over?"

"No problems," George Mason replied. "By the way, this is Faye Walford, Maxine's half-sister."

The Frenchman rose and made a stiff bow, but did not shake hands. Faye half rose and settled back into her chair, expectantly. The gendarme then crossed to a filing cabinet, drew out a small buff-colored folder and placed it on his desk. Consulting it for a few moments, to refresh his memory, he said:

"For some time before you contacted us, Inspector Mason, my department has been looking into the case of the English visitor, Maxine Walford. We hope that you can assist us in our enquiries."

"We shall certainly do whatever we can," Mason assured him, realizing that what was to him a new case was not so to the French.

"Let me bring you up to date," the captain said, as Faye leaned forward attentively, to make sure she caught his foreign accent. "Maxine Walford owned a timeshare for the month of August at Les Palmiers. According to the resort manager, Guy Kervella, she was due to settle her account for use of utilities - water, power and so on - and check out by 10 a.m. on the morning of August 31st, so that her apartment could be readied for the next occupant."

"And she failed to show up?" Mason speculated.

"*Exactement, Inspecteur,*" the other emphasized. "You have hit the nail…how do you say in English?"

"…on the head," the detective finished for him.

"Around 11 a.m. that same day," Lemaitre continued, "Monsieur Kervella, thinking that she may simply have overslept after a night out, rang through to her apartment. Receiving no reply, he used his master key to effect entry. He found it empty. Since then, there has been no trace of Maxine Walford. We contacted the British Embassy in Paris, without success, to help locate her son Marcus, in case she had been in touch with him."

"Next of kin would be listed by the timeshare company," Mason surmised, "in case of emergency, such as sudden illness or - he hesitated before saying it - death?"

"*Exactement, Inspecteur,*" the gendarme confirmed. "His address is in north London."

"My nephew Marcus would not have been at his home address," Faye said, anxious to be of help.

The two men turned towards her, expectantly.

"He is a second-year student at King's College, London," she explained. "He spent the long vacation as a sports instructor at a summer camp for children near Dayton, Ohio. Following that, he will be spending the new academic year on a student exchange program at the University of Maine."

"*Merci, mademoiselle,*" the officer said. "That at least settles one point."

"I take it," George Mason said, "that you have thoroughly examined the apartment in question, for possible leads?"

"Indeed we have, *Inspecteur*," Lemaitre replied, his face clouding somewhat. "And what we did find may, I am afraid, be of small comfort."

"What exactly did you find?" Faye pressed him, fearing the worst.

"There is clear evidence," the Frenchman went on, "that Maxine entertained someone in her apartment towards the end of August."

"What sort of evidence?" Mason asked.

"Remains of a light meal for two, most likely a salad, with white wine and a liqueur."

"Fingerprints?"

"Not clear enough to be of much practical use," the other explained. "But we did obtain DNA samples from traces of saliva on the wine glasses. And that is not all that we found."

"Go on," the detective urged.

Lemaitre glanced rather circumspectly in Faye's direction, shifted his position and said:

"There were traces of ricin powder on one

of the dinner plates. Further tests showed that ricin had also been added to the salt cellar."

Faye Walford and George Mason exchanged concerned glances.

"Are you implying that my half-sister was poisoned?" the dental hygienist asked, in evident dismay.

"I am relating the facts as we know them, *Madamoiselle,*" Lemaitre coolly replied. "Our official position, pending further evidence, is that Maxine Walford is missing."

"Ricin has a rather interesting history," Mason observed.

"Quite so," the Frenchman agreed. "It is produced from castor beans, the source of castor oil. A mere few grains can be lethal."

"I seem to recall," the Scotland Yard agent said, "that it was used in London some years ago to kill a Bulgarian dissident who had published books critical of the Soviet regime. A pellet containing ricin was shot into his leg."

"I was not aware of that particular incident," Lemaitre replied. "But I did once read that Aleksandr Solzhenitsyn, the author of *Gulag Archipelago*, who spent some years living in Vermont, suffered traces of ricin poisoning and survived."

"Lucky for him!" came Faye's vehement comment.

"How much do you yourselves know

about the missing woman's plans?" the captain then asked.

"Only that she was due to take up a new appointment in September at a boys' boarding school in the north of England," George Mason explained. "Another woman, apparently posing as Maxine Walford, arrived at the school instead. She has since absconded with a large sum of money from the school building fund."

Jules Lemaitre slowly nodded his head as he took in this new information. He spent a few moments noting it down in his folder before remarking:

"That puts an interesting question mark against Maxine's dinner guest," he said.

"I don't suppose you have anything specific on that?" Mason asked, tentatively. "Whether male or female?"

"As a matter of fact," the French officer said, as he rose from his chair and crossed to the window to let in the sea air, "we may have something of significance. Her guest was definitely a woman."

"How can you be sure of that?" an increasingly alarmed Faye Walford asked.

"Because your sister received a telephone call from a woman at 4.05 p.m. on August 27th. All incoming calls to Les Palmiers are routed through the manager's office. Guy Kervella confirms that a woman rang that afternoon and that he connected her with Maxine's extension number. Around six o'clock, just as he was going off duty, he noticed a tall brunette enter the timeshare on the ground floor and walk up the short flight of steps towards Maxine's apartment."

"Putting two and two together," George Mason said, "it is beginning to seem possible that the dinner guest and the imposter at St Dunstan's School could well be one and the same person."

"An inference most plausible," Jules Lemaitre agreed.

"That is just too fantastic to imagine," Faye Walford objected. "What possible motive could such a person have?"

"That remains to be seen," Mason said. "First, we have to trace this woman and discover her true identity. That may be no easy task. At least, if she and the imposter are one and the same person, we are circulating a Wanted poster with a clear image. It is a start in the right direction, unless you, *Capitaine*, have some specific knowledge of this visitor?"

The Frenchman regretfully shook his head.

"She could be anybody," he said. "So many tourists visit Nice in the high season. Many more pass through on their way to the Riviera resorts of Antibes, Cannes, St. Tropez and even to San Remo on the Italian side. It is impossible to keep tabs on them all. But I do have some further information which may assist you."

He consulted his folder again briefly, as the English pair looked on expectantly.

"Our technical expert has traced the phone call in question to a telephone booth on the Promenade des Anglais."

"The English Promenade," Mason said, translating for his companion.

"That particular facility accepts only phone cards. That is helpful, because each card is embedded with a serial number that registers with the telephone company whenever it is used."

George Mason leaned forward attentively, as the significance of the Frenchman's words sank in.

"After the call to Les Palmiers," Lemaitre went on, "three further calls were made with the same card. Two of them went to England, the other to Germany. These are the numbers dialed."

He wrote them on a slip of paper, which he then passed across his desk.

"At last, we may be getting somewhere," a more optimistic George Mason said. "We can trace these numbers through British Telecom when we get back home and find out who this person has contacted."

"Glad to be of assistance," Jules Lemaitre said, rising from his chair to indicate that the interview was over.

"I should like to visit the timeshare," Faye said, "before we leave Nice."

"That is easily arranged," the gendarme

said, placing a quick call to the manager. "I am heading that way myself in a few moments. I shall be most happy to drop you both off."

"You have been very helpful, Capitaine Lemaitre," George Mason said. "We shall keep in touch."

As they made their way towards the timeshare, Mason remarked to Faye Walford:

"I was not aware that your half-sister had a son. Was she once married?"

Faye returned a wry smile.

"Maxine never married, Inspector Mason, nor did she wish to," she replied. "She became a single parent by choice. Marcus is not her natural son. She adopted him from an orphanage in Cheshire."

CHAPTER 5

The following Monday, George Mason was on his way north to historic city of Chester, taking the same rail route as that used by Faye Walford when he had bidden her good-bye at Euston Station on their return from Nice. She was heading back to her home at Knutsford to resume her employment in dental care, pending further developments in her half-sister's case, while he himself had taken the remainder of the previous week off, to spend time with Adele. Meanwhile, technical staff at Scotland Yard had traced through British Telecom the destination of the two calls made to England in late August with the phone card used by Maxine's dinner guest. The first was made to Deeside Hotel, Chester, presumably to book a room; the second was to a florist's shop called Green Fingers, in the cathedral precinct of that historic city. Faye Walford, he mused, as the train sped through the countryside of Staffordshire and into the county of Cheshire, was hoping against hope that Maxine would be found alive. His own reading of the case left little room for optimism. Only a person with specialist knowledge of poisons would use a substance like ricin, placing a very sinister question mark against its user.

On arrival at his destination, he soon located the hotel on the banks of the Dee, a major river running through central Wales to its outlet in the Irish Sea. The foyer was fairly quiet just before midday, permitting the receptionist to give him his full attention.

"Inspector George Mason," he said, introducing himself, "of the Metropolitan Police."

The clerk, a balding individual with wire-rimmed spectacles, glanced up in some surprise.

"You wish to book a room, Inspector?"

"Er, no," the detective replied, with a bland smile. "I need some information in connection with a current investigation."

"What sort of information might that be?" the other warily enquired.

"I should like a list of single females who booked a room, on or around August 30th. It would have been booked by telephone, rather than by mail or online."

"That would have been around the time of the Deeside Carnival," the clerk explained. "We were fully booked and there are over a hundred rooms."

"Perhaps I could leave it with you and call back later?" Mason suggested.

"I shall have the back office run through

the computer records for you, Inspector," the clerk obligingly offered.

"How long do you think it will take?" Mason asked, thinking he would grab a bite to eat after his train journey and then visit the florist.

"Could you call back at, say, two o'clock, Inspector? We should have it ready by then."

Mason thanked him and left the hotel, seeking out the sandwich bar he had noticed a few blocks back. Judging the October air still warm enough to eat outdoors, he found a bench where he could eat his ham-and-salad roll while observing the activity on the river. There were a few small children using pedalloes close to the bank and two college rowing crews, probably in training for an inter-varsity event, powering downstream. He almost envied them their carefree lives, recalling his own student days and the pique he had felt, from being slightly overweight, at not making the rowing team. He had taken up sailing instead, a sport he still sometimes enjoyed with Bill Harrington, who had recently bought a yacht. In due course, the cathedral clock struck the hour of one, drawing his attention to its impressive medieval outlines. He would use it as a marker to locate Green Fingers.

Quitting the riverside, he walked back into the city center, keeping the cathedral in view. Within ten minutes, he had gained the precinct, a pedestrianized area where he soon found the florist's, situated between a store selling antique instruments suitable for the performance of baroque music and an evangelical bookshop. He paused just long enough to scan the window displays, never having been quite sure exactly what a sackbut was. Apparently, it was a vintage trombone, nestled there between a beautifully-inlaid clavichord and a string instrument he took to be a vintage viol. Plaster busts of Bach, Handel and Vivaldi gazed back harmoniously through the glass.

The girl behind the counter of Green Fingers smiled up at him with her dark eyes as he entered the premises. She wore a leaf-green apron over a pale top and dark jeans, and was busy trimming the stems off a bunch of gladioli, brushing the discards to one side with her free hand. Mason produced ID and explained his errand, causing her dark eyes to widen and her brow to pucker.

"A telephone order for flowers on August 30th?" she asked, hesitantly.

"I should think it would be for that purpose," he said, before a rather lugubrious thought struck him. "Unless it was for a wreath."

The girl gave him an odd look at that remark and consulted her sales ledger. He watched in keen anticipation as her small hands skimmed backwards through the pages. This was the only real lead he had.

"August 30th was a special day," she said, eventually. "It was the occasion of our annual flower show. Percy Trimble, the television gardening expert, came up from London to judge the entries."

"Did you win a prize?" he enquired.

The girl flushed slightly and said:

"I am not a grower, Inspector Mason, but Green Fingers always books a display stand to promote our wares. My uncle, however, won second prize for his dahlias."

"Good for him," the detective said, much impressed.

"Now, as regards telephone orders," she went on, "we received a request from a woman for white peonies in the late-afternoon. All other sales, and they were few on account of the children's parade which precedes the flower show, were made directly over the counter."

The detective's spirits rose.

"Do you have a name?" he asked. "Or credit card details?"

"The customer would not give a name," the girl explained. "Said she would drop by and settle with cash, which in fact she did two days later."

"She just turned up, you mean, and collected the flowers?" he asked.

The salesgirl shook her head firmly.

"The peonies were not for herself," she explained. "They were to be sent by special delivery to Valley Care Home at Llandudno, just down the Welsh coast from here."

"You shipped them before receiving payment?" he asked. "Very trusting of you."

The girl smiled, disarmingly.

"Not especially," she assured him. "The woman said that the care home would vouch for her. She seemed genuine enough to me and it was a good order. Peonies are expensive blooms."

"Can you describe this person to me?"

The girl pondered for a moment.

"It is some weeks ago now," she replied. "So many people visit Green Fingers."

"But you must recollect something," Mason insisted, regretting that he had not brought the Wanted poster with him.

"I have a vague impression of someone in her mid-forties," the other at length replied. "Smartly dressed, with a forthright manner."

"Color of hair? Height?"

"Taller than me and generously built. She had dark hair, I seem to recall."

"Your recollection is quite good, after all," the detective said. "Thank you very much for your assistance."

He left the premises and hurried back towards the railway station, calling at Deeside Hotel on the way. The clerk handed him a sealed envelope, which he did not open until he was seated in the 2.40 p.m. train to Llandudno. As the express gathered speed along the banks of the Dee estuary and crossed into North Wales, he slit the envelope open and scanned the list of the half-dozen or so single females who had booked accommodation at the hotel in late-August. Part-way down, his attention riveted on the name Maxine Walford. He whistled aloud, peered at it again for confirmation and fell to musing on the implications. They were not very reassuring, at least from Faye Walford's point of view. It now seemed fairly clear to him that this unknown person had fully assumed Maxine's identity and may still be using it, even after her sudden departure from St. Dunstan's School.

He relaxed for the remainder of the journey, taking in the captivating scenery as the train followed a route through the coastal towns of Abergele and Colwyn Bay, offering views of the ocean on the right and the mountains of Snowdonia on the left. A great area to spend a vacation, he considered, thinking he would suggest it to Adele as a possible alternative to the Lake District. It was good hiking country, with picturesque sandy coves for beach-lovers and quaint country pubs to restore the inner man with a plowman's lunch and local ales. A poster on the platform of Colwyn Bay station advertised the noted Welsh Mountain Zoo. He recalled reading somewhere that they kept golden eagles there, along with typical local fauna.

Just over an hour later, he reached his destination. At Llandudno Junction, he took a taxi that drove the length of the promenade between Great Orme, a large promontory with a lighthouse overlooking the southern end of the bay, and Little Orme to the north. There were still tourists about, even this late in the season. Isolated family groups dotted the beach, playing ball games and building sandcastles with moats to be filled by the incoming tide. A few hardy retirees, knees well-wrapped in travel blankets, relaxed in deckchairs, pretending it was still summer. The waterfront hotels and restaurants were in a mid-afternoon lull. The observant detective had time to take in these facets of the coastal resort before his driver turned off the main drag just short of Little Orme and continued a short distance along a tree-lined country lane, setting him down outside a large Victorian mansion. A rather faded sign advertised its name, and a handful of elderly residents occupying wicker chairs on a screened veranda revealed its purpose. He soon located the matron in her compact office close to the entrance and introduced himself. She was more than a little surprised to see him.

"Please do take a seat, Inspector Mason," she said, shuffling some paperwork on her desk. "How can I assist you?"

"I am conducting an enquiry," George Mason informed her, "concerning a missing person."

"And what could that possibly have to do with Valley Care Home?" the matron asked, in some surprise. "None of our residents has gone missing."

The detective smiled blandly back at her. She was a woman of mature years, with chin-length graying hair and an air of no-nonsense efficiency.

"It does not, I am happy to say, concern one of your residents," he assured her. "At least, not directly, insofar as I am aware."

"Please do go on," the woman urged.

"I believe," he continued, "that a bunch of white peonies was sent to this address by special delivery from a florist called Green Fingers at Chester. It would have been around the end of August."

The matron pondered his remarks for a moment, and said:

"That is correct, Inspector. I remember them distinctly. They were very beautiful flowers."

"Destined, I presume, for one of your residents?"

"Quite so, Inspector," the matron said. "They were for Gertrude Kramer, from her daughter, who sent them in lieu of a promised visit."

"The daughter's name?" Mason eagerly asked, his spirits rising.

"Mrs. Kramer, in her more lucid moments, always refers to her as Ros. I imagine that is short for Rosamund, or possibly Rosalind. Or even Rosemary."

"Ros Kramer," the intrigued detective repeated, half-aloud. "Tell me, matron, have you ever met the daughter?"

"Unfortunately not," she replied. "I was on annual leave on the Devon coast when she booked her mother in as a permanent resident last June."

"As recently as that?" the detective remarked.

The matron curtly nodded.

"The assistant matron at the time, Sheila Ogden," she added, "would have received the Kramers. But Ogden left us in July to start a new life in New Zealand."

"I should like, if it would be convenient," Mason then said, hoping to get an indication of the daughter's current whereabouts, "to exchange a few words with this Gertrude Kramer."

The matron returned a rather cryptic smile, rose from behind her desk and led him along a short corridor to a spacious lounge, where residents who preferred the indoor warmth were sitting in easy chairs, either reading or sleeping. To one side, a livelier group was playing bridge at a mahogany card table.

"Card games are very popular with some of our guests," the matron said, noting his interest.

She then indicated a frail-looking woman

wrapped in a shawl sitting towards the back of the room, by a leaded bay window. An open book lay across her lap. To the visitor, she looked sound asleep.

"I would not wish to disturb her," he said, considerately.

"I doubt it would help you very much if you did," the matron ironically remarked. "Mrs. Kramer, unfortunately, is losing her memory. I suspect that is why her daughter sent flowers in lieu of a personal visit. She might have been afraid her mother would not recognize her."

George Mason felt a twinge of disappointment, as well as sympathy. There might have been any number of issues the mother could have enlightened him on, yet that chance was now gone. At least, he felt, he had a definite link to Maxine Walford's dinner guest on that fateful evening at Les Palmiers, as well as an authentic name.

"I do hope your long journey has not been a waste of time, Inspector Mason," the matron said, sensing his reaction.

"By no means," he quickly replied. "On the contrary, it has been most productive."

"Afternoon tea is about to be served in the dining-room," she continued. "You are welcome to join us and perhaps chat with some of our residents. They have little contact with the wider world, in the normal run of things, apart from occasional visits to the theatre. The Welsh National Opera visits

Llandudno during the summer months, for example."

"I shall be happy to accept your hospitality," the detective said. "I am an opera fan myself, which should give us a few talking points."

"Please do not also mention that you are a policeman," she cautioned. "That might only alarm them."

"Point taken, matron. Is there anything else about Gertrude Kramer that you could tell me?" he asked, as they went through to the dining-room. "Some little detail that may have struck you as odd?"

"She speaks, when coherent, with a rather heavy accent," the other replied. "I would say she is probably not a native of Britain."

"Most interesting," George Mason said, "and also possibly very significant."

*

Chief Inspector Harrington was waiting for him when George Mason reported back to base first thing the following morning.

"Had a useful trip?" he pointedly enquired.

"A step forward, hopefully," his colleague replied.

"Glad to hear it," Harrington said, approvingly. "The Aurelian Brothers have been on to me about the missing funds. Brother Aelred, whom for reasons best known to themselves they refer to as the Visitor, was most eager for the monies to be recovered at an early date. He blames himself partly, for being too trusting."

"People in his calling are often not very wise in the ways of the world," Mason commented.

"Because they spend so much of their lives sheltered from it," his senior added, grinning as he filled his briar pipe with a Dunhill mixture.

"If they do not recover the building funds very soon," Mason added, "they will have to take out a loan from the diocese, to keep on schedule. That is something they are very reluctant to do, apparently, having substantial debt already."

"So what have you come up with so far?" Harrington asked, expectantly.

"I traced the suspect to a hotel and also to a florist at Chester, from the numbers dialed from Nice with the phone card. She checked in on August 29th, having booked the room two days earlier. It could well have been a stop-over on her way to Dovestones."

"Why Chester, of all places, Inspector?"

"Because her mother resides at a care home in Llandudno, North Wales. She may have intended to visit her, but the matron there thinks she decided to send flowers instead, fearing that her mother would not recognize her."

"Alzheimer's?" his senior asked,

betraying an uncharacteristic streak of sympathy.

"At a rather advanced stage," Mason said, "unfortunately."

"Is that all you have to report?" Harrington testily enquired.

"By no means," his colleague replied. "Maxine's dinner guest was a certain Ros Kramer, who is possibly of European origin. But at Deeside Hotel she registered as Maxine Walford and may still be going under that name, which does not look too promising for the real Maxine."

"You think she murdered her," the other said, "at that timeshare in Nice, and assumed her identity?"

"If Capitaine Lemaitre does not locate Maxine soon, Chief Inspector, it will begin to look very much that way, I fear."

"But why?" Harrington pondered, toying with his pipe. "What could be the motive for such a heinous crime?"

"That is something we shall have to discover," Mason said, "once this is definitely designated a murder enquiry."

"For that, we would need a body," his senior said. "And if this Ros Kramer, as you call her, is as foxy as you claim, she may have carefully disposed of it. That is, if she is in fact guilty of the crime."

"Traces of ricin powder," Mason continued, "were found at Maxine's apartment. That suggests a killer with specialist knowledge of poisons."

"And how to obtain them," Harrington ruefully added. "What do you aim to do now, as a useful next step? The Wanted poster has gone out to police stations around the country. We have had no response to it, as yet, to my knowledge."

"I am of a mind to follow up the call made to Germany with the phone card at Nice," George Mason said, "on the off-chance that it proves as useful as the Chester numbers."

Harrington slowly nodded agreement.

"I shall get one of our technical staff to check it out with Deutsche Telecom," he said. "It should not take more than a couple of days."

He then applied a match to his briar pipe, sending a cloud of aromatic smoke in Mason's direction, to signify that their brief conference was over. George Mason returned to his own office, quietly confident that things were beginning to move forward, if only slowly.

CHAPTER 6

Roslinda Kramer finished packing her two suitcases in the room she had occupied at Queen's Hotel, Bayswater since her arrival in London. She then crossed to the wall mirror to apply dark eye shadow and adjust her new hairstyle. Two days ago, while walking down Queensway on her way to Kensington Palace Gardens, she had been amazed to see her own image staring back at her from the window of Bayswater Police Station. The Wanted poster conveyed a good likeness, she had to admit, but she could not for the life of her imagine how the police had obtained it, and in so short a time. Her reaction, after the initial shock, was to book an appointment at The Cut Above, as upmarket beauty salon in Leinster Square, a few blocks from her hotel. She had it bobbed and dyed several shades lighter, with good results. The face that now looked back at her from the bedroom mirror bore little enough resemblance, she felt sure, to the police portrait.

Concerned that the police would obtain the serial numbers of the banknotes she had withdrawn from Pennine Bank, Dovestones, she had converted the stolen money into euros in separate parcels at travel agencies, post offices and mainline stations, forfeiting some of its value in commissions. She checked that it was safely tucked away in large Manila envelopes beneath items of clothing, before locking her luggage and descending by elevator to Reception to settle her bill. It was then a short walk on a blustery autumn day to Bayswater Underground, where she took the Circle Line to Paddington Station.

Figuring that police enquiries would center mainly on major cities, she had decided to settle for the immediate future in the West Country, confident that the authorities had only an outdated photograph to go off, and no valid name. As far as they were concerned, she was Maxine Walford, who had absconded from St. Dunstan's School with a large sum of money. She would now drop her alias and revert to her maiden name. Her aim was to cross the English Channel at some point and convert the euros back to Sterling at various facilities, to cover her tracks. She would then open a deposit account at a small country bank, one that had little exposure to money laundering and would therefore not question a substantial deposit.

On arrival at the mainline station, she crossed the busy concourse to join the short queue at the ticket office, where she found herself standing for a few minutes behind a middle-aged gentleman wearing a dark-blue suit. Out of idle curiosity, she appraised the man carefully, marking him as a senior civil servant or perhaps a bank manager, noting also the initials G.M. on his leather briefcase. Having purchased his ticket, the man turned and glanced at her, with a half-smile.

"Sorry to take so long," he apologized. "Service is a bit slow today, on account of the one-day strike by one of the trade unions."

"Their objective is to cause maximum disruption to the traveling public," Roslinda Kramer remarked, noting as the man turned away that he was quite good-looking, the maturer sort of male she was determined to cultivate on arrival in Devon. Courteous too, she thought. How many people, in this day and age, would apologize for something like that?

Now that it was her turn, she bought a one-way ticket to Dartmouth, using the money she had earned during her brief stay at St. Dunstan's. Gripping her suitcases, she proceeded to the newspaper kiosk to buy the current issue of *The Lady*, repairing with it to Platform 2 to board the 11.35 a.m. express to Exeter, where she would switch to a local train to continue her journey through rural Devon. Settling into a comfortable window seat, as she waited for the train to pull out of the station, she reflected with some satisfaction that everything so far had gone according to plan. If she was half hoping that the polite gentleman at the ticket office would be catching the same train, she was disappointed. He was nowhere to be seen.

An hour later, the train was speeding through the Berkshire countryside, making scheduled stops at Reading and Newbury. She had already skimmed through the classified section of *The Lady*, but not with the intention of seeking paid employment. She had other fish to fry, circling in biro an item in the Personal column. It read: 'Retired naval officer, with broad cultural and sporting interests, seeks active, like-minded companion in age-range 45-55. Reply to Box 352, preferably with recent photograph.' All thoughts of the polite gentleman back at Paddington receded from her mind, as she began to compose mentally a reply to the box number, thinking she would have a new photograph of herself taken soon as she had found accommodation at Dartmouth and enclose it with her reply. She would book into The Devonshire Arms for a few nights and visit the real estate agencies, thinking there should be a good selection of long-term rentals available, now that the main tourist season was over. An apartment overlooking the River Dart would be ideal, she reflected, having carefully researched the area on the Internet at Bayswater Library. She had been pleased to note that Dartmouth had strong naval associations, being the home of the Royal Naval College.

*

George Mason had spent most of that morning at Maida Vale, on routine enquiries into a case one of his colleagues was leading. At just turned eleven o'clock, he took the Bakerloo Line the short distance to Paddington Station, to renew his commuter rail-pass. Even without industrial action, that procedure always took a while in these times of heightened security. His identity and credit card status were checked, drawing from him a brief apology to the person patiently standing behind him in the queue. His brief recollection, as he took the Circle Line to Whitehall, was of an attractive, forty-something woman, with short blond hair, toting two suitcases, as if bound for a long vacation.

Chief Inspector Bill Harrington was on the point of leaving for lunch by the time Mason arrived back at Scotland Yard shortly after midday. The senior officer did not like interruptions to his gastronomic routine, making a point of normally reaching Isola Madre, an upscale Italian restaurant farther down Broadway noted for fresh pasta dishes, just as Big Ben struck half-twelve. He scowled at his colleague's late entrance and sat down again heavily in his swivel-chair, his professional instincts overcoming the rumblings in his stomach.

"I expected you half an hour ago," he remarked irritably, as George Mason took a seat facing him.

"Had to call at Paddington Station, to renew my rail-pass," Mason explained. "It took longer than I expected, owing to limited industrial action."

Harrington grunted impatiently and quickly consulted a folder lying on his desk.

"Strikes by public servants should be outlawed," he protested, "for all the inconvenience they cause to the general public. But some good news, at least. Deutsche Telecom have traced the number dialed from Nice with that phone card you mentioned."

"That did not take them very long," Mason remarked, impressed at their efficiency. "So where does it lead us to?"

"To an area east of the Rhine, known as Sauerland," the chief inspector explained. "The number dialed belongs to Die Blaue Kugel, a night club in a suburb of Wetzlar, an historic town on the River Lahn."

"Interesting," his colleague observed. "What kind of night club might that be?"

"I searched the town's website, which seems mainly designed to attract tourists to the region. Ever been that way, Inspector, on your extensive travels?"

George Mason shook his head.

"It is apparently a sparsely populated area," his senior continued, "with steep, densely-forested valleys and little in the way of modern industry. It is so wild, in fact, that they are thinking of reintroducing the European bison there."

"Wildlife of all types is staging a strong comeback across the Continent," Mason remarked. "I wonder what sort of connection our friend Ros Kramer has to that particular region?"

"That is something for you to find out, old chap," Harrington said, in an uncharacteristically affable vein.

"You mean...?"

"Precisely, Inspector. I have had one of the technical staff draw up a route for you. Help Detective Sergeant Benson clear up those robbery incidents at Maida Vale for the remainder of this week and book yourself a flight to Cologne for next Monday. From Kolner Hauptbahnhof, you take the mainline train to Wetzlar."

"You still have not told me what kind of club it is," Mason protested, a little taken aback at the suddenness of this new development.

"The usual sort of thing," his senior replied. "Cabaret, dancing, escort services and so on."

"Escort services being a euphemism for…?"

"Call girls, Mason, to put it bluntly," Harrington said, with a hint of disdain, as he passed the folder across the desk for his colleague to read.

George Mason carefully noted the travel details the technical staff had jotted down for him and passed the folder back.

"Anything wrong?" the other then asked, noting Mason's look of concern..

"Isn't there the slight matter of police protocol involved here, Sir?"

"You mean we should contact the German authorities, the Kriminal Polizei, ahead of your visit?"

"Exactly," Mason replied. "In something so serious as a murder investigation, should we not liaise with the Kripo, as they style themselves?"

"It isn't officially a murder case, at least not yet," Harrington brusquely retorted. "In the first instance, go to the night club as a private individual and see if you can turn up something useful as a regular member of the clientele. If the situation calls for it, you can then present yourself with credentials to the local Kripo, as you call them, but watch out for the Gestapo."

"Are you serious, Chief Inspector?" his colleague asked, with raised eyebrows.

"Just testing your reflexes," his senior said, with a mischievous twinkle in his eye. "Have a good trip, Inspector. Try the Thai cuisine they boast of, mix with the locals as a regular tourist and find out what you can. If you go there as a police officer, you will get nowhere. Now, if you will excuse me, luncheon at Isola Madre calls, and not before time."

Mason returned to his own office to concentrate on outstanding business. By the end of the week, he had helped Sergeant Benson wrap up his investigation into a series of robberies at jewelry stores in the Maida Vale and St John's Wood areas. They were apparently motivated, as was often the case nowadays, by the need to finance drug addiction. He was now free to devote his undivided attention to the Maxine Walford case, spending most of Friday afternoon making preparations for his journey and brushing up his rusty German. He aimed to take Adele out to dinner at the Savoy Grill, as a sweetener in case she felt neglected by his frequent absences. He had been away from home several times of late, in the line of duty. Although she rarely complained, he was aware that she was not over-enthusiastic about that aspect of his job.

*

Some two hundred miles from the Masons' London home in West Ruislip, Commander Ralph Markland, R.N. Retd, as he liked to style himself, also had a dinner engagement in mind, as he drove his Audi at a leisurely pace along the coastal road between Torquay and Dartmouth. He turned over in his mind the assorted replies he had received from his advertisement in *The Lady*. They were, as he had anticipated, mainly from widows leading solitary lives in the quieter resorts along the south coast, but the one that intrigued him most was from a certain Roslinda Kramer, who had enclosed a recent photograph of herself revealing an attractive blonde, with chin-length hair and dark eyes. Her letter had expressed interests that corresponded closely to his own, including classical music, opera, fine dining and travel, tastes which indicated a person of substantial means, someone accustomed to the good life. To Ralph Markland, a bon viveur, she sounded the ideal sort of companion. But did she, he wondered, also have marriage in mind? That was an important consideration for him, at this juncture in his life.

Eventually veering off the coastal road, he headed northwards along the valley of the

River Dart, through small market towns and villages with thatched-roof cottages, taking in the lush Devonshire scenery on the way. It was his favorite among the English counties, for its deep countryside and tasteful coastal resorts. He was prone to congratulate himself on his move a few years ago from his native Birmingham to Torquay, Devon, where he stayed at a modest boarding house a few streets back from the busy seafront. His objective now was Bridge Hotel, in a village just north of Kingsmere, where he had booked a table for two. He checked his Rolex wristwatch, given to him by one of his previous wives, and eased his foot off the pedal in order not to arrive ahead of time. His contact was already sitting in the foyer of the small riverside hotel as he parked his car and strode smartly inside. He recognized the woman at once from her photograph and approached her in expectant mood.

"Miss Kramer?" he enquired, offering his hand as she rose to her feet with a look of pleasant surprise. Not knowing quite what to expect, she was inwardly gratified to greet a handsome, sixty-plus gentleman suavely dressed in nautical blazer, gray flannel slacks and polka-dot cravat. He conformed perfectly to her image of an English gentleman, even if that had been formed mainly through novels and older films featuring the likes of David Niven or George

Saunders.

"Commander Markland?" she enquired in her turn, briefly shaking his hand.

"None other," he replied. "Delighted to meet you at last."

The initial courtesies completed, he took her arm and led her through to the dining-room at the rear of the hotel, where they were assigned a table for two by a window overlooking the upper reaches of the Dart. They sat facing each other and studied the menu, furtively appraising each other at the same time.

"Have you been living in Dartmouth long, Miss Kramer?" he genially enquired.

"Just a few months," she replied untruthfully, not wishing to give the impression that she had just arrived. "By the way, my friends call me Roslinda."

Ralph Markland smiled.

"And I usually answer to Ralph," he said.

"Well, Ralph," an impressed Roslinda said. "I imagine you are a long-term resident, what with the Royal Naval College just down the river."

Markland smiled evasively.

"For most of my career I was stationed at Portsmouth," he said, "where the naval shipyards are."

"And you have lived here since you retired?"

"On and off," he replied. "It is a most attractive area. The best of both worlds, in fact. We have the countryside and the sea, in good measure, and the Navy connection as well."

The waiter appeared to take their order.

"I think I shall try the rainbow trout," the commander said.

"And I shall have…I think…the pepper steak," his companion said, a little uncertainly.

"And for starters?" enquired the waiter.

"Prawn cocktail," both diners replied, almost in unison.

"And we should like a wine list," Markland added.

"The trout will be from the River Dart," he went on, the moment the waiter had left. "It should be very fresh."

"I enjoy seafood," his companion said, thinking back to the *Morue Atlantique* she had enjoyed two months ago at the old harbor in Nice. "River fish less so."

"An acquired taste, I suppose," he replied, "like so much else. Now tell me, Roslinda, what brought you down to the West Country?"

Roslinda Kramer tensed slightly; it was not a question she had anticipated.

"The need for a change," she quickly improvised. "Had enough of city life, the hectic pace, the pollution, the crime."

"I know what you mean," he said approvingly, wondering at the same time what her financial situation was. She seemed too young to be drawing a pension. "The rising crime rate is a very disturbing trend. But tell me, is this a permanent move you have made?"

"Is anything permanent, in this life?" she replied, evasively.

"A rather philosophical point of view," the other admiringly commented. "I like that. *Nil permanet sub sole,* as the Romans put it."

Roslinda returned a blank look at his use of Latin. The starter arrived at that point, occupying their attention. Ralph perused the wine list and opted for a pinot noir.

"Red wine also goes very nicely with fish," he said. "Especially the lighter varieties."

"And even better with a steak," she remarked. "I would normally choose white Burgundy with seafood, preferably Chablis."

"You dine out often?" the commander asked. "Or do you prefer home cooking?"

"It very much depends on my mood at the time," Roslinda truthfully replied. "Dining out is much more sociable than eating alone at home."

Ralph Markland thought he was beginning to see the way ahead more clearly. Here was a woman in genuine need of companionship, he considered, confirming the impression he had received from her response to his advertisement in *The Lady*.

"In your letter, you said you enjoyed opera," he remarked.

"I like all kinds of music," she replied, between forkfuls of garnished prawn.

"Last year, I was in Llandudno for the Welsh National Opera's summer season, or at least for part of it."

"Indeed?" she asked, immediately interested, while calling to mind the Valley Care Home in that same resort. It prompted feelings of guilt that she had not visited her mother, but she soon dismissed them so as not to seem preoccupied.

"I booked for two separate performances," Ralph went on, enthusiastically. *The Magic Flute* and *Der Rosenkavalier.*"

"Among my very favorites," Roslinda enthused in her turn, warming considerably to her host for his appreciation of German culture.

At that point the entrées arrived. Ralph Markland began boning his trout, while his companion tucked into her juicy steak with peppercorns.

"If you like Richard Strauss," she observed, after a while, "you would enjoy *Salome.*"

"That is one of the few operas I have yet to see," he replied, noting that she ate with good appetite.

He liked women who enjoyed their food. There was something reassuring about them, homely even. It suddenly struck him as he watched her that she was not English, though her accent was near-perfect, as if she had been well-trained or a long-term resident. It was her pronunciation of Richard, affording the *ch* the same guttural value as in Scottish 'loch', that gave her away. He feigned ignorance of her slip. In fact, it might suit his purposes better, he mused. If she was, as he was beginning to suspect, a fairly recent arrival from Germany or Austria, she would be unfamiliar with British ways and therefore more dependent on his judgement than a British or American woman might be.

"Enjoying your steak?" he asked, politely and rather superfluously, since it was already half-eaten.

"I normally prefer it a little rarer," she replied, with a broad smile. "But it is a first-rate cut."

"Aberdeen Angus," the suave navy man remarked.

"Tell me," Roslinda suddenly said, "what types of ships you served in. I have always been fascinated by the sea and ships."

Markland hesitated before replying, covering himself momentarily by removing the skin from the underside of his trout, which he placed fastidiously at the edge of his plate.

"Er…minesweepers, mainly," he then said. "That is what I started out on after the war. Later, I switched to shore duties."

"At the Admiralty?" she asked.

"Er...no," he replied. "Mainly provisioning and logistics, at Portsmouth Naval Base."

"And you have since retired," she continued, "on a service pension? I really am impressed."

"It keeps the wolf from the door," Ralph observed, with mock modesty. "You yourself, I imagine, are still some years short of retirement? I would take you for a successful career woman. The fashion industry, perhaps?"

Roslinda Kramer glowed inwardly at the implied compliment, but slowly shook her head.

"I have independent means," she said, "and the time to indulge my special interests."

"Which you outlined very well in your letter," the other noted. "And which, may I add, coincide to a large extent with my own. Did you know, for example, that the London Philharmonic are touring the West Country this month? They are booked to play at Exeter Town Hall next week."

"I should love to hear them," Roslinda eagerly replied.

"Then perhaps we could go together," he suggested. "I shall need to book tickets in advance, to avoid disappointment. We could have an early dinner here at the Bridge

Hotel again, before driving up to Exeter."

"I should enjoy that very much," she said, nudging her glass forward for a refill of red wine.

"Then that is settled," Ralph said, with evident satisfaction. "Care for a dessert?"

"I might just barely squeeze some in," she replied.

"I can recommend the cheesecake, from previous experience. It is made with local strawberries and fresh Devon cream."

His companion briefly consulted the menu.

"I think I shall try the home-baked crumble," she said, "as I have never tasted gooseberries."

Another giveaway, Ralph thought, but he did not mention it. Every Englishwoman would have eaten gooseberries at one time or another. They were practically a national tradition, like rhubarb pie.

"I think you may find them rather tart," he said, with an indulgent smile.

When their appetizing meal gradually drew to its close, the last rays of the sun dimpled the surface of the river, casting a romantic aura over this unspoiled part of rural Devonshire. Ralph Markland promptly picked up the tab and offered his guest a lift back to Dartmouth. To his mind, it had been a most successful evening.

CHAPTER 7

The following Monday, George Mason reached Wetzlar in the early evening, after a two-hour train journey through the forested valleys of Sauerland, thinking that wild boar rather than bison would be more at home in such rugged terrain. Alighting from the train, which was continuing to Kassel, he crossed the stone bridge over the River Lahn to reach the cobbled main square. He paused for a few moments to admire the floodlit cathedral and the half-timbered buildings lining the remaining three sides of the medieval enclave, before locating Hotel zum Hirsch along a side-street. A large sign displaying the head of a stag soon drew him in the right direction. He checked in at Reception, climbed the narrow staircase to the second floor and entered his room. It was equipped with heavy wooden furniture and a double bed with a firm mattress. Tapestries representing woodland scenes hung on the walls, offset by what he took to be a Monet print.

Feeling rather tired after his trip, he stretched out on the bed to relax in the soft glow of the table lamp, which cast the woodland scenes in deeper shadow, so that he half-imagined a boar about to emerge. Not wishing to fall asleep, he aimed the remote control at the television set. It was the early evening news, which he half listened to, picking out the odd phrase in German that was familiar to him. As far as he could tell, they were discussing problems arising from reunification, now that the Berlin Wall was down; and in particular whether to grant the Ostmark, the currency of the former East Germany, parity with the Deutschmark. It was a weighty matter, prompting a heated exchange between opposing parties in the studio, focusing on the uneven economic development of the two parts of Germany.

Half an hour later, at just turned seven o'clock, he rose from the bed, took a quick shower to freshen up and went down to the foyer to book a taxi. Within minutes he was on his way to Die Blaue Kugel, with the prospect, since he had not eaten since breakfast, of a gourmet Thai dinner. An illuminated blue globe advertising its name hung over the club doorway. He paid the entrance fee, eased past the stocky bouncer and paused for a while in the narrow vestibule to examine the signed photographic stills of current and former artistes. Exotic dancing seemed to be the main attraction, he mused, as he made his way through to the dimly-lit interior. It was set out much like any restaurant, its tables covered in dark-red linen cloths with a small lamp in the center. There was no overheard lighting. A few of the tables were already occupied as he took his place towards the back of the room, in order to get a good vantage-point without being too visible himself. A young waitress of vaguely Oriental appearance immediately approached him.

"*Guten Abend*," she said, with a friendly smile. "*Zum essen?*"

The intrepid detective nodded. At this moment, food was definitely the first thing on his mind, which invariably worked better on a full stomach. Scanning the elaborate menu printed in German that she left with him, he chose a pork dish, opting for a Mosel wine to accompany it. The young woman, slender as a birch-tree, soon reappeared to take his order, as his eye traveled round the room and fixed on the small, unlit stage. Not much activity up front, he mused, thinking that the cabaret would probably not start until later in the evening, when the clientele filled out more. Bill Harrington had slyly mentioned hostesses, but perhaps these would also appear at a later hour, after the serious business of eating. In the meantime, there was piped music of a vaguely Oriental flavor, to help create the desired atmosphere.

When his meal arrived, he was pleased to note that, while resembling Chinese cuisine in some ways, Thai food had unique characteristics of its own, including portions of exotic vegetables and fruits. He was on the point of finishing it, having poured himself another glass of chilled Riesling, when a brunette with heavy eye make-up and wearing a low-cut silk dress took the seat opposite him. He was a bit taken aback at the suddenness of the move, but soon recovered his poise.

"You would like to buy me a drink?" she artfully asked, in German.

"Be my guest," Mason gallantly replied, motioning the waitress to bring an extra glass, which he promptly filled.

"You are on a visit to Sauerland?" she asked pleasantly, after a couple of small sips, perhaps taking him for a businessman.

"In a manner of speaking," he neutrally replied.

"But you are not from Germany, are you, even though you speak good German?"

"Actually, no," he replied.

"From America, perhaps? I like Americans." Her dark eyes lit up.

George Mason resignedly shook his head

"English, then," she said, after a while. "You are here on business? I can help you unwind."

"As a matter of fact," the detective said, nudging his plate aside, "I was hoping to meet someone recommended to me by a colleague of mine who visited this area early last year."

"A person who works at this club?" she asked, with a perceptible frown, as if afraid of losing a well-heeled foreign client to someone else.

"As a hostess, possibly," the visitor said. "Or perhaps even as a bartender or a waitress."

"We have many hostesses," the young woman said, with an indifferent shrug. "They come and go, mainly from East Europe."

Illegal immigrants came to Mason's mind, probably on short-term assignments or contracts arranged by a minder. That might make it all the more difficult to track down any given individual. Yet, he reasoned, if a phone call was placed here from Nice last August, there must be some valid link with Maxine Walford's dinner guest and this pseudo-Oriental club.

"She was called Roslinda Kramer," he then said, putting his cards on the table.

The hostess's face registered genuine surprise. She sipped more wine and appraised him closely, with a kind of curious sympathy.

"You did not hear about Roslinda?" she

enquired, in rather solemn tones.

"I am afraid you have the advantage of me," the detective remarked.

"Roslinda Kramer is dead," she said. "She drowned last summer in a yachting accident off the North Sea island of Sylt. But you are only passing through Wetzlar. How could you know something like that?"

"I certainly was unaware of that," George Mason replied, as astonished as he was intrigued. "Was she a friend of yours?"

The woman emphatically shook her head.

"Her good friend was Ilona," she said. "She used to perform at this club, mainly songs by Hans Eisler, which were very popular a while ago. Eisler also composed the East German national anthem, which became defunct last October."

"Following reunification of the two Germanys?"

The hostess nodded.

"I take it that Ilona is no longer with you?" he then remarked.

"She went back home to Bucharest earlier this year," came the pat reply.

"Do you have details of the drowning incident?" Mason then asked. "My colleague who knew her would surely wish to know."

"I shall fetch the proprietress, Margit Breuer," the young woman politely offered. "She knows far more about the incident than I do."

George Mason savored his wine in the

meantime, mulling over this unexpected bit of news that had also yielded the name Roslinda. To add to the mystery, Roslinda Kramer, by all accounts, had passed on. His musings were suddenly interrupted by the arrival of a group of young Americans, who entered the establishment with the air of regular patrons. He thought they were most likely servicemen in civilian dress from a nearby U.S. base, as he observed them occupy the foremost table of the restaurant, just below the stage, no doubt to get a good view of the cabaret. His initial surprise soon faded. There were still, almost fifty years after the war, a number of American bases in Germany, with large contingents of troops needing to relax off-duty. The club owner approached his table, accompanied by the hostess. She eyed him coolly.

"What precisely do you wish to know about Roslinda Kramer?" she asked, with thinly-veiled hostility.

The detective shrugged rather helplessly and pursed his lips.

"I am just curious to learn how she met her death," he replied.

Margit Breuer's features softened a little as she said:

"Roslinda was a skilled yachtswoman. She set out alone from the island of Sylt, where she kept her boat. A sudden squall came up on the North Sea. The coastguard she checked with before setting out informed the police that her yacht was washed ashore twelve hours later. There was no sign of its skipper, nor has her body so far been recovered. Does that answer all your questions, Herr…?"

"Smith," he quickly improvised, to conceal his true identity.

"Sit down, Ilse," the proprietress then said to her employee, "and entertain our client in a fitting matter. Enough of tragedy."

"A very unfortunate circumstance," Mason said to Breuer, somewhat insincerely. "I imagine you were very close."

"She was like a daughter to me," the other said. "Enjoy your evening, Herr Smith, and let her rest in peace. No more questions."

Ilse sat down expectantly, warming to this new client, who seemed somehow different from the club's normal run of clientele. She put that down to his being from England, a country she had often, in common with many of her compatriots, often admired but never actually visited.

George Mason, for his part, ordered a second bottle of Riesling and prepared to stay the course for the evening. The price of liquor doubled after eight o'clock. If he plied Ilse with enough drinks, he figured, she would probably be content at the amount of money she was making for the club, whatever additional services she might have in mind. She might also reveal all sorts of interesting information about the way the establishment operated and especially about Roslinda Kramer's former associations with it.

*

He awoke late with a thick head the following morning, putting it down to the quantity of wine he had drunk the previous evening. He eased himself gingerly out of bed and rang room service to order strong coffee, reflecting as he drank it on his evening with the talkative Ilse. She had told him practically her whole life story, how she had been raised in an orphanage at Bad Schandau, in the former East Germany, making her way to the West through Hungary when that country opened its borders prior to the collapse of the Berlin Wall. Unprepared for the higher cost of living here, she did not earn enough from menial employment to cover even basic expenses and had turned to hostessing as a last resort. He formed the impression that she quite enjoyed the work. More to the point, she told him that Roslinda Kramer was also raised in the DDR, in the city of Cottbus, north of Dresden. Kramer had originally trained as a librarian at Dresden University and had apparently lived in West Germany for some time before reunification. He also learned that she had been widowed and that, at Die Blaue Kugel, she worked what was known as the American market, which he took to mean servicemen from the nearby military base.

Draining his coffee, he dressed quickly and went down to the hotel restaurant just in time to catch the end of breakfast service. They did a cold buffet heavily geared to modern health fads, with a range of organic cereals, yogurts, fruit, nuts and juices. He took fairly generous portions, while muttering to himself that ham-and-eggs would be a better cure for a hangover. With his tray full, he crossed to a window table whence he could observe the sporadic activity in the narrow street outside, while also glancing at the headlines of *Die Welt*, a national broadsheet left by a previous guest. He remained contentedly in his place until ten o'clock, enjoying the ambience of the well-appointed, oak-paneled restaurant and the vicarious companionship of the handful of other late risers. By the time he got up to leave, he was more or less fully alert again. The duty waiter, who supervised the self-service area, gave him directions to Wetzlar Kriminal Polizei, the storied Kripo.

He found it easily enough after crossing the main square and negotiating a narrow street with half-timbered buildings, the Schillergasse, which led to a quiet pedestrianized area behind the imposing cathedral. The duty officer, a pert young woman in a dark-green uniform, was surprised to see him.

"Inspector Mason, from Scotland Yard?" she asked in some surprise, inspecting his ID. "Whatever brings you to Sauerland?"

"An enquiry concerning Die Blaue Kugel night club," he replied.

The young officer returned an odd look, half of disapproval, half of curiosity.

"Then you should speak with Oberkommissar Otto Weiss," she said. "I shall check if he is available."

She put a quick call through to another office, while George Mason stood waiting. Replacing the receiver, she said:

"He will see you straight away, Inspector Mason. Follow the short corridor to the left and knock at the second door on the right."

The detective thanked her and did as he was bid. A burly officer in shirt sleeves Mason estimated to be in his early forties opened his office door even before the visitor had time to knock.

"Please step inside," the officer said, pleasantly surprised, "and take a seat."

Mason's practiced eye took in the details of the small office. It was furnished much like his own quarters in London, except that it had a mineral water dispenser by the window and a more modern computer on the desk. A large color photograph hung on one wall.

"The Harz Mountains," the

oberkommissar said, noting Mason's interest.

"It reminds me of Snowdonia," his visitor remarked, appreciatively, "in North Wales."

"You are a long way off your regular beat aren't you, Inspector?" Otto Weiss then said. "To what do we owe the honor of a visit from the Metropolitan Police?"

George Mason cleared his throat and said: "I am conducting an investigation concerning a woman named Roslinda Kramer, who I believe has connections with this area."

"Roslinda Kramer," Weiss repeated after him. "The name seems to ring a bell. Wait a minute while I consult my files." He crossed to a large filing cabinet, turned and said, "By the way, can I offer you a glass of mineral water? It is all we have I am afraid at the moment. The coffee machine is temporarily kaput."

"I can help myself, thanks," the other said, rising and crossing to the dispenser.

"Rather odd that you should be investigating Kramer," Otto Weiss remarked, on regaining his seat.

"Why do you say that?" his visitor asked.

"Because our records show that she died last year in a yachting accident."

"Then she *is* on your books?" the intrigued detective said, leaning forward attentively.

"She was indeed, very much so," Weiss

replied, "up until her untimely death. She was wanted by the Kripo for blackmail activities against a senior U.S. Army officer. A colonel, if I remember rightly."

"That figures," the adroit Mason said, "since she worked at a night club frequented by army personnel."

"Die Blaue Kugel!" the other exclaimed, with a broad smile. "We raid it from time to time, on suspicion of drug-pushing and hiring illegal immigrants."

"Now what would a qualified librarian, trained in Dresden, be doing working as a night club hostess, when there would surely be many opportunities in her chosen profession?" George Mason pointedly asked.

"Most likely because she was a Stasi agent," the other replied.

"You don't say so!" George Mason exclaimed.

"It is a fact, nonetheless, Inspector," Weiss assured him. "The East German secret police were disbanded late last year, after the fall of the Berlin Wall. Most of their numerous agents simply walked off the job, but not before they had destroyed most of their records, held in many miles of secret files. Fearing recrimination, they sent them out to industrial shredders called *papierwolfs.* Luckily for us, we managed to retrieve some of those containing profiles of personnel."

"And Roslinda Kramer's name came up?"

"It did indeed, Inspector. She was initially approached while still a student at university, but she at first resisted. The Stasi recruited people from all walks of life to inform on friends and even relatives. They were much more subtle than the KGB, spreading rumor, insinuation and general paranoia among the population. After a period as librarian in her native Cottbus, she became a full-time Stasi agent, probably in her mid-thirties."

"Specializing in pillow-talk with American officers?"

"Quite so, Inspector. But also, unknown to her Stasi minders, who would not have condoned it, she had a profitable sideline in blackmail."

"So that is why, when most Stasi agents simply disbanded and merged into the normal day-to-day life of a unified Germany, Roslinda Kramer was being actively sought by yourselves, by the Kriminal Polizei?"

"Right up until the time we were notified of her death by the police and the coastguard service at Sylt."

"What would be your reaction, Oberkommissar, if I were to tell you that she quite recently placed a telephone call to the night club, from Nice on the French Riviera?"

The German officer rose to his feet and

exclaimed:

"*Mein Gott,* Inspector Mason! You cannot be serious."

"But I am," the detective calmly replied, sipping his chilled drink, which reminded him of Vichy water. "A call was made to the night club late in August using a traceable phone card. The same card was also used around the same time to order flowers for one Gertrude Kramer, a resident at a care home in North Wales. The matron there was quite clear that they came from the woman's daughter, whom she referred to as Ros."

Otto Weiss eased himself slowly back into his chair and looked hard at his visitor.

"You are quite certain of this?" he asked, with evident concern.

The Scotland Yard agent nodded.

"This puts an entirely new complexion on the case," the oberkommissar said. "As I recall from subsequent reports of the incident in the press, no woman's body was discovered in the aftermath of the wreck. The yacht washed up on the north shore of Sylt."

A knowing smile spread across George Mason's features.

"You are suggesting, Oberkommissar," he said, almost conspiratorially, "that she faked her own death?"

"That would seem to be a plausible inference, Inspector," Otto Weiss replied, "based on the evidence we have. The waters off Sylt are notoriously treacherous, with huge breakers constantly pounding the shoreline. Few victims of boating mishaps, I regret to say, are ever recovered."

"That may well be, Herr Weiss," George Mason conceded. "And since I have never had the good fortune to visit your celebrated North Sea resorts, I shall take your word for it. But I still think Roslinda Kramer is alive."

"And somehow now domiciled in England?"

"Where she has resumed her life, possibly under a new identity, which may in fact be a stolen identity."

"Can you clarify that?" a puzzled Otto Weiss requested.

"She arrived at a boys' boarding school in the North of England at the beginning of September, posing as Maxine Walford, the new bursar the school had recently hired. She may still be going by that name, but I rather doubt it, as Maxine had relatives living in England. She would be risking exposure."

The German pursed his lips and pondered the matter.

"Quite often," he at length observed, "European emigrants to Anglophone countries like England, the United States and Australia anglicize their names so that they blend in better with the local population. Abramovitch becomes Abrams, for example."

"Or Grunewald becomes Greenwood," Mason suggested.

"Exactly," the other said. "You see my point, Inspector. Kramer may have altered her name in some way. Just a thought, Inspector, but in any event, you have a very resourceful and ruthless former secret agent to reckon with. I wish you the best of British luck."

"It seems we may need it, in the circumstances," his visitor remarked, amused at the other's turn of phrase. "And for your part, what do you intend to do?"

"This is evidently no longer a cold case," Otto Weiss explained. "We shall reopen it and continue our inquiries into her blackmail activities. There may well be more than one victim, in addition to the officer I mentioned. But while Kramer remains in England, the main onus of this investigation must be on Scotland Yard."

"If anything useful should turn up at this end, meanwhile," his visitor said, "please do get in touch with us at without delay."

"Rest assured, Inspector," the German said, "that your people will have our full cooperation. Before your leave Wetzlar, by the way, you should take the opportunity to look in at Lotte's Haus."

George Mason returned a puzzled look.

"It is one of our main tourist attractions," Weiss continued. "Johann Wolfgang von

Goethe did some of his courting there as a young law student. The house is now a museum containing memorabilia of the young couple, as well as early editions of his books, translated into many languages."

"A famous author, in point of fact?" the detective said.

"Our answer to William Shakespeare, Inspector."

"I shall take your word for that, Oberkommissar," George Mason remarked, rather skeptical of the comparison with his celebrated fellow-countryman.

"The duty officer you met in the front office will be happy to give you directions, if you so wish. The house is quite central, just across the main square."

"Thanks for the tip," Mason said, rising to take his leave. "Since I have some time to kill before catching my train back to Cologne, I shall make a point of visiting it. *Guten Tag, Oberkommissar.*"

"*Guten Tag, Herr Mason,*" came the reply, with a warm handshake. "*Und gute Reise.*"

*

Around the time George Mason was heading out to Koln-Bonn Airport in the early evening, following an educational visit to Lotte's Haus, lunch at an inn and a return rail-trip from Wetzlar, Roslinda Kramer was sitting on the foredeck of the cross-Channel ferry observing the retreating skyline of Cherbourg on her passage to Southhampton. Early the previous day, she had flown across to Paris from the provincial airport at Bristol expressly to avoid major checkpoints, and had mainly spent her time in France converting the euros she had acquired in London back into pounds Sterling. Beginning at Orly Airport, she also made use of facilities at mainline stations, travel agencies and currency boutiques, exchanging her money in relatively small amounts, so as to seem like a regular tourist. If by this roundabout procedure she forfeited around twelve per cent in total commissions, she reassured herself that the banknotes she was now carrying with her, which she aimed to add to the account she had opened at Wessex Bank, Dartmouth, were completely untraceable. She was looking forward to adding substantially to this deposit in the not-too-distant future.

It was a calm autumn day on the English Channel, allowing her to take full advantage of the thin sunshine and the sea breeze on the two-hour crossing. She was in a buoyant frame of mind, confident that she had covered her tracks successfully since leaving Dovestones. The police could have no idea whom they were really looking for in connection with the disappearance of St.

Dunstan's funds; they would no doubt be seeking an individual named Maxine Walford. After years of covert work for the East German secret police, she could now look forward to settling down to a quiet civilian life on the English coast. Before leaving Cherbourg, she had mailed a picture postcard of the port in a plain envelope to Margit Breuer, her one remaining connection with the disbanded Stasi, instructing her to address any future communications *poste restante* to Dartmouth Post Office. It would be unwise perhaps to telephone her again so soon, following her earlier call from Nice, much as she would have liked to hear Margit's familiar, almost motherly, voice.

When the ferry eventually docked at Southampton a little after six o'clock, she disembarked and took the regular Green Line bus to the nearby resort of Highcliffe. Commander Ralph Markland would, by prior arrangement, be waiting to meet her there, with a surprise venue in mind for a special evening dinner. Not entirely sure, but reasonably confident, of what the gallant retired naval officer had in mind, she could hardly wait for the country bus to complete its journey along the Hampshire coast road, with stops at picturesque villages and hamlets on the way. At 7.30 p.m., the transport finally reached its destination, coming to a halt in the main square of

Highcliffe, where all passengers alighted.

The debonair retired officer was waiting in the fading daylight to greet her, escorting her towards the spot where his rented Audi was parked. They soon left the quaint market town to motor down narrow country lanes bordered by tall hedgerows and wildflowers, delving deep into the Hampshire countryside, on the edge of the New Forest.

"Had a good trip?" he enquired, secretly wondering why his new acquaintance had made a sudden visit to France.

"Just business," Roslinda replied, in neutral tones. "And yes, it was a good trip from the point of view of the weather and the food. I have always loved French cuisine."

Ralph Markland took it as a good sign that she had business interests across the Channel and did not press her to go into details. He switched the car radio to the Third Program so that they could enjoy the evening concert broadcast by the BBC as they drove, and also to remind her of the recent visit they had made to Exeter to hear the London Philharmonic. Fine dining and good music were key elements of his courtship tactics; they had rarely failed him in the past.

"Beethoven?" Roslinda asked, thinking that she recognized the music.

"Schubert, as a matter of fact," her escort

knowledgably replied, as he in due course steered his car through ornamental wrought-iron gates bearing a family crest. Beyond was extensive parkland with manicured lawns sporting stands of beech and oak. Roslinda held her breath as he drove for some distance towards the main entrance of an imposing mansion, parked carefully and hopped nimbly round to the passenger side to open the passenger door.

"Where on earth are we, Ralph?" she enquired, stepping out with an unfeigned sense of awe.

"At Chewton Glen," her companion replied, pausing to admire the broad sweep of the estate and to point out two large pheasants grazing the lawn. "It is one of the top ten restaurants in England, according to the Michelin guide."

"Simply magnificent," she said, genuinely impressed and warming considerably to her new beau. "Almost like visiting a member of the Royal Family."

"A minor royal perhaps," Ralph Markland allowed, touched by her naivety while leading the way up a flight of stone steps, across a paved terrace and through French windows to the reception area. A gentleman in formal attire greeted them courteously and led them to the table booked in advance. A waiter soon followed with elaborate menus.

"Actually," Ralph went on, expansively,

"this is the former home of the author, Captain Marryat, a naval officer during the Napoleonic Wars. He may even have seen action at the Battle of Trafalgar."

"A navy man, just like yourself," Roslinda enthused. "So that is why you brought me here, you old sea dog!"

Her companion smiled complacently, well-satisfied with the impression his choice of venue had made. He drew her attention to the shelves of books lining the walls of the alcove where their table was placed. The restaurant was divided into small, interconnecting rooms, much the way it would have been had it remained a private home. This gave it an aura of intimacy.

"These are original editions and foreign translations of his novels," he explained. "He was quite a celebrity in his day."

"And lived, evidently," Roslinda remarked, "like a landed aristocrat."

"But what an inspiration," Ralph continued, "to turn the house into a restaurant, so that the general public can now enjoy its amenities to the full."

"I am all in favor of democracy...and egalitarianism," his guest said, recalling the years of service she had devoted to Communist ideology and the myth of a classless society.

The commander frowned perceptibly at that remark. Egalitarianism was way down his list of civic virtues. He had not assiduously cultivated the persona of a retired naval officer to be placed on an equal footing with the general public, even though his origins were quite humble. His father, after all, had been a chauffeur and his mother a supermarket cashier. Roslinda meanwhile had been studying the menu and did not divine the drift of his thoughts.

"Think I shall try the Chilean sea bass," she said, at length.

Ralph Markland, who had been here on previous occasions, invariably opted for Dover sole, when available. He gave their order to the waiter.

"And for the starter?" the latter enquired.

"We should both like the French onion soup."

"And to drink?"

"A bottle of Mersault," the commander said, aiming to make an impression on his guest.

Roslinda smiled to herself at her host's wine order, quickly revising upwards her estimate of his means. A regular Riesling, such as she had often enjoyed when dining out in Germany, would have suited her fine, but she was not about to complain. She would not look a gift horse in the mouth.

"Pushing the boat out a bit, aren't we?" she observed, humorously employing a nautical metaphor.

"A special occasion such as this calls for special treatment," Ralph Markland replied, fully appreciating her wit.

"Indeed?" she remarked, in mock-innocence.

"Successful relationships are firmly based on trust," he went on, suddenly changing tack.

"I can hardly argue with that," Roslinda said, adding a touch of pepper to her soup and briefly stirring it to help it cool.

"Were you aware," the commander continued, in the same vein, "that most marriages that founder do so over questions of money?"

"No, I was not aware of that," his guest disingenuously replied. "But I am fully prepared to take your word for it, Commander."

"Husband and wife, in my view, should have no secrets from each other," he rather pompously went on, "especially those of a financial nature. Everything should be open and above board."

"You mean, as in a joint bank account?" she enquired, as if the idea was quite new to her.

"Absolutely," Ralph Markland emphasized. "How could it be otherwise, if complete openness and trust are to be maintained?"

Roslinda Kramer took that as a rhetorical question and made no reply. She commenced tasting her soup, urging him to do likewise while it was still warm and feeling much intrigued that her host was raising the notion of combining financial interests. She relaxed completely and enjoyed the gourmet seafood and expensive wine in the delightful ambience of Chewton Glen, deep in the Hampshire countryside. She was fully aware that, before the evening was out, perhaps somewhere between dessert and coffee-with-liqueurs, Commander Ralph Markland, R.N. Retd. would pop the question. At that point she would, to use an angling rather than a nautical metaphor, have him hooked.

"Tell me more about Captain Marryat," she said, as she was finishing the entree.

"He wrote the first sea-adventure novels," came the pat reply, "based on the variety of naval actions he saw while serving on British warships. *Mr. Midshipman Easy* comes to mind, although perhaps his best-known novel has nothing to do with the sea. It is called *Children of the New Forest.*"

"I think I may have heard of that," his guest said, without adding that she had studied English literature at school in Cottbus, as on her course in librarianship at Dresden University.

"Apart from that, I know little about him, except that I believe he was a friend of Charles Dickens and very likely knew other Victorian writers."

"Have you read any of his books, Commander?" his guest was curious to learn.

"Afraid not, Roslinda. But perhaps I shall get round to it one day, now that we have both visited his former home."

"A very beautiful home it is, too," she remarked, nudging her finished plate aside.

CHAPTER 8

Faye Walford had been attending a refresher course for dental hygienists at St. Bartholomew's Hospital, Smithfield. When the proceedings drew to a close after lunch on the third day, she took the Underground to Westminster and stepped briskly down Broadway towards Scotland Yard, arriving there at just turned two o'clock. Uppermost in her mind, and this had nagged her continuously during the hospital sessions, was the fact that she had had no further news from the police regarding the fate of her half-sister, Maxine. She now aimed to find out why, entering the suite of offices occupied by Special Branch just as Inspector George Mason was getting a briefing from Chief Inspector Bill Harrington.

"Surprise, surprise," Mason said, genially turning to greet her. "What brings you to the great metropolis?"

"A residential course at Barts," she

replied, rather tersely.

"Please take a seat," Harrington said, offering her the only spare chair. George Mason remained on his feet.

The visitor sat down and said, in a determined voice:

"I am very concerned that there has been no news about Maxine. Have you not heard anything further from the French police, from Capitaine Jules Lemaitre?"

The two police officers exchanged ominous looks, Mason nodding to the senior man to break the news.

"No, we have not, Miss Walford," the chief inspector said. "But a few minutes ago, I did receive a telephone call from a senior member of M.I.6."

"The Secret Intelligence Service?" the young woman asked, in disbelief. "How can they possibly be involved?"

George Mason cleared his throat and said:

"You were not aware, evidently, that your half-sister did undercover work for M.I.6 while she was living in Paris?"

"And how would this young woman be aware of something like that?" Harrington impatiently interposed. "Intelligence work, by its very nature, is hush-hush."

The visitor merely looked back at him in amazement, tinged with concern.

"I am afraid there is negative news," Harrington then said sympathetically, as Mason placed his arm on her shoulder to lend moral support.

"You are telling me that Maxine is dead," Faye said, anticipating him.

"A body was recently recovered from a marshy area screened by pinewoods bordering the seafront at Nice. It was so decomposed as to be unrecognizable, but viable DNA was extracted from a molar. It matched that recovered from one of the wine glasses at Les Palmiers. There were also traces of ricin in the stomach."

Faye Walford bowed her head, fighting back tears. Quickly composing herself, she said: "I think I always suspected as much, ever since we made that trip to the Cote d'Azur."

She glanced wistfully up at George Mason, for confirmation.

"I did try to be as realistic as possible," he said, "to prepare you in advance for a tragic outcome."

"Are you absolutely certain about the DNA match?" she asked, as her final throw. "Are such tests one hundred per cent reliable?"

"According to the forensic laboratory just outside Nice," Harrington explained, "the profiles are identical. The amount of DNA recovered from the wine glass was minimal, but even small amounts can yield useful results. And each person's profile is unique, as is his fingerprints."

"The French also have a DNA profile of

her suspected killer," Mason added, "from the second wine glass."

"But, of course, you have no idea who that person might be?" Faye cynically remarked, yet with a hint of expectation in her voice.

"Ah, but we do," Mason confidently announced. "Her real name is Roslinda Kramer. She is a former Stasi agent, widowed and living somewhere in England, as far as we know."

"The Stasi being the former East German secret police," Harrington explained to her, "who quietly disbanded after the fall of the Berlin Wall and merged into normal civilian life."

"After shredding most of their files," Mason wryly added.

"It sounds to me like there may have been some political motivation behind all this," Faye thoughtfully suggested. "But how could that be, if the two Germanys are now reunited?"

The two officers exchanged baffled looks; they had no ready answers.

"That is something M.I.6 is working on," the chief inspector explained. "They will keep us abreast of any developments."

"But you are no nearer to establishing the whereabouts of the killer, are you?" their visitor remarked.

"I am now engaged full-time on the case." George Mason assured her.

"Interestingly enough," Harrington added, "Kramer is also being sought by the German police, by the so-called Kripo, in connection with the blackmail of a U.S. Army colonel.

"She was at one time employed as a hostess at a night club in the city of Wetzlar," Mason explained, "which was often visited by American servicemen."

"What do you propose to do now," Faye Walford challenged, "to bring her to justice? She is presumably going about freely, as a guest of Her Majesty the Queen, enjoying all the benefits of a British subject."

"We have several ongoing lines of enquiry," Mason replied, with a show of optimism. "Kramer, if she is going by her real name, has recently sent flowers to her mother at a care home in North Wales. The salesgirl at Green Fingers, Chester has undertaken to note the time and date of any similar orders made in the future. She will pass the information along to us."

"And we have circulated a Wanted poster to every police station in Britain," Bill Harrington added. "It shows a good likeness of the woman, captured by a commercial photographer as she happened to glance through a ground-floor window at St. Dunstan's School."

"Then let us hope somebody recognizes her and turns her in," Faye said, with feeling, as she rose from her chair. "And now I have to explain all this to her son, studying at Maine University."

"You have my deepest sympathies, Miss Walford," Harrington said. "The French authorities would normally dispose of Maxine's remains, unless you have other preferences."

The young woman glanced down and thought about that for a few moments, before saying:

"I think it is probably better, Chief Inspector, all things considered, for the French to deal with that. I shall arrange for a memorial service at our local church in Knutsford, after speaking with Marcus."

"That is probably a wise decision, Faye," Mason added, "and rest assured that we shall catch up with her killer sooner or later and bring her to justice."

Their visitor seemed willing to accept the detective's reassurance for the time being.

"My train north leaves Euston Station within the hour," she said, with a heavy sigh. "I must really be getting a move on."

"I am going in that direction myself," Mason said, thinking he could offer her some small degree of comfort on the way. "I could accompany you as far as Euston Square."

Faye seemed pleased at the suggestion, bidding good-bye to Bill Harrington. The pair left the building together, stepping briskly across Broadway to avoid the busy traffic.

"Now, how do we reach Euston?" she asked, frowning at the complex route map in Westminster Underground entrance.

"We take the eastbound Circle Line to St. Pancras," the detective explained. "We then switch to the Northern Line, for just one stop."

"It is really quite amazing," she remarked, as the train sped beneath the Thames embankment towards Blackfriars, "how little you really know about your own kin."

"You mean you had no inkling about Maxine's involvement in M.I.6?"

Faye shook her head, emphatically.

"Frankly," she replied, "that is just about the last thing I would ever have suspected."

*

Roslinda Kramer took a bus that morning to the outskirts of Dartmouth, to visit the branch of Wessex Bank where she and Ralph Markland had opened a joint savings account prior to their coming union at a civil ceremony at the Registry Office. To celebrate their forthcoming marriage, they had recently driven down to Penzance in neighboring Cornwall to board the *Scillonian* for a three-hour sail through choppy seas to the Isles of Scilly. As the bus made slow progress through the busy town center on account of market day, she reminisced with pleasure on the highlights of that trip. It had been a real eye-opener to her to visit this group of subtropical islands off the south-west coast of England. They had spent most of their three days there island-hopping by boat, wandering at leisure round the famous Abbey Gardens on Tresco and at Carreg Dhu on St. Mary's, with frequent visits to isolated sandy beaches.

Evenings were spent at outdoor restaurants, sipping wine and enjoying fine seafood as they watched the yachts tacking across the bay and the ocean liners leaving the English Channel on their way through the notoriously choppy Bay of Biscay for late-season Mediterranean cruises. Ralph had been most attentive, with all the aplomb of an English gentleman and naval officer. He had an intimate knowledge of the islands from previous visits. It seemed almost a pity to bring such a promising relationship to an abrupt end, but his departure yesterday for what he had described as a reunion dinner at the Royal Services Club in London's Maida Vale presented the perfect opportunity. She would withdraw the balance of the joint account and return to her apartment to finish packing her few belongings, having given advance notice to terminate the lease. A Green Line bus would then take her as far as Bristol, where she would transfer to the National Express service to Caernarvon, North Wales.

The teller regarded her with disbelief,

when she presented a withdrawal slip for 100,000 pounds on arrival at the bank.

"Commander Markland was here only yesterday morning, the minute we opened," the young clerk explained. "He withdrew 95,000 pounds, leaving a balance of just five thousand."

Roslinda Kramer felt on the point of collapse, steadying herself by firmly gripping the edge of the service counter.

"You can't be serious," she said, inwardly gutted.

"I assure you that is the current state of your joint account," the teller replied. "Commander Markland explained that he needed the sum to pay off a loan he had taken out at our Torquay branch, farther up the coast. The original reason for the loan, I believe, was for a deposit on a bungalow at Blackpool Sands, just down the coast from here."

"It must be a misunderstanding," Roslinda said, laughing nervously while putting on a brave face in order not to arouse the teller's suspicions that something might be amiss.

Biting her lip, she quickly made out a new withdrawal slip for the balance, thinking that at least the cad had not left her completely penniless. A nice gentlemanly touch, she mused, with the devastating awareness that she had unwittingly fallen victim to her own game. Small wonder he was in favor of joint accounts. He had evidently needed to withdraw funds from the Torquay branch of Wessex Bank to match her deposit into the new joint account, so that they would start out on an equal footing. As a retired naval officer, his bogus reason for the loan would not have been questioned and he would readily have been given a large line of credit. He could now repay his loan at Torquay and retain the balance of the hundred grand, all of which was her money down to the last penny. She would never see Commander Ralph Markland, R.N. Retd again, she was sure of that, and felt almost inclined to contact the police, so profound was her disgust.

"You are closing the account so soon?" the teller asked, in some surprise.

"We are leaving the area," Roslinda coldly replied.

"Very well, madam, if that is what you wish."

He counted out five thousand pounds in large-denomination bills and handed them across the counter, watching as she tucked them securely into her purse.

"Have a nice day," he bade her, as she turned to leave.

Once outside the bank, she nearly collapsed again, but managed to make her way to a nearby café, where she ordered strong coffee to steady her nerves. She reviewed her situation. It was not too rosy. The amount of money she now had in her purse would last a few months at most. After that, she would have no dependable source of income. Sipping the coffee slowly at the sidewalk table, she watched the training vessel from the Royal Naval College slip down the River Dart towards the sea. The uniformed cadets lining the deck waved to her, but she did not respond; she had had her fill of the British Navy. If Ralph Markland had been a bona fide commander in it, then she was Mata Hari.

By degrees, a plan of action formed in her fertile mind. She would return to her apartment and compose an urgent letter to Margit Breuer, giving as her return address the Lleyn Hotel, Caernarvon. Margit had been like a mother to her during the time she had spent at the night club. She would be sure to have useful advice for an alien in English society, for someone who could claim no welfare benefits or public assistance of any kind and who could never, in any circumstances, complain to the authorities. She would then complete her packing and leave for North Wales, to arrive by nightfall. Tomorrow, she would make the short trip along the coast to Llandudno, to pay a visit to Valley Care Home. The matron there had never met her, and she could pose as someone vetting the establishment for a relative seeking institutional care. Under no circumstances would she reveal her true name.

If she were to arrive shortly after lunch and expressed a wish to view the residents' amenities, she could be pretty sure of catching a glimpse of her mother, either dozing in an armchair or doing her knitting. Gertrude would not recognize her, of course, but at least she would have the satisfaction of seeing her mother again, and of knowing that she was well-cared-for. That meant a great deal to the former Stasi agent, who recalled with deep gratitude the sacrifices her mother had made during the early years of the Communist regime, when her father had spent long periods away from home on military service.

Finishing her drink, she returned on foot to her apartment. It was a fine day and the exercise would help relieve the stress and tension that had built up over her visit to the bank. Nor was she completely destitute, she reflected. She still had 90,000 Swiss francs, roughly equivalent to 35,000 British pounds, stashed in an account away from the taxman's prying eyes, at Bank Irmgold in Zurich. It represented the proceeds of her blackmail activities against American servicemen over a period of years. A problem there was that it was mainly in the form of four-year investment bonds which would not mature until 1995. Withdrawing them now would incur financial penalties, as well as a costly trip to Switzerland. If, with Margit's help, she could successfully negotiate the next few years, she would be home and dry. Perhaps she would rent a small cottage on one of the less-frequented Isles of Scilly, with its bracing sea air, palm trees and subtropical gardens. If she had gained anything of worth from her brief acquaintance with the contemptible, self-styled Commander Ralph Markland, it had been her introduction to this remote and idyllic outpost of the British Isles.

*

Ralph Markland, for his part, had left Dartmouth early the previous day and driven to Torquay to return his rented Audi to the Hertz agency, and to pay off the loan he had taken out at Wessex Bank, explaining to the manager that the property deal at Blackpool Sands had fallen through. He paid a fortnight's rent to his landlady in lieu of notice, packed his few belongings - he was used to living out of a suitcase - and took a taxi to Torquay Station, where he caught the late-morning express to London. When in the capital, he invariably stayed at his sister's place at Herne Hill. Mildred was a few years younger than he, but already a widow, with two married daughters living not very far away in Dulwich. She thus had ample room in her small terraced house in a quiet cul-de-sac and was always glad when her elder brother turned up after one of his mysterious escapades. She had no idea of how he made his money and never asked, accepting at face value his claim that business interests involved him in frequent travel. He was also generous, contributing handsomely towards his keep when in residence and assisting her with property taxes and other running expenses that her state pension was hard put to meet.

When the train pulled in alongside the platform, Ralph Markland had hopped aboard, congratulating himself over his successful venture in the West Country. When he failed to show up within the next few days, Roslinda would almost certainly call at Wessex Bank to check the balance of their joint account. What a shock was in store for her, he mused, feeling rather pleased with himself at leaving a modest balance to provide for her immediate future. He felt he owed her something in exchange for the genuinely enjoyable time they had spent in Dartmouth and Highcliffe and on their brief trip to the Scillies. He had no doubts that, being still relatively young, she would find gainful employment in the service industries of the Devon and Cornish Rivieras. But would she contact the police? That was a calculated risk on his part. He was inclined to think not, on the grounds that she would be too embarrassed by the whole episode. The fact that she was quite possibly a recent immigrant might also deter her, from lack of familiarity with the way things worked and how to deal with British officialdom. Not everyone had confidence in the authorities; some individuals even had things to hide.

When his train eventually reached Paddington Station, he took a London Transport bus service to Herne Hill, pleasantly surprising his sister by his unannounced arrival. She was about to pay a visit to her elder daughter, Rachel, inviting her brother to accompany her. Markland used the opportunity to add his ill-gotten gains to his deposit account at the local branch of Westminster Bank, a short walk from his niece's village home. He then browsed through the bookshops for a while, before joining his folks for afternoon tea, regaling them, as they enjoyed freshly-baked scones with strawberry jam and Devon cream, with an account of his trip to the Isles of Scilly. He made no mention, however, of his brief association with someone he viewed as a recent immigrant from Germany. On eventually returning to Herne Hill, Mildred prepared a late dinner of broiled fish. They filled out the evening watching an Inspector Morse mystery on television.

The following morning, after a leisurely breakfast reading the London *Times*, he selected a dark-blue blazer, service tie and light-gray trousers from the wardrobe he kept permanently at Herne Hill, so that he could travel with minimum luggage. He dressed with typical care, bade Mildred good-bye and took the bus outside the post office to Maida Vale. On arrival there, he strolled down the high street towards the premises of Royal Services Club, which he had not visited since the New Year celebrations. These random visits were an essential part of his guise as a naval officer, a Walter Mitty-esque role he enjoyed acting out and one which invariably brought him success with the fair sex, always well-represented at club functions. It also compensated him to some extent for the rejection on medical grounds of his application for a naval commission decades ago. An expert forger in Bethnal Green had produced a membership card for him, whose validity no official at the club had so far questioned. So it was with his habitual cockiness that he strode through the portal, to be confronted by a senior official flanked by an armed marine.

"I.D." the official curtly requested.

Markland complied, producing his membership card with a fairly recent photograph and handing it over. The marine looked straight ahead, with a fixed stare, while the official did a quick computer check.

"Please step into the adjoining room, Mr Markland," the latter said, after several rather tense moments, nodding towards the marine to accompany them.

With an uneasy feeling, the bogus commander did as he was bid. As the door closed firmly behind them, the club official rang Scotland Yard.

"Royal Services Club, Maida Vale," he said, on making contact. "We are conducting a spot check all this week on club members, as part of a security drive."

"I shall put you through to Chief Inspector Harrington," the operator said. "That will be his province."

"Harrington," the chief inspector soon boomed down the line.

"Good day, Chief Inspector," the official said, quickly repeating his message.

"You are concerned that the club may be a target for extremists?" Harrington enquired.

"We have to take strict precautions," the other replied, "in view of attacks recently made against service personnel. We have here a visitor who claims to be Commander Ralph Markland, R.N. Retd. We have, in fact, no match for the name on our recently-installed and updated computer file of naval officers, current and retired. He did, however, present what appears to be a valid membership card."

"Interesting," Bill Harrington remarked. "Are you now catching up with modern technology?"

"Not before time," the official wryly conceded. "A retired quartermaster, Geoffrey Parsons, had been operating a card index system for the last several years. The part-time work helped boost his service pension, so we decided to wait until he called it a day - last Easter, in fact - before modernizing our systems."

"It may be a good idea to interview this Commander Markland here at the Yard," the chief inspector then said.

"I have placed him under guard, temporarily," the official said. "How soon can your people get over here?"

"Maida Vale is Detective Sergeant Clifford's beat," came the reply. "I shall get him to drop by straight away."

"We should be much obliged for your help in clearing up this matter, Chief Inspector."

"No problem," Bill Harrington replied, replacing the receiver and filling his briar pipe.

CHAPTER 9

On the following Saturday, George Mason took the train northwards, as Faye Walford had done two days earlier. He departed from King's Cross on the old north-eastern line, one of whose locomotives, *Mallard*, held the world record for steam. He could picture its streamlined contours designed to cut wind resistance, as the modern and far less romantic diesel engine pulled slowly out of the station and gathered speed through the north London suburbs. On his mind were Faye Walford and her half-sister Maxine, following the new piece of information that the latter had been an agent of M.I.6. It suggested another possible motive for Maxine's murder, something linked to the shadow world of espionage, not that the intelligence services would volunteer any helpful insights on that score. They guarded their activities closely, and rightly so. It would be up to him, George Mason, to find out what he could using his own resources.

Switching trains at Leeds Central, he arrived at Skipton in good time to help his mother celebrate her birthday over dinner at their favorite inn, The Dalesman, where he had also booked a room for the night. Early the following morning, he set out by cross-country bus for the Pennine village of Dovestones, to pay a second visit to St. Dunstan's School. The Brothers, alerted to his trip northwards by telephone the previous Friday, were expecting him and had cordially invited him to lunch. After a brisk walk along the tree-lined avenue leading out of the village, the intrepid detective rang the bell beside the solid oaken door shortly before noon. Brother Austin, the principal, answered it.

"Good to see you again, Inspector," he said, warmly shaking his visitor's hand and leading the way to his private office. "Had a good trip?"

"The local bus service is a little trying," Mason replied. "It must have stopped at every town, village and post office between here and Skipton."

"I know, I know," Austin sympathetically agreed. "The pace of life up here is much slower than in the metropolis. You have to make allowances for it."

The good Brother, Mason reflected, might well use such transport as a form of penance, in addition to the fastings and hair shirts he thought monks were accustomed to wear. But he kept such musings to himself. An older member of the teaching order, whom the detective had not met before, was already seated in the principal's office when he entered it. The stranger rose to greet him.

"May I introduce Brother Visitor Aelred?" Austin said. "Aelred, this is Inspector Mason, from Scotland Yard."

The two men shook hands, to complete the formalities.

"We are very pleased you could drop by, Inspector," Aelred said, affably.

"Brother Visitor and I were hoping you could bring us up-to-date on the progress of your enquiries," Austin said. "But first, let me offer you a drop of sherry as an appetizer before lunch."

The visitor offered no objections to that, recalling now that the senior man present had been the one who had originally recommended Maxine Walford for the position of bursar. Bill Harrington had already met him, when the Visitor had called at Scotland Yard.

"A most unfortunate business," Brother Aelred remarked, as the seated trio nursed hand-cut crystal glasses filled with Harvey's Bristol Cream.

"You may not have heard the latest development," the detective said, "regarding Maxine Walford, the person you originally engaged as bursar after meeting her on the

Eurostar."

The two monks looked expectantly towards him, waiting for him to elaborate.

"I trust that she is safe and well," Aelred said with feeling, even as the expression on Mason's face told him otherwise.

"It has now been confirmed," Mason said gravely, without mentioning M.I.6, "that Maxine Walford is dead. Her body was recovered from a marshy area close to the main beach at Nice. DNA tests have confirmed her identity as the owner of a timeshare at Les Palmiers."

"This is truly appalling," the Visitor said, wringing his bony, ascetic hands. "Are you quite certain of this?"

"The French police team, led by Capitaine Jules Lemaitre, seem quite confident of their findings," Mason said. "It is up to us here in England to hunt down the murder suspect."

"You are referring to that same individual who arrived here in Maxine's stead," Brother Austin said. "Who took all of us in with her cunning and deceit. You would have thought butter would not melt in her mouth."

George Mason nodded in agreement.

"How has Faye Walford taken it?" the Visitor solicitously enquired.

"She is naturally very upset, particularly since she has had to convey this terrible news to Maxine's adopted son, who is currently following a university course in

America."

"Very distressing indeed, Inspector Mason," Aelred said.

"Is there any real prospect of recovering the stolen funds?" the principal asked, after the bad news had sunk in. "We hardly wish to be put in the position of borrowing from the diocese, to complete our building project."

"Or shelve it indefinitely," Aelred added.

"That depends on a number of factors," their visitor said, thoughtfully sipping his sherry.

"You have to track down the criminal first, obviously?" Aelred said.

"Then we have to determine the disposition of the stolen funds," Mason said. "All of which, I am afraid, may take a considerable amount of time."

"Looks like we shall have to apply to the diocese after all," Brother Austin said, resignedly, "if we are to be anywhere near ready for the increased pupil intake in September."

"There must be a good chance," George Mason said, encouragingly, "that we shall recover the money, or at least a good part of it, once we have located the culprit."

"Let us fervently hope so," Brother Visitor Aelred said.

As the loud school bell signaled the hour of noon, the vice-principal, Brother Clement, knocked and put his head round the office door, acknowledging the detective's presence with a friendly nod.

"Have three places set for lunch in the guest room," Brother Austin instructed him.

"I shall attend to it at once, Brother Principal," Clement replied.

"And be so good, Brother Clement, as to supervise the boys in the main refectory," Austin added, "so that we three can enjoy a degree of peace and quiet."

"The pupils are permitted to talk during weekend meals," the Visitor explained to George Mason. "And they make quite a din, I can tell you. On school days, by contrast, it is our custom to take the meals in silence, accompanied by readings from well-chosen books."

Mason smiled at that remark. Boys will be boys, he mused, whether at an East London comprehensive school or at an exclusive boarding school like this, which would be comparable in its own way to Eton or Harrow.

"Something I have to show you," the principal remarked to him, leading the way out of his office and down the short corridor to the comfortable guest room. He waited until the trio were seated at table, beneath a large framed portrait of the order's medieval founder, before handing the detective a printed slip of paper. George Mason studied it carefully and was about to comment when he was forestalled by his host making the sign of the cross and launching into Grace before Meals.

"This is a fairly recent statement of account," George Mason said, as soon as the blessing was concluded, "from a bank at Zurich. It gives a client number, but no name, to preserve privacy."

"We thought it was some kind of financial statement," the unworldly Brother Austin said.

"And I think I can guess who it was intended for," Mason said.

"You can actually come up with a name?" the intrigued principal asked, as he commenced ladling a thin-looking vegetable soup into small porcelain bowls.

"I haven't been entirely idle," Mason pointedly remarked, "in the course of the last few weeks. Your bogus bursar is, in fact, a German national suspected of blackmail in her own country. Her name is Roslinda Kramer, presumed by the Kriminal Polizei at Wetzlar to have drowned in a yachting accident off the island of Sylt. We have reason to believe, however, that she faked her death and subsequently struck up an acquaintance with Maxine Walford at Nice. Having disposed of your intended bursar, she assumed her identity, with the aim of establishing for herself under a new identity in this country."

He did not elaborate on the rider he had privately been considering, that Maxine's death might also have had some connection with her undercover work for M.I.6.

"Our new bursar, just recently hired," Austin said, "found the document in her room. It had fallen down the back of a drawer. Presumably, this Ms. Kramer, as you call her, overlooked it in her hurry to quit these premises."

"It indicates a deposit of 90,000 francs," the detective explained, "in what seems to be a private Swiss institution, Bank Irmgold. Whether you could recover part of your stolen monies from it, given Switzerland's strict laws on banking secrecy, remains to be seen."

"Let us fervently hope that might prove to be the case," the Visitor said, addressing his now lukewarm soup with good appetite.

"Amen to that," Brother Austin said.

The soup was followed by roast fowl with garden vegetables, accompanied by a single glass of Valpolicella. Conversation turned on more general themes, on the autumn weather and on the season's prospects for Blackburn Rovers, the local soccer team, which was keenly supported by the staff at St. Dunstan's, Austin and Clement attending most of the home games, teaching duties and monastic routine permitting. As they were finishing a typical school dessert of stewed prunes and semolina, accompanied by milky tea, the principal suddenly said:

"We hope, Inspector, that you are in no

particular hurry to be on your way? You did say that you came north on a private visit."

George Mason suspended the last spoonful of semolina in mid-air, as he awaited further explanation, noting a certain twinkle in Brother Austin's eye.

"Brother Austin is referring to the Senior Art Competition," Aelred said, "which is to be adjudicated this afternoon, promptly at two o'clock."

"And we should be most grateful, Inspector," the principal added, "if you would consent to act as adjudicator."

George Mason felt an inner panic. What on earth did he know about modern art? His personal tastes had progressed no further than the Impressionists. Yet, having just been the beneficiary of the Brothers' hospitality, he did not see how he could possibly refuse. He swallowed the last mouthful of dessert and sipped his orange pekoe tea, as he considered the proposal.

"It would only take up a few minutes of your time," Austin explained, noting his hesitation. "But it would mean a great deal to us to have a complete outsider with an educated taste and an impartial point of view."

"Usually," Brother Visitor explained, "the school invites the bishop's secretary, Monsignor Hugh Delargy, to do the honors. But the good man, I am afraid, is currently indisposed with a bout of flu."

"It is doing the rounds," the detective sympathized. "Several of my colleagues at the Yard have gone down with it."

"Then that is settled," the principal announced, checking his watch. "It is now 1.15 p.m. If you would like some fresh air meanwhile, Inspector, you might care to take a stroll through our extensive gardens behind the school."

"We shall meet you back in the school hall at 1.40 p.m.," Brother Aelred suggested, "so that you can preview the paintings before the senior boys assemble. Brother Austin and I, in company with the other members of our community, will be in the chapel meanwhile reciting the midday office."

George Mason took the hint that they needed time for their spiritual exercises. He rose from the dining table and found his own way, by means of meandering passages, out of the rear door of the building. A rambling garden opened before him, with sunken paths, rather unkempt flower beds and trellises overhung with climbing roses, clematis and hydrangea vines. Beyond that, goal posts indicated playing fields for both soccer and rugby, before the landscape beyond them merged into the wooded hills farther north, the dim silhouette of the Cumbrian Mountains completing the skyline. How beautiful the northcountry was, he mused, and how far removed from the bustle and strife of the metropolis. An ideal setting for an education in the round, he considered, as he found a wooden bench to sit on while he smoked a small Dutch cigar out of sight of the pupils noisily letting off steam in the playground. At the appointed time, he retraced his steps back indoors, to fulfill the unusual task the Brothers had cavalierly assigned him. It could only be a matter of personal preference, after all, he reflected. He was no expert and would select the three paintings that appealed most to him, irrespective of the arcane considerations often associated with art shows and competitions. In the event, after admiring the high standard of the entries, he chose a watercolor of Dovestones village for first prize, awarding second and third slots to a still life and a woodland scene, respectively. He then congratulated the winners and made a few encouraging remarks to the assembled pupils, who were much intrigued when the principal introduced him as a senior police officer from Scotland Yard. Brothers Aelred and Austin thanked him profusely afterwards, accompanying him to the main entrance. He cordially took leave of them and strolled back down to the village, basking in his new role of art critic.

*

He had not been long at his desk on Monday morning, having taken the Sunday evening express from Leeds following dinner with his mother, when he received a call from Germany. Oberkommissar Otto Weiss was on the line.

"*Guten Tag, Inspektor*," he began.

"*Guten Morgen*," the detective replied, in his best German. "What can I do for you?"

"I promised to let you know if we turned up anything at our end with regard to Roslinda Kramer," Weiss continued. "It is about her former husband, mainly. Our research department has identified him as a former senior Stasi agent."

"A man-and-wife team," an intrigued George Mason remarked. "Does that not strike you as significant?"

"They had a common commitment to the cause of Communism, that is all," the German officer explained, "but their spheres of activity were poles apart."

"Can you expand on that?"

"The husband, Wolf Breitman, had apparently infiltrated the European Commission's Anti-Fraud Office at Paris."

"The same city where Maxine Walford lived," George Mason noted, thinking it an interesting coincidence.

"Exactly," returned the German. "Breitman had accessed the Pericles Program designed to safeguard against currency counterfeiters. According to the

French authorities, he aimed to flood the market with fake ecus and destabilize the economies of the Common Market."

"Wasn't the ecu the forerunner of the euro?" Mason asked, jogging his memory.

"It was indeed," came the reply. "Up until 1999, when it was replaced by the euro."

"Did Breitman succeed in his objective?" Mason asked.

"There was a full report on the case in the French daily, *Le Monde*, at the time. Wolf Breitman was exposed by a double agent working for both the Stasi and the C.I.A. The C.I.A. may have passed on his name to the French authorities."

"Or the Americans may have passed the information to M.I.6," George Mason said, "in view of the close cooperation they have established since World War 11. And their contact in Paris may well have been Maxine Walford. But we may never know that for certain, since the intelligence services will not reveal the names of operatives, either living or dead."

"Then I suggest you could use it as a working hypothesis, Inspector," Weiss helpfully suggested, "if you think it may assist you in your enquiries."

"It is something to bear in mind, certainly," Mason said. "I imagine the French wasted no time closing in on Breitman."

"They eventually traced him to a rooming

house in a suburb of Marseilles popular with North African immigrants," Otto Weiss explained. "There was a siege of the premises and exchanges of gunfire. It is all here in *Le Monde*. I could fax you the article, if you like."

"No need for that," Mason said, feeling that he had already gotten the salient features of the case. The less paperwork, the better, as a general rule.

"He was shot dead resisting arrest," the oberkommissar remarked, in conclusion. "But there was no mention of a wife at any stage, including at the obsequies."

"Nor would there necessarily be," the detective shrewdly observed, "since Kramer was going by her maiden name. By the way, does Bank Irmgold ring a bell for you?"

"It is a private Swiss bank, I believe," Weiss replied at once. "Of the type used by tax evaders from around the globe, particularly from Germany and France. Tax avoidance is legitimate in Switzerland. You will not get much information out of them."

"Not even with the name of one of their clients?" Mason pointedly asked.

"Go on, Inspector," the intrigued Kripo officer replied. "I'll buy it."

"Roslinda Kramer," Mason announced, with aplomb.

"How on earth did you come across information like that?" the astonished oberkommissar demanded.

"Confidential sources," the detective replied, not wishing to bring the Aurelian Brothers into it, out of respect for their calling and their expressed wish for as low a profile as possible in any police investigation. They also naturally wished to protect the image of St. Dunstan's School.

"Our Federal Tax Office will be most interested to hear about that," Weiss said. "But they may require documentary proof."

"Would a recent numbered bank statement be sufficient?" the detective asked. "When we finally track the suspect down…"

"*If* you do so," the German interrupted. "Bear in mind, Herr Mason, that she is a very resourceful former agent, probably with friends in high places."

"In the event," Mason said, "I shall be most happy to forward this document to your office, as proof of her title to a substantial deposit in Swiss francs. Any funds eventually recovered by your tax people, after appropriate fiscal deductions of course, could go towards compensating the Brothers."

"I think you are moving ahead a little too quickly, Inspector Mason," the other cautioned. "Roslinda Kramer will - how do you say in English? - be a tough…"

"…nut to crack," the Scotland Yard agent said, smiling to himself at the German's attempt at English idiom.

"And I do not suppose you are any nearer to locating her?"

George Mason detected a faint note of skepticism in the oberkommissar's voice, suggesting that the German was privately backing Kramer in a contest of wits.

"At this moment in time," he replied, rather curtly, "I do not even know what name she is going by, let alone her present whereabouts."

"Then I wish you the best of British luck," Weiss replied, now with a strong hint of irony. "We shall keep in touch. *Aufwiederhoren.*"

The moment George Mason replaced the receiver, shrugging off his counterpart's reservations, Bill Harrington called him into his office.

"How are things moving on the Walford case?" he immediately asked.

"Moderately well," his colleague replied.

"Which means no break-through as yet, I suppose," the chief inspector rather caustically remarked.

"We are slowly building up a profile of the suspect," Mason said, as much to bolster his own confidence as to mollify his superior.

"In the meantime," Harrington went on, "see what you can do to assist Detective Sergeant Clifford. He recently apprehended a certain Commander Ralph Markland at Maida Vale. The Royal Services Club he

173

was aiming to enter have no record of him on their newly-computerized files."

"You mean Markland could be an impostor?" George Mason suggested.

"That is for you to establish, Inspector," came the reply.

"Where is he now?"

"In temporary custody at Mile End police station, under the Anti-Terrorism Act," his senior replied. "We can hold him without charge for twenty-one days."

CHAPTER 10

Roslinda Kramer was moderately enjoying her stay at the Lleyn Hotel, Caernarvon, if more than a little anxious about her dicey financial situation. The hotel was typically Welsh, with heavy traditional furniture in the public rooms and tapestries depicting scenes from the life of Owen Glendowr, the medieval nationalist, on the walls. The restaurant served local dishes, among which she had especially enjoyed brook trout stuffed with seaweed and the English white wine that accompanied it. She had not thought of England as a wine-producing country, yet the hotel's offerings in that area compared favorably to a good Mosel. To occupy her time, she took long walks along the seafront, in the teeth of strong autumn winds gusting in over the bay, whipping up the waves. She also visited the famous castle built by Edward 1 in 1330 A.D. to subdue the Welsh, and had already taken the bus to Llandudno to call at Valley

Care Home. How touched, as well as reassured, she had been to observe her mother sitting in an armchair by the bay window. Unobserved by the matron, she had engaged her in conversation, painfully aware that Gertrude did not recognize her, and had asked her what she was knitting. She learned that it was a Welsh shawl. In a little while, when she felt on a more even keel, she would send more flowers, those lovely white peonies that were her mother's favorites.

The letter she had been expecting from Margit Breuer arrived on the Wednesday morning. Its contents left her with mixed feelings, but at least it seemed to offer a way forward. She read it again as she poured herself a third cup of coffee in the charming, old-world restaurant, after most of the hotel's late-season guests had finished their breakfast and ventured outdoors. Margit advised her to go as soon as possible to Portsmouth, a key naval base on the south coast. Once there, she was to present herself at The Gull's Nest, a social club frequented by naval personnel. The proprietor, Quentin James, would be expecting her and would offer her a job as hostess. Within days of taking up her new post, she would be contacted by a Russian agent, Boris Lyadov, who would explain to her the sort of information she should try to gather. Refolding the letter, she smiled ironically to herself at the thought of returning to her old way of life, when she had confidently considered that was all in the past. She realized, of course, that she had no realistic alternative. A regular salary would be paid by the club and extra amounts would follow from Lyadov, depending on the value of the information she was able to provide.

Finishing her coffee, she left the hotel and walked to the town center to enquire at National Express the times of bus services to Portsmouth. There was only one service each day, leaving Caernarvon at 9.05 a.m., via Bristol. It had left an hour ago, but she was not averse to spending another day in this charming coastal resort. The sea air was helping restore her poise from the setback she had received at the hands of that bogus naval commander, a shock compounded by the awareness of having been beaten at her own game. She thought she would spend most of the day visiting the famous Bodnant Gardens she had passed on the way to Llandudno. She would pack her suitcases on her return and enjoy a leisurely dinner in the hotel restaurant. She would then watch the television news in her room, in case there were any developments in the Walford case, especially any indications that the police had developed useful leads. She would have an early night, in order to be up at first light for the early breakfast sitting. Afterwards, she would take a taxi to the bus station and would soon be on her way to a new life at Portsmouth. Or was it her old life?

It was of little surprise to her that she was to be handled by a Russian agent. While still working for the Stasi, she had often heard rumors that the Russians, even in the twilight of the Communist era, were planting increasing numbers of spies in America and Western Europe, rumors that were routinely denied by Moscow. But her understanding had been that they were mainly after industrial secrets, particularly those new technologies that gave the advanced democracies a distinct edge in the international trading arena. No doubt that interest also extended to the latest military technology and the latest spyware. For cover, Boris Lyadov probably held a senior post in some unrelated business such as oil exploration, renewable energy or the rare earth metals so much in demand for modern technologies.

*

Around the time Roslinda Kramer was boarding the bus to Bristol, Inspector George Mason and Sergeant Owen Clifford arrived at Mile End police station to confront Ralph Markland, who was led out of his cell to an interview room accompanied by a woman constable. He wore a look of aggrieved innocence.

"What was your objective," Mason asked, "in attempting to gain entry into Royal Services Club?"

"I showed valid ID," came the adamant reply.

"The Royal Navy has no record of a Ralph Markland," the detective wryly remarked, "either as a rating, a commander or an Admiral."

The interviewee shifted his feet nervously, averting his gaze.

"It will save us both a lot of time if you come clean," Mason continued. "You have no valid standing at Royal Services Club, so what was your purpose in attempting to gain access to it?"

"I have always enjoyed associating with military personnel," a chastened Ralph Markland replied, sensing the game was up.

"Do you have connections to any group whose activities may threaten the security of the United Kingdom?" Mason pointedly asked.

The bogus commander returned a wry smile.

"If you are referring to terrorist organizations," he replied, "you are barking up the wrong tree, Inspector. Nobody could be a more loyal subject of Her Majesty the Queen than I."

"What evidence can you offer in support of that claim?" his skeptical questioner asked.

"My unblemished service record from 1943 onwards."

George Mason turned to Owen Clifford.

"Does that square with your check on his background, Sergeant?" he asked.

The junior officer quickly consulted his notes.

"The subject enlisted at the age of eighteen as a private in East Sussex Light Infantry. That was in March, 1943," he explained. "Fourteen months later, he was recommended by his commanding officer for promotion to Lance Corporal and honorably discharged in 1948."

George Mason nodded appreciatively, looking directly at Markland.

"You served your country well," he said, "over a period of several years. That is a mark in your favor and I commend you for it."

Ralph Markland returned a self-satisfied smile. There was no way, he felt, that they could now charge him under the Anti-Terrorism Act, which he assumed had been the reason for his arrest.

"But your subsequent career has not been so admirable, has it?" Mason quickly pointed out.

Markland's face dropped. He now wondered if they really had something on him, or whether they were bluffing. Owen Clifford soon put his mind to rest on that score.

"It appears, Mr. Markland," he said, "that you were already on police files prior to your recent escapade in Maida Vale."

He passed a police photograph across the desk.

"In 1985, you were charged at the Old Bailey," Clifford continued, "with fraudulent deception and the theft of twenty thousand pounds from a joint bank account you shared with a woman named Constance Fleet."

A crestfallen Ralph Markland shifted position uneasily and fidgeted with his tie, but made no reply.

"You were released on bail before sentencing," the sergeant reminded him. "But you jumped bail and disappeared off the radar. Until, that is, your abortive attempt to gain entry into Royal Services Club. Do you deny any of this?"

The subject glowered back at the police officers, saying nothing.

"Of course, you have the right to remain silent," Clifford then said, "and to retain legal counsel, if you so wish."

"But if you cooperate fully with the authorities," Mason interposed, "it will probably go easier for you in court. You already have the Fleet case hanging over you. Skipping bail, may I remind you, is a very serious offence in itself."

Ralph Markland weighed the detective's

remarks carefully, helping himself to a glass of water from the flask provided. He was in a bind and he knew it, but he calculated that at least there should be no record in Britain of the time he spent in Canada during the nineteen-seventies. He had used the alias Lionel Trevelyan, based on his mother's Cornish surname.

"Is there anything else you wish to tell us?" Mason prodded, noting the more cooperative expression on the other's face.

Markland deliberated with himself for a few more moments. It was probably only a matter of time, he considered, before the police became aware of certain recent events in Devonshire. It would be in his interest to come clean about it all, while revealing nothing of his dubious activities in Toronto and Vancouver.

"In addition to Constance Fleet," he reluctantly replied, "there is a certain Roslinda Kramer, of Dartmouth."

George Mason sprang to his feet at mention of that name.

"Could you repeat that for me?" he asked, in considerable astonishment.

"K-r-a-m-e-r," the bogus commander spelled out. "Forename Roslinda "

The detective paced the room, quite beside himself at this unexpected breakthrough in the Walford case. That was how police work often proceeded, he was well-aware, through links between seemingly unconnected events.

"It seems you have been making a lucrative career out of preying on women, Mr. Markland," he remarked, regaining his seat. "In short, you are an unscrupulous conman."

Ralph Markland cast his eyes downwards, but made no response. It was humiliating to admit to himself that his interrogator had put things in a nutshell. He was not particularly proud of his record, yet his lack of qualifications had debarred him after military service from entry into a well-paid profession. He could not support his taste for the high life in any menial occupation and had chosen to live outside the law, trusting to his wits to escape exposure. Now the game was up, and he well knew it.

"How did you meet this Roslinda Kramer?" a much-intrigued George Mason asked.

"I placed a notice in the personal columns of *The Lady*," the other replied. "She was among the dozen or so single women who responded. We arranged a meeting, had dinner together and things seemed to move forward quickly from there."

"You established that she was a woman of substantial means," he prompted, "and cultivated a close relationship, before taking her to the cleaners?"

The conman slowly nodded.

"Describe her to us."

Ralph Markland leaned back in his chair and pictured his recent victim, a whimsical smile playing about his lips as scenes from their brief association came to mind, especially protracted dinners on the Isles of Scilly, in garden restaurants fronting the ocean.

"She was an attractive woman, if with slightly-masculine features," he began, expansively. "She had short blond hair, a full figure and rather heavy eye make-up."

"Approximate age?" Sergeant Clifford asked.

"Mid-forties, I should say," came the prompt reply.

George Mason felt a little puzzled at the unexpected description. He withdrew from his briefcase a copy of the Wanted poster and passed it across the desk to gauge the other's reaction. Markland gasped in surprise.

"Might this person be the Roslinda Kramer you knew?" he asked.

The detainee studied it carefully, puckering his brow.

"Same shape of face," he remarked. "But the eyes and the hair seem quite different. I would say this might be the person I met, but I could not be one hundred per cent sure."

Mason replaced the poster in his briefcase, recalling how Oberkommissar Weiss had described his quarry as a resourceful and cunning individual. It occurred to him that Kramer could have noticed the poster along the high street of almost any town in England and modified her appearance accordingly.

"Is there anything else you can tell us about her?" he asked. "Some tell-tale feature or mannerism?"

Ralph Markland did not wait long to reply.

"She had a German accent," he said, "so slight as to be almost imperceptible."

The detective gave a broad smile of satisfaction. There was now little doubt in his mind that they were discussing the former Stasi agent and not some other person going by the same name.

"What makes you say that?" he asked.

"We were discussing opera over dinner one evening at an inn by the River Dart," Markland explained. "A delightful setting, with excellent cuisine…"

"Skip the periphera," Mason rapped. "Please keep to the point."

"She was commenting on an opera by Richard Straus - *Salome*, I think it was - and she pronounced *ch* as in the Scottish 'loch'. That was a sure giveaway to me."

"So you concluded that she was of mid-European origin and, for that reason, an easier target?"

Ralph Markland glanced downwards, his silence answering for him.

"Do you happen to know her current address?" the detective then asked.

"On our return from the Scillies, where we spent a few days together," Markland replied, "she was residing at a rental apartment in Dartmouth. Number 5, The Lanyards, I believe the address was."

George Mason made a note of it, before saying:

"You will remain in custody, Mr Markland, until formal charges are pressed against you by the Crown Prosecution Service. I shall include in my report, for whatever benefit it may be, that you cooperated fully with our enquiries. Good day to you, and good luck."

The Scotland Yard agents got up to leave as the detainee was led back to his cell.

"What do you make of that, Inspector?" Owen Clifford asked, as they halted momentarily at the traffic lights on Mile End Road on their way back to Westminster.

"The man is a cad of the first order," his colleague remarked. "And he is facing a lengthy prison sentence. But he has also given me, I am fairly certain of it, a valuable lead in the Maxine Walford case."

"So what do you propose to do now?"

"You will see soon enough, Sergeant," came the non-committal reply.

As soon as he arrived back at base, George Mason gave a verbal report of the morning's events to Chief Inspector

Harrington. He then contacted Devonshire C.I.D.

"I want you to put the occupant of 5 The Lanyards, Dartmouth under surveillance, with immediate effect," he instructed. "Report back to me her typical movements during the day and evening, whom she meets and where. I also need as exact a description as possible of her age, appearance and mode of dress."

"Something brewing, Inspector?" enquired Superintendent Walter Breakell, head of Devonshire C.I.D.

"You can stake your pension on it," Mason replied.

"I shall put an experienced woman officer on the case straight away," Breakell promised, knowing full well that Special Branch would offer no further explanation at this stage as to what this was all about. He had had dealings with them before.

George Mason then put a call through to
· the dental practice at Knutsford, where Faye Walford was employed. By good luck, she was taking a brief respite between patients.

"Just wanted to let you know, Faye," he said, "that there has been a breakthrough in Maxine's case."

"Wonderful, Inspector," Faye replied. "I have been hoping against hope for some encouraging news."

"We think we may have traced your half-sister's elusive timeshare guest to a rental apartment at Dartmouth," he explained. "I can't go into details just now, however. Hopefully, I shall have more positive information to relay shortly."

"This is the best news I have heard in weeks," Faye said, with gratitude. "Do keep up the good work, Inspector!"

*

As church bells pealed the noon hour, a youngish woman clad in a dark two-piece suit left the premises of Bank Irmgold on Kellergasse in downtown Zurich and strode briskly towards the Hauptbahnhof, the city's main railway station. She made a brief call at a pharmacy on Limmatquai, a busy thoroughfare running alongside the River Limmat, to buy a couple of personal items, crossed the central tramlines to the embankment and fed the remains of her lunch to the circling gulls. From there, she accessed the escalator that took her beneath the busy tram intersection into the lower-level station concourse. She then purchased a return ticket to Stuttgart and a copy of *Zurcher Zeitung,* the city's main broadsheet, to read in the train, approaching the barrier to Platform 4 five minutes ahead of the Schnellzug's scheduled departure.

Freni Zollweger relaxed in a comfortable window seat, bought a small bottle of mineral water from the refreshment trolley, unzipped her leather document case and drew out a typed list of names she was careful not to let nearby passengers overlook. She soon persuaded herself, once she felt the motion of the train slowly pulling out of the station, that she was justified in taking this course of action. It was her way of getting back at an organization that had, in her view, treated her shabbily after several years of devoted service. She had joined the bank's back-office staff soon after her son Anton had entered elementary school, having obtained her divorce from a Swissair pilot two years previously. Uppermost in her mind now was continuity of education and a settled environment for Anton, following the traumas of the divorce settlement.

She felt she had been with the bank long enough to dig her feet in and resist the transfer they had in mind to a branch at Engadin, where many wealthy foreign clients lived. Had the move been a promotion, she might not have minded so much. In fact, it was a kind of demotion, in accordance with the new chief executive's rationalization plans. Efficiency was all these people cared about, she reflected. The lives and daily needs of their employees were of much less concern. The bottom line was all that really mattered, as well as returns to shareholders in higher dividends and bonuses to senior executives. If Bank

Irmgold could place her on two weeks' notice simply because she had expressed cogent reasons for remaining in Zurich, they would reap the consequences. Acting in complete anonymity, she would sabotage their business and quietly leave, aware that in the current economic climate it would be no simple task to obtain a new position at the same level of compensation. She was counting, however, on a substantial whistle-blower fee.

Sipping her mineral water in a contented frame of mind, as the train sped northwards towards Lake Constance and the German border, she scanned the list of names. They were all German nationals from the highest income strata. It included politicians, businessmen, entertainers and sporting personalities, especially tennis and soccer stars. All held secret deposit accounts at Bank Irmgold and, for all she knew, at other private banks as well. The Tax Buro she was now heading for at Stuttgart would be most interested in these names, and in the measures taken by Bank Irmgold to shield them from public scrutiny. They would quickly pass the information to the Federal Tax Buro at Bonn, who would then begin the long process of recovering the millions of euros owed to them in the form of income taxes evaded over several decades. Freni Zollweger felt, in fact, that she was performing a public service, in view of the

additional welfare amenities the recouped
funds would provide. Replacing the list
inside her case, she took up her newspaper,
smiled blandly at the too-curious elderly
gentleman sitting opposite, and commenced
reading a timely article on equality of
opportunity in the workplace.

CHAPTER 11

Roslinda Kramer arranged her hair, applied dark eye shadow and finished dressing, choosing a sweater and a heavy wool skirt for venturing outside on a blustery November day, to face the strong south-westerly wind blowing in from the English Channel. For the past three weeks, she had lived quite comfortably at this family-run bed & breakfast on Solent Road, which she had located on arrival from Wales. It was quite close to the bus station and just beyond the perimeter of the dockland and naval shipyard. She now felt that it was coming time to look for a place of her own, a small apartment perhaps, a bit farther out in a more genteel residential area. She would visit the real estate agents in the center of Portsmouth, to see what they had on their books and what was affordable, before repairing to The Sea Urchin, a quiet pub near the harbor, for her meeting with Boris Lyadov.

She had been much intrigued, while watching television news in her bed sitting-room on the evening after her arrival, to learn of the arrest of Ralph Markland, on a charge of masquerading as a naval officer to gain entry to Royal Services Club at Maida Vale. According to the news, he was a conman who preyed on gullible women of means, often proposing marriage and voiding their joint bank accounts to finance a high-end life-style, before disappearing from their lives. How gratified she had felt that the bounder had been so speedily exposed, that he could now look forward to a lengthy period behind bars, which was where he undoubtedly belonged. She felt that justice was being served and was still mulling the pros and cons of contacting the police in her role as victim, relying on the fact that they could not possibly recognize her as the individual in the Wanted poster, so artfully had she changed her appearance. Not even Margit Breuer would know her, if she were to step right now inside Die Blaue Kugel.

Proceeding on foot to the main shopping center, she had time to collect fliers from a handful of estate agents and study them briefly over coffee at The Corner House cafe, before deciding it was time to meet her Russian handler. It was a fair distance down to the harbor. She preferred to walk, to save money and take in the sights and sounds of this bustling sea-faring city. Lyadov was expecting her promptly at noon. He would not appreciate being kept waiting.

"My dear Roslinda," he cordially greeted her, as she joined him at their alcove table. "What will you have to drink? Your usual?"

Roslinda nodded and watched his short, slim figure cross to the bar to order her a gin-and-tonic. Russians, she had always imagined, were people of big build, rather bear-like and capable of holding large quantities of vodka. But not this rather puny little man. He ran quite counter to national type, his favorite tipple being English beer.

"How are things going at The Gull's Nest?" he enquired, on regaining his seat. "Is Quentin James treating you well?"

"As well as can be expected, in the circumstances," she rather languidly replied. "It is the hours that are so killing, often till two or three in the morning. I had had my fill of that back home in Wetzlar. But at least he is paying me off the books, with no tax or social insurance deductions. I have therefore no official identity as far as the British authorities are concerned."

"Margit assured me that you were particularly good at your work," Lyadov said, "and that you were able to obtain valuable information for the Stasi."

"I was younger then and idealistic," she

wryly remarked, "working for a cause I believed in. Things are not quite the same after German Reunification. We are all capitalists now."

Her handler sipped the froth off his beer and regarded her curiously, yet not without sympathy.

"Whereas now your sole motivation is money?" he remarked.

Roslinda nodded, unapologetically.

"The Cold War is grinding to an end," Lyadov admitted, in a voice tinged almost with regret. "But that does not mean the end of espionage as we know it. Far from it, Roslinda. Business as usual, in fact."

"Can you expand a little on that?" she asked, much intrigued at the notion.

"What we hope you can come up with for us," he replied, "using your considerable charms, is information on the Vanguard Class nuclear submarines that have recently come into service with the Royal Navy. Even if the information seems insignificant to you, it may be meaningful to us. Of particular interest, I might add, are their scheduled itineraries, range, maximum speed and manpower levels."

"You want me to target the officers," Roslinda cannily observed, "ply them with drinks and pander to their self-image as defenders of the free world?"

"Not just the officers," Boris Lyadov said, with an indulgent smile at her choice of words. "Ratings may be equally forthcoming, if you appear to show due regard for their more subordinate roles. Always approach topics in as roundabout a way as possible, to avoid arousing suspicion."

"You can count on my professionalism and tact for that," she assured him. "But what is the information worth, in terms of hard cash?"

Lyadov took a large swig of ale, smacking his lips in satisfaction. For a man of small stature, he had a surprisingly good capacity for ale.

"I do like English beer," he remarked, emphatically. "It has a fine malty tang to it, far more refreshing than those insipid lagers on sale everywhere today."

"You are evading my question," Roslinda pointedly remarked.

"That is not something I am at liberty to answer," the other replied. "It depends very much on how my superiors assess the value of your information."

"But you could pay me a retainer?"

Lyadov shrugged disarmingly, and broke into a disingenuous smile.

"It is not our practice to do that," he replied. "It is not as if our survival depended on the quality of your intelligence. It is not now a question of war and peace, but of keeping ahead of the game. The main focus of interest in the coming years will undoubtedly be the Middle East. Any information you could come up with on naval maneuvers in the Persian Gulf, for example, would be highly valued by my superiors. I know that for a fact."

"That is a tall order, Boris," Roslinda rejoined. "But if it translates into hard cash…"

"I am sure you will do your utmost," the other said, interrupting her, "to meet our requirements."

"The truth is," she added, "I am almost broke, apart from some modest savings in Switzerland, which are longer-term investments I cannot access at the present time without incurring a penalty. Quentin James pays just enough to cover basic living expenses. I am counting on you to help supplement that."

"One of the older-type submarines is docking here at Portsmouth this very evening," the Russian said. "A whole bunch of submariners of all ranks will be converging on The Gull's Nest later on, to take full advantage of shore leave. A perfect opportunity for you, my dear Roslinda."

The former Stasi agent sat back in her chair and took the first sip of her gin-and-tonic, savoring it slowly as she thought about what she would wear for her debut as hostess that evening. Boris Lyadov, she decided, was not a bad sort, unlike some individuals she had come across in the shadow world. He meant for her to do well, and would doubtless pay adequately for good results. Too bad he would not pay a retainer.

The Russian, having laid things out for her as plainly as he could, quickly drained his glass and rose to his feet.

"The same date and hour next month," he said, conspiratorially. "Meanwhile, the very best of British luck."

Roslinda Kramer raised her eyebrows at that parting remark. Was he being serious, she wondered, or merely ironic?

Left to herself, as she nursed her drink and quietly observed the midday clientele of the pub, her thoughts returned to Maxine Walford. She congratulated herself on having killed two birds with one stone. She had had the British agent in her sights for some time, holding her largely responsible for betraying her husband to the French authorities in Paris. Eliminating her and using her identity to establish herself in England had been a master-stroke. Even if she had been taken for a ride by the dastardly Ralph Markland – the Devil take him - she was still a free agent in a free country, with her future before her, quite possibly in the Isles of Scilly.

*

George Mason was a few minutes late

arriving at his desk that morning, an unusual occurrence that did not escape the notice of Chief Inspector Harrington. He had dropped his wife Adele off at Paddington Station, where she was taking a train to visit an old school friend in Berkshire, and had got caught up in heavy commuter traffic. He glanced apprehensively through the open door of Harrington's office, half expecting some caustic remark, but the latter held his peace. It was approaching the hour of the chief inspector's regular meeting with the superintendent, and he had weightier concerns than time-keeping on his mind.

Mason had not been long at his desk when the telephone rang. It was Oberkommissar Otto Weiss ringing from Wetzlar.

"*Guten Tag, Inspektor,*" he began. "I trust I find you well?"

"Never better, Oberkommissar," the detective replied, having recently completed a health check from the police physician at Harley Street. Even his cholesterol level was down, but he was advised to keep taking his pills.

"An interesting development at our end," Otto Weiss said, cutting to the point of his call.

"Indeed?" Mason replied, expectantly.

"It concerns our mutual friend, Roslinda Kramer."

"I am all ears," the detective said.

"The background is a little complex," the

German officer continued. "It may take a little while to explain."

"Take all the time you want, Oberkommissar," Mason generously allowed. "There is nobody breathing down my neck, not for the moment at any rate."

Otto Weiss cleared his throat audibly and said:

"It seems that a former employee of Bank Irmgold at Zurich has furnished our Federal Tax Buro with a list of names of the bank's confidential clients. They are well-heeled individuals, both male and female, who have been salting their money away for years to avoid federal taxes. It is a matter of millions of euros, Inspector, which our government is determined to recover on behalf of the taxpayers."

"A worthwhile objective," Mason agreed.

"You are aware, Herr Mason, that Kramer has funds on deposit at Bank Irmgold. It was you yourself who informed me of the fact."

"I did indeed," came the reply. "And I still have in my keeping the dividend voucher that turned up at St. Dunstan's School, Dovestones. I can forward it to you, if you wish."

"That would be helpful, Inspector," his German counterpart said, "as corroborative evidence, since her name is included on the whistle-blower's list."

The detective smiled to himself on hearing that.

"That does not surprise me at all, Oberkommissar," he said. "I shall mail the voucher to you today."

"Thank you, Inspector," Otto Weiss said. "But that is not the main reason for my call."

"Which is?" Mason guardedly asked.

"Most of the tax-dodgers are highly-placed individuals in business, political and sporting circles. The authorities here are having little difficulty tracing them, except for those that have moved abroad."

George Mason felt he caught the drift, and shifted uneasily in his chair.

"They have traced Kramer to Wetzlar," Weiss continued. "to the address supplied on her initial application for a Swiss bank account. But, of course, she has long since left this area and was, in fact, presumed drowned. The tax authorities are relying on the Kripo to track her down. Which is where your good self, Inspector, enters the picture."

George Mason could not help admiring the German officer's nerve. Not very long ago, he had been backing Roslinda Kramer against Scotland Yard in any battle of wits, as if members of the Stasi, by dint of training or dedication, were automatically superior to agents of the Metropolitan Police. Now, surprise, surprise, he was asking for the assistance of the C.I.D.

"Sorry to disappoint you, Oberkommissar," he replied. "But, frankly, your guess is as good as mine as to Kramer's present whereabouts."

The stunned silence at the other end of the line lasted several moments.

"But you are Special Branch," Otto Weiss remonstrated. "Surely, in all this time, you have been able to close the gap with your quarry?"

The hint of irony in the other's voice did not escape the detective. Nor did it elude him that what to the Germans was a tax-evasion and blackmailing case, was to Scotland Yard a calculated and cold-blooded murder.

"We recently thought we had nailed her," he admitted, as much to justify his own record as to placate the Kripo agent. "But we missed her by days, after tracing her to an address in Dartmouth, where she had entered into a brief relationship with a self-styled naval officer. He was a conman who cleaned out their joint bank account, so I figure she could be hard-pressed for money and will one day, perhaps quite soon, make a false move."

"You missed her by days, Inspector!" Weiss exclaimed. "So now, you are saying, the scent has grown cold?"

Did George Mason detect that same streak of irony in the other's voice, as if he were still backing the former Stasi agent to outwit Special Branch? Hard to tell with a foreigner like Otto Weiss, whose nuances of speech were more difficult to gauge than a native speaker's. He gave him the benefit of the doubt.

"We are as anxious as you are, Oberkommissar, to recover funds, which in our case are stolen funds, not secret bank accounts," he said. "The money belongs to the Aurelian Brothers, a monastic order of educators. The case is top priority at this office, and it will remain so until we make an arrest."

"Then you have my best wishes for your success," the other said, now without a trace of irony. "And you will no doubt keep me informed of developments?"

"Gladly, Herr Weiss," the detective assured him.

Replacing the receiver, George Mason mulled over the information Walter Breakell had given him. The Devonshire superintendent had sent a woman constable to keep an eye on any activity at 5 The Lanyards, Dartmouth and report back. After two days, having observed no comings and goings, the constable approached the landlord. He informed her that the tenant, who had registered with him as Roslinda Kramer, had given notice to terminate the lease some days before she moved out. In the event, she had left alone and in some haste, without leaving a forwarding address. He had had few dealings with her apart from collecting the rent and did not know whom she associated with, nor her future plans.

That led Mason to suspect that Kramer had laid out her designs some time before her break-up with Ralph Markland, implying that she may have planned a financial deception similar to the one he had perpetrated on her. Markland had, it seemed, beaten her to it. There was a certain poetic justice in that, he reflected, smiling wryly to himself as he turned his attention to the file on the arrested conman. He had not been so occupied more than a few minutes when the telephone rang again. This time, it was Faye Walford on the line.

"Good morning, Inspector," she began. "How are things with you?"

"Busy, as ever," he replied, with mock ennui.

"The last time we spoke, you seemed on the verge of a breakthrough," she continued. "I have been expecting to hear from you almost daily."

George Mason nervously cleared his throat. It was not the most opportune time to give a progress report.

"We succeeded in tracing the suspect to the Dartmouth area," he explained. "But she had already left by the time the Devonshire Police located her address. Missed her by a few days."

"So you are back to square one, Inspector?" Faye remarked, with a strong tinge of disappointment.

"Not entirely," he extemporized. "I am coordinating enquiries with the German police, at a town called Wetzlar in the Sauerland. Too early to say anything definite, but there *have* been significant developments."

What more could he say, he wondered, in the circumstances? The bird had flown, and it was quite possible that his quarry had outsmarted him, as Otto Weiss seemed fully confident that she would.

"The main reason for my call," Faye explained, "is to let you know that we are arranging a memorial service for Maxine at St. Olave's Church, Knutsford."

"And when is that event to take place?" George Mason courteously enquired.

"Mid-January," Faye replied. "just before her son Marcus returns to the University of Maine after the Christmas break. He was of a mind to quit altogether when I broke the news of his mother's death, but I persuaded him to stay on and complete his exchange year, for the sake of his future."

"You did the right thing," the detective said. "That is exactly what Maxine herself would have wished."

"If you are going to be in the North of England around that time, the fifteenth, perhaps visiting your mother again, we should be very pleased if you could attend."

"I shall certainly do my best," he replied, thinking it was the least he could do.

"The choir will be singing some of her favorite hymns, and the vicar, Canon Plimpton, will give the homily."

"Would you like me to read one of the lessons?" Mason offered.

"That is very kind of you, Inspector," she replied. "But I have already made the necessary arrangements. Marcus will read the first lesson and Brother Austin, the principal of St. Dunstan's, has kindly agreed to drive over from Dovestones to attend the service and read the second lesson."

"That is very decent of him," George Mason remarked.

"I think so, too," Faye said. "He thought it would be a nice ecumenical gesture, too, for a Catholic monk to take part in an Anglican Church service."

"Undoubtedly," Mason replied, thinking ecumenism was all the rage these days. "I shall pencil the date in my diary. I am sure I shall be able to find a good excuse to come up north again."

"By which time," Faye said, "I hope you will have more encouraging news."

"I hope so, too!" he rejoined, with feeling.

CHAPTER 12

Roslinda Kramer moved into her new accommodation on December 1st. She had found it through an agency in an older part of the city, where Victorian mansions had been converted into apartments. If the area had a rather seedy aspect, and was not quite as genteel as she would have hoped, it was relieved to some extent by mature poplars growing at intervals along the sidewalks. She had deliberately targeted the most economical rentals available, settling in the end for a small suite with bathroom and kitchenette at the front of the building, from where she could keep an eye on the comings and goings of the other residents of the quiet neighborhood, often seen walking their dogs. She would have liked to own a small dog, mainly for company, but did not feel it practical in her current circumstances. For that, she would wait until she had made her final move to the Isles of Scilly, the ideal destination ever at the back of her mind.

Her job at The Gull's Nest turned out to be much like her previous role at Die Blaue Kugel, except that she was now dealing with British servicemen instead of American. Her new clients were more reserved and generally drank less, apart from the bibulous Scotsmen, whose brogue was music to her ears. She had acquired enough background knowledge about naval affairs from Ralph Markland to converse intelligently, while at the same time trying to slip in an innocent-sounding query about technical matters. So far, no luck at the sort of game Boris Lyadov was expecting her to play. For that, she would need to develop a much closer relationship with one of her clients than mere chit-chat over drinks. Back home, that had been easier, since the Americans were permanently stationed at a base not very far from the club. Whereas here, the mariners and submariners were ashore only a few days at a time, before setting off for far-flung destinations round the globe. Longer-term relationships were therefore problematic.

It was with a sense almost of relief that she received a second letter from Margit Breuer later in the month, informing her that Boris Lyadov had been ordered to leave the United Kingdom by the end of the year, in a tit-for-tat response to the expulsion of a British diplomat from Moscow. That was the way the biscuit broke in east-west relations. Part of the accredited staffs at embassies were engaged in espionage of one form or another, and what might appear on the surface as a straightforward political or commercial mission could have several ulterior objectives. Quite possibly, Boris had long been under surveillance by M.I.5. She wondered if she would ever see him again, or if he would even turn up at their next scheduled meeting. On balance, she thought that was unlikely. But his withdrawal from the scene brought other questions to the forefront of her mind.

Foremost among these were financial considerations. She could no longer fully depend on supplements from the Russians, even in what seemed to her the unlikely event of her providing the sort of key information they required. It was conceivable, of course, that she would eventually be assigned a new handler. But she knew from her years in the Stasi that the wheels of international espionage ground slowly, that it was often a question of priorities. She did not realistically see her role at The Gull's Nest fitting into that category and it may well be months before any new arrangements came into play, assuming she wasn't bypassed completely. Could she wait that long, eking out a bare existence on a hostess's pay? She thought not. It was time, she considered, to pay another visit to the personal columns of *The Lady*, using a pseudonym as a precaution. Ralph Markland was surely an exception to the general rule. Most older men who advertised for companionship in women's magazines had to be genuine lonely hearts, there was no doubt about that. They were also likely to be quite well-off and seeking women of comparable status. By the law of probabilities, unscrupulous conmen like the bogus naval officer should be one in a hundred, at most. She was determined not to be taken for a ride a second time. She was also bent on an early exit from the hostess game.

The uneasy thought crossed her mind that Markland, following his arrest, might have given the police details of their brief time together, including her address at Dartmouth. But on second thoughts she dismissed her concerns, figuring that the bogus commander would be unlikely to own up to a financial scam, thereby increasing the charges against him in court. It had been a good move in any event, she decided, to relocate to Portsmouth. Not that the police would, in a month of Sundays, succeed in linking her to Maxine Walford and St. Dunstan's School. Poor Maxine, she mused. She had quite enjoyed her company during her short visit to Nice, having discovered the Englishwoman's holiday destination by routine enquiry at the private girls' school in

Clichy, where she knew her victim was then working. Too bad in many respects that Maxine had betrayed her husband to the French authorities, as the key suspect in a major currency scam. This had led to his untimely death in a shoot-out with the French police at Marseilles. There could be no regrets, in retrospect. Maxine had a lot to answer for and had been repaid in full.

Margit Breuer had also mentioned in her recent letter that a middle-aged Briton had called at Die Blaue Kugel asking after her, claiming that a business associate had recommended her services. Margit had given him short shrift, explaining that the person he was seeking had drowned in a yachting accident off the North Sea island of Sylt. The enquirer had seemed satisfied with that. Roslinda puzzled for a while over this unexpected piece of news, trying to recall if she had in fact entertained English clients during her several years at the Wetzlar club, feeling sure that she would have remembered doing so, since Britons visiting the area were few and far between. The truth was that she had met scores of individuals there, mainly Germans, American servicemen and the occasional tourists from other European countries. She could not place an Englishman among them and, although the fact bothered her somewhat as a loose end, she resolved to dismiss it from her mind. She had enough to occupy her for the time being.

The Gull's Nest was going to be very busy over Christmas and New Year, with lots of Navy personnel on shore leave. She must remember, ahead of the festival, to contact Green Fingers at Chester and order a bunch of peonies to arrive at Valley Care Home, Llandudno by December 24th. She would also mail a seasonal greetings card to Margit Breuer.

*

By the end of December, George Mason was at last beginning to feel a degree of optimism. Late the previous week, just before Christmas, he had received a phone call from Green Fingers, the Chester florist he had visited some time ago, informing him that they had just processed a new order for white peonies destined for Valley Care Home, Llandudno. The request, apparently enclosing a money order from a Portsmouth post office, had arrived by mail. It did not escape the detective's notice that the city was a key naval base, and that Roslinda Kramer had a previous history of entertaining military personnel. There now seemed to him to be two possibilities. Either Kramer had recently moved to that city, or she was merely passing through. He leaned towards the former view, seeing Portsmouth as a logical move from Dartmouth, which also had strong naval associations.

The trail had seemed to grow cold when the Devonshire police had drawn a blank at 5, The Lanyards, the suspect's last known address. It had placed him in a delicate position with Faye Walford and Brother Austin, both of whom were daily expecting results. Thinking fast, he had followed up his interview with Ralph Markland by placing in the personal column of *The Lady* a notice similar to the one the bogus commander had employed. Before him on his office desk were the unopened responses, all twelve of them, some in lilac-scented envelopes, others in plain white. He shuffled through them, examining the postmarks from different parts of the country, from as far afield as Durham and the Scottish Borders and from as nearby as Chelsea and Dulwich Village. None of them bore a Portsmouth postmark, inducing feelings of disappointment, before he noticed a letter from Chichester, a medium-sized town due south of London and just along the coast from the naval base.

"What have we got here?" Bill Harrington challenged, picking up the scent as he passed Mason's desk. "A lonely hearts department?"

George Mason grinned, rather sheepishly.

"Something along those lines," he replied. "It is a gambit based on information provided by Ralph Markland. I must admit, though, I wasn't expecting scented stationery."

"This one smells a bit like peaches to me," his senior said, lifting it from the desk and examining the postmark. "From Evesham too, a major fruit-growing area."

"They come from all over the country," Mason said, rather pleased with himself.

"Does Adele know about all this?" Harrington teased. "Female correspondence; secret assignations?"

"Not unless you spill the beans," the detective rejoined, enjoying a joke at his own expense. It was a rare-enough event to catch the chief inspector in jocular mood.

"My lips are sealed," Harrington conspiratorially remarked, perching briefly on the corner of Mason's desk. "Any likely lassies, though, with long auburn hair and trim figures, introduce them to me."

"With pleasure," Mason said, smiling to himself at the other's predilections regarding the fair sex, something he certainly would never have guessed, while recalling that his senior's wife, Cynthia, had auburn hair. Banter at the Yard generally avoided such topics, owing to the presence of female officers. Sexual innuendo could be taken as a form of harassment.

"This is rather a novel departure for the Metropolitan Police, Inspector," Harrington continued. "You say you got the idea from Ralph Markland?"

"I did indeed, Sir," came the reply. "And I have been wondering why a woman with Roslinda Kramer's background in the secret police would consent to opening a joint bank account with a comparative stranger, whom she first met through the personal column of a women's magazine. I just cannot see her being so gullible."

"An interesting question, Inspector," the other remarked.

"In fact, Chief Inspector, it seems completely out of character. Unless..."

"Unless what?" came the immediate query.

"Unless our suspect planned to perpetrate the same scam on Markland as he had worked on her. In other words, he beat her to it."

The chief inspector stood back from the desk and glanced out of the office window, musing on his colleague's remark. A slow smile spread across his astute features as, turning back, he said:

"A very interesting reading of the situation, Inspector, I must admit. So what are you up to now?"

"I figure that people who buy magazines like *The Lady,*" Mason replied, "probably do so on a regular basis. If my reading of the case is correct, Roslinda Kramer may well be on the look-out for a new victim, if only to even the score. So I placed a notice myself in the personal column of last month's edition. I drew a blank, perhaps because I mentioned that I was a Londoner. This month, I made my notice specific to the Portsmouth area, on the off-chance that she might read it. I know for a fact that she has recently been in the Portsmouth area."

"How did you learn that?" the chief inspector was curious to learn.

"Kramer sent a money order from Portsmouth to a florist at Chester, to order flowers sent to Valley Care Home, Llandudno."

Bill Harrington judiciously nodded.

"Full marks for ingenuity, Inspector," he said, crossing from the window to the office door. "It seems a long shot to me, but you never can tell."

"The Wanted poster has produced no results, unfortunately." Mason remarked, "as the suspect may alter her appearance from time to time. Ralph Markland described her as blond, for example. There is so much a woman can do in that area, what with hair-dos, dyes, cosmetics and apparel. This is one resourceful lady, Chief Inspector, as Oberkommissar Weiss informed us. But she has an Achilles heel."

"Which is?" an intrigued Bill Harrington immediately asked.

"Devotion to her mother."

"The flowers?"

George Mason nodded.

"Excellent detective work, Mason," his

senior then said, as a parting shot. "At last, we seem to be getting somewhere."

Left to himself, George Mason read each letter carefully, feeling he owed his correspondents that much. They included the fairly predictable contingent of widows and divorcees, all of whom gave convincing accounts of themselves. A few of them gave rather harrowing details of health problems, marital breakdowns, disappointments and sheer bad luck. Mason felt his sympathetic inner self responding. He would genuinely have liked to help some of these people out of their predicaments, but there was little he could do in reality. He felt like an interloper into their private worlds, but the minor qualms he had on that score were overcome by the pressing need to solve a major crime. The letter from Chichester intrigued him most of all. It was from a woman who signed herself Gertrude Winter, who claimed to have broad experience in the hospitality industry. Did that include working as a night club hostess, he wondered? He recalled that Roslinda's mother was named Gertrude, as he looked for some indication of possible European origins. But the English idiom was perfect. He could not have written a more natural-sounding letter himself, noting with increasing interest that it included a box number at Chichester Post Office.

On picking up the letter again to re-read

it, he noticed a horizontal bar through the stem of the figure seven in the box number provided. An English person would never write a seven in that fashion, he considered, but a European almost certainly would. Brother Austin had noticed the same characteristic, from figures the bogus bursar had provided. Had Roslinda Kramer taken the bait, he wondered, quite beside himself at the notion? Pouring himself a fresh cup of coffee, he composed a brief reply suggesting a meeting in the near future. Chichester would suit him even better than Portsmouth, being easier to reach by road. When he got down to the south coast, he would check in at The Windlass Hotel, where he and his wife Adele had previously stayed on vacation. He recalled with pleasure its fresh seafood, putting-green and Finnish sauna.

*

Three days later, George Mason was on his way to Chichester, a noted yachting center in Sussex. He recalled Otto Weiss mentioning that Kramer had been a keen yachtswoman, and that she had supposedly drowned in the North Sea off Sylt. If Kramer was indeed the author of the letter, could there be some special reason she had answered his advertisement from Chichester? It was close enough to Portsmouth to get there and back comfortably in less than half a day. Perhaps she had developed naval contacts who used Chichester marina for social and recreational purposes. Or perhaps she had found employment there, commuting from Portsmouth by bus or train. Arriving at The Windlass Hotel shortly before seven, he parked his car in darkness in the hotel lot, strode through the lobby and asked the receptionist if he could speak with the manager.

"Is there a problem, sir?" the clerk asked, with concern.

The detective shook his head, dismissively.

"Just a personal matter," he explained. "Confidential."

The young woman picked up the house phone and spoke a few words into it. Then, turning to the visitor, she said:

"Mr. Ivens will be with you shortly, sir. Please take a seat."

Mason chose a hard chair in the reception area, observing the guests checking into the hotel for the night, intrigued to note newly-affluent Chinese tourists among them. His gaze then turned towards the watercolor paintings on the lobby walls, recognizing scenes of the Sussex Downs he had passed through at one time or another on his various travels. His brief reverie was soon disturbed by an elderly gentleman with a white goatee beard emerging from the corridor to the left.

He paused to have a quick word with the young receptionist before turning to the detective.

"Stanley Ivens," he announced, affably. "You wish to have a word?"

The detective rose to his feet, to grasp the outstretched hand.

"George Mason," he said. "Is there somewhere we can talk in private?"

"Step this way," Ivens replied, "into my private office."

As he made to follow the manager, Mason noticed a youngish-looking woman entering the building alone. She was wearing a cocktail dress beneath an open topcoat, had bobbed blond hair and rather heavy eye shadow. That's her, was his immediate reaction, as he disappeared from her line of vision down the short, thickly-carpeted corridor leading from the hotel foyer. She has obviously taken some pains over her appearance, he thought, and she means business. He smiled to himself at the way he had engineered the meeting. It was a bit like bearding the lion - or was it the lioness? - in its den.

"How can I assist you, Mr. Mason?" Stanley Ivens asked, once the office door closed behind them.

The detective produced ID, drawing a look of surprise mixed with concern from the manager.

"I need to enlist the aid of the hotel staff

in furthering my investigations," Mason explained.

"But how can we possibly help you, Inspector?" Ivens asked, with some concern. "We have a business to run, and we must constantly consider the welfare of our guests."

George Mason returned a reassuring smile.

"It is really a very simple and straightforward matter, Mr. Ivens," he replied. "But it will be of invaluable assistance to me."

The manager's rather tense features relaxed, as he awaited further explanation.

"This evening," Mason continued, "I am entertaining a young woman - well, a fairly young woman - in your dining-room at seven o'clock. In fact, she has already arrived and is probably waiting for me right now in the lounge."

The manager's eyes took on a knowing look at mention of entertaining ladies to dinner.

"You made a good choice," he said, encouragingly. "Our seafood menus have received a special commendation in the Egon Ronay guide. May I this evening especially recommend the Dover sole?"

"You certainly may, Mr. Ivens," Mason replied at once.

"And a bottle of 1988 Muscadet, perhaps, to help it down?"

"No contest," the detective said, thinking that, at the very least, he was in for a gourmet meal.

"Red carnations for the table décor can also be arranged," the manager artfully suggested, with an eye to good business.

"That, Mr. Ivens, will not be necessary," Mason said. "But the small additional service I should like you to undertake on my behalf is to have my guest's wineglass removed with extra caution at the conclusion of the meal. The waiter should grasp the glass by the stem and on no account leave fingerprints anywhere else on the glass, which should be taken directly to the kitchen and left untouched for me to collect after my guest has departed."

Stanley Ivens listened to all this with growing incredulity. Then a rather conspiratorial smile began to spread across his lean, weathered features.

"Everything shall be done in accordance with your instructions, Inspector," he said. "I wish you a pleasant evening and *bon appetit!*"

George Mason emerged from the manager's office in a buoyant frame of mind, striding purposefully towards the hotel lounge, where he soon espied his dinner guest sitting in an armchair with legs crossed, leafing through a glossy magazine. Approaching her at a tangent, so that she was not immediately aware of his presence, he realized that she was of slighter build than he had anticipated, but hardly petite. He also noticed that the roots of her hair were dark, indicating that she was not a natural blonde. On sensing his approach, she turned at once, presented him with an engaging smile and rose to her feet.

"Miss Winter?" he amiably enquired.

"Gertrude," she replied at once. "And you must be...?"

"George Mason," the detective replied.

"Pleased to meet you," she continued. "You must have had a long drive."

"A little over an hour from London," Mason said.

"I do not own a vehicle," she explained. "Otherwise we could have met half way."

"No problem," the detective said, dismissively. "I reserved a table for seven o'clock, and it is already ten minutes past. Shall we go through to the dining-room?"

"With pleasure," Gertrude eagerly replied. "I have been so looking forward to this, I have hardly eaten all day."

"Then we must make up for lost time," he quipped, escorting her from the lounge.

The maître d'hotel led them to a window table, whence they could overlook the lights of Chichester Harbor, leaving elaborately-printed menus with them. The two diners studied them carefully.

"I am quite spoilt for choice," Gertrude said, "between the rib-eye steak and one of the seafood dishes. Turbot garnished with roast almonds sounds most appealing."

"I think I shall opt for the Dover sole," her host said, without mentioning the source of the recommendation.

"Don't think I have ever tried that," his guest said, "so I shall play safe and choose the turbot."

"How about a bottle of Muscadet to go with it?" Mason suggested.

"I should prefer a German wine," she countered. "A good Mosel, perhaps?"

The detective noted this possible indication of her true nationality and at once agreed to her request. He could hardly quarrel with a Mosel Riesling.

"Cock-a-leekie soup to begin," he continued, as he had always enjoyed leeks.

"And I think I shall have wild mushrooms in garlic," Gertrude said, setting down the menu with a look of satisfaction and turning her attention to her interesting host, who certainly knew how to entertain. No doubt, she considered, that was owing to his apparent background in the hotel industry.

"You mentioned in your letter," Mason said, as soon as they had placed their order, "that you have experience in hospitality."

"That is correct," his guest replied, having invented a suitable background in advance of their meeting. "I run the catering side at a well-known pub called The Sea Urchin."

"Here in Chichester?" Mason enquired.

Gertrude shook her head.

"In Portsmouth," she replied. "Before that, I was in industrial catering, but I found the pace too hectic. It is for younger people."

"I know what you mean," her host replied with mock sympathy, at the same time admiring his guest's inventiveness. He doubted very much that she would tell him her true profession, which would have been far more interesting to hear about than pub meals.

As he spoke, Gertrude Winter experienced a nagging feeling that she had seen him somewhere before, but she was hard put to remember where. The wine waiter arrived to serve the chilled Riesling, which was soon followed by their first course. George Mason unfolded his napkin and commenced eating with good appetite. Chicken-and-leek soup was his all-time favorite, one too rarely included nowadays in restaurant menus. His guest observed him closely for a few moments while he was so engrossed, determined to place him.

"Excellent wine," he remarked. "Mostly, people choose Liebfraumilch. I believe it is by far the most popular German wine, in England at any rate."

"There are many excellent wine regions in Germany," Gertrude said. "And did you know that they also produce first-class reds?"

"I was not aware of that," Mason admitted. "From which part of Germany?"

"From the Ahr Valley, mainly," she explained.

"You have me there," the detective said.

"The River Ahr flows from the Eifel Mountains on the border with Belgium," she explained, "to join the Rhine, just north of Bonn."

"You know Germany well," he disingenuously remarked. "Have you visited it often?"

"The odd vacation," she replied, forking the last of the wild mushrooms. "I never much cared for popular tourist destinations. They tend to be much too crowded for my liking."

"You mean such places as the Costa Brava and the French Riviera?" he asked, to gauge her reaction.

Gertrude Winter merely sipped her wine, glancing round the room as if curious about the other diners. It was as if she had not even heard his question. The waiter returned to serve the main course with due ceremony, and they both became absorbed in the serious business of eating. George Mason could not recall when he had last eaten Dover sole; it was even rarer than cock-a-leekie soup on modern menus. It made his drive down from London all the more worthwhile.

After a short while, his guest said: "I

prefer to travel off the beaten track. And, in general, I prefer mountain resorts to coastal ones."

Much like his wife Adele, Mason noted; who was especially fond of the English Lake District and the Scottish Highlands. At the same time, it struck him as typically German, picturing to himself hikers in *lederhosen*, with Tyrolean hats and knapsacks. He observed her closely as she ate, trying to reconcile her features with the poster now displayed at police stations. The general shape of her face, particularly the line of the jaw, which was more square than pointed, seemed to tally. Her blonde hair was dyed, another giveaway. Eyes, however, were always the most revealing feature, but she disguised them with make-up.

Was he looking, he asked himself, at the face of a killer? At someone who could take out another human being in a cold-blooded, calculated fashion? When she glanced towards him with her engaging smile, he found that hard to believe. In English law, a person was innocent until proven guilty. That was a principle established as far back as the Middle Ages, when the system of open courts or assizes was created by Henry 11. It was the envy of Europe, where the opposite held true: a person was guilty until proven innocent. Until he had obtained definite proof, he felt duty bound to give Gertrude Winter, assuming that was her real name, the benefit of the doubt. It made it easier for him to entertain her to dinner.

At that point, the hotel manager, who had been circulating briefly among the dinner guests, stopped by their table.

"Everything satisfactory, Mr. Mason?" he enquired.

"Excellent sole," the detective replied. "Freshly caught today, I imagine?"

"Landed this very morning, like all our seafood. Except for the king prawns, which are specially imported," Stanley Ivens happily explained.

"The turbot, too, was quite delicious," Gertrude Winter said. "I shall be asking the chef for his recipe."

"Which he will guard with his life!" Ivens said, bidding them a good evening before moving on to the next table.

The odd dining couple smiled at each other, and it was then that Roslinda Kramer, alias Gertrude Winter, realized where she had seen her host before. It came almost as a revelation that this was the gentleman who had been so courteous to her in the ticket queue at Paddington Station all those weeks ago. How she had wished then that he would be boarding her train. Now, amazingly, he was sitting opposite her, treating her to a handsome dinner. She felt her star was rising after recent setbacks, first with Ralph Markland then with Boris Lyadov. The fact that the manager knew him by name spoke well of his status. What a good catch he would be, if she succeeded in hooking him. An image of Tresco, one of the larger islands in the Scillies, came to mind. It no longer seemed such a distant prospect, a mirage on the horizon of her inner longing.

"Room for a dessert?" George Mason asked, as the main course was cleared away.

"Something light," his guest replied. "Perhaps the lemon sorbet."

"With coffee and a liqueur?"

At that moment, his guest suddenly and unexpectedly placed a heavily-ringed hand on his arm, a gesture the surprised but alert detective was careful not to rebuff.

"You are so generous, George," she enthused. "I cannot remember when I had such a delightful meal."

"My pleasure," he amiably replied. "Coffee with liqueur, or perhaps a straight brandy?" To his mind it was the perfect way to round off a good meal.

"I think I would like a Drambuie," she replied.

When the waiter cruised by, he ordered sorbet for his guest and raspberry flan for himself, while mulling over his next move. She was definitely expecting - he could tell from her affectionate demeanor - a follow-up meeting. The question was how to gain time until the test results from her wineglass came through, without seeming to hold her off.

"You mentioned in your letter that you enjoyed music," he said, on a different tack.

"It is my life's blood," she replied, removing her hand from his arm to address the sorbet. "Especially on quieter evenings at home. Opera is my overall favorite."

Mason had taken the trouble to educate himself a little on that subject before arranging this meeting, having learned something of the woman's tastes from the bogus naval commander, who was anxious to cooperate with the police. He had consulted Grove's *Dictionary of Music* at Westminster Library, particularly the entries on Mozart and Richard Strauss, noting all major works attributed to them.

"I have always enjoyed the Mozart operas," he said, with partial truth. Although he would not go far out of his way to watch a live performance, he had much enjoyed television presentations and films like *Amadeus*.

"You have a favorite?" she asked, with keen interest.

"*The Magic Flute*," he came back at once. "In fact, some years ago I watched Ingmar Bergman's film version of it, sung in Swedish, at a little art cinema in Chelsea. Quite marvelous. I would say it is the best film he ever made."

"You have the advantage of me there," his guest replied, wistfully. "I have to rely on CD recordings, in the absence of live performances."

"You should try Llandudno," Mason said, again to gauge her reaction. "The Welsh National Opera do a summer season there, at a theatre on the sea front."

Gertrude's features betrayed nothing. It was as if she were gazing far beyond him, perhaps picturing Llandudno, where her mother lived. Or some town in Germany. Or her next idealized destination, Tresco in the Isles of Scilly.

"I beg your pardon?" she said, as if she had scarcely heard his last remark.

"Nothing," Mason said. "It is not that important."

"You must excuse me," she then said. "I was thinking of my mother."

"Is she still living?" the detective asked, feigning ignorance.

His guest sadly shook her head.

"She died some years ago," she untruthfully replied. "Mozart was her favorite composer, too. Her best-loved work was *Don Giovanni*. Your remark reminded me of her."

"And *your* favorite?" he asked solicitously, tackling his raspberry flan.

She laid her dessert spoon momentarily aside, sat back and struck a pensive pose.

"That is a hard one," she replied. "I have in fact a number of favorites, but my most favorite opera of all has to be, I suppose, *Der Rosenkavalier*."

"Richard Strauss," the well-briefed detective came back at once.

"Then you know it too!" she exclaimed. "I am so glad to hear you say that."

"Only from television," Mason replied. "I can't say I know it all that well. A romantic comedy set in eighteenth-century Vienna, if I remember correctly?"

"Exactly right, George, and it gives us something very special in common," she continued, hoping he would take the hint that a new romance could be in the air.

George Mason almost choked on a piece of flan. Clearing his throat, he said, without looking directly at her:

"How would you feel, Gertrude, about a follow-up meeting?"

"I should like that very much," she instantly replied. "Especially if we can meet again here, at The Windlass."

"That may or may not be possible," the detective said. "At least, not for a little while. I have to travel north in the next few days to wind up some private business there. If you can give me a telephone number, I shall call you as soon as I get back to London."

His guest immediately complied, jotting the number down on her paper napkin and passing it to him. He recognized at once the Portsmouth dialing code.

"Your home or work number?" he asked.

"It is my home number," she replied. "It

will be easier to reach me there."

"I suggest we take our coffee and liqueurs in the lounge," he then suggested. "They keep a log fire going in the hearth, and it is getting quite cool in here."

"That is because they have partially opened the windows in the smoking area," Gertrude said.

"A typical British compromise," the detective replied, "to reserve half the dining-room for smokers. I smoke too - small cigars, in fact - but never while dining."

"You could have a smoke by the fire in the lounge," Gertrude said. "They would permit it, and I like the aroma of cigars."

With that, George Mason settled the bill and they rose from table to transfer to the lounge, where his companion leafed through a travel magazine and engaged him in sporadic conversation, while he enjoyed a Dutch half-corona and ducked questions of a too-personal nature. About an hour later, they parted company, promising to meet again early in the New Year. Gertrude Winter, without mentioning her destination, had indicated that she would be away over the Christmas break, leaving the detective wondering if she would be at Llandudno or in Germany. He summoned her a taxi on the forecourt, bade her good-night and proceeded to the kitchen to retrieve her wineglass. On second thought, he returned to the lounge and also removed her coffee cup and liqueur glass.

CHAPTER 13

The weather was so cold that George Mason thought it was about to snow as he emerged from St. Olave's, Knutsford after the memorial service for Maxine Walford. Brother Austin stood close to him, as Faye thanked Canon Plimpton for his services and bade good-bye to the relatives and friends who had braved the bleak January morning to attend. She then warmly embraced her nephew Marcus and watched him climb into his girlfriend Linda's car, inviting them both to her place for dinner that evening. She then turned to the two non-family members of the small congregation.

"I think a spot of lunch is called for," she said. "Something warm after sitting so long in a cold building."

"We might try The Wheatsheaf," Mason suggested. "I passed it on the way here. It's a nice-looking pub."

"With a reputation for good food," Faye said. "Are you joining us, Brother Austin?"

The cleric consulted his watch.

"I think I may just have time," he said, evidently taken with the idea. "My car is parked behind the church. I shall catch up with you both inside the pub."

George Mason, who had walked to the church from the railway station, climbed into the passenger seat of Faye's Mini-Cooper for the short drive along Applegate Road. The Wheatsheaf was beginning to fill for the lunchtime trade from nearby shops and offices. They were lucky to find a table close to the fire, sitting down to warm themselves while waiting for Brother Austin, who minutes later hailed them from the far side of the bar lounge.

"I think I shall have the chili," Faye said, deciding quickly.

"And the chicken pot pie for me," Mason decided, passing the menu card to Brother Austin as the latter took his seat.

"Not often I treat myself to a pub lunch," Austin remarked, carefully pondering the options. "It will make a nice change from the school refectory. And I think I shall try the steak-and-kidney pie, with roast potatoes."

"Terribly cold outside," Faye said. "Looks like snow."

"Winter seems to be arriving bang on time this year," George Mason remarked,

. rising from his seat to place their orders at the service counter.

"I expect I shall make it back to Dovestones without too much difficulty," Austin said, leaning towards the fire for warmth, "if the weather holds."

"Thank you very much for taking part in the service," Faye said. "You read the second lesson beautifully."

"From habituation," the other modestly replied. "Though we are not ordained priests, we take a full part in religious services and often preach sermons as well, when requested by local parishes. I thought the memorial went admirably. Such lovely hymns and the vicar, Canon Plimpton, gave an excellent address. I had no idea, for example, that your half-sister was involved with M.I.5."

"Nor had I," Faye replied, with feeling. "Nor did any member of her family."

"I suppose that is all in the nature of secret service work," the cleric continued, "and I began to wonder as Plimpton was speaking whether there could be some connection between that and her untimely death."

"Only Inspector Mason could answer that," the young woman observed. "And he keeps his cards very close to his chest."

At that point, the detective returned from the bar with a round of drinks, placed them on the table and sat down.

"The food should arrive shortly," he said. "I explained that we were pressed for time. I for one have to catch the 2.28 p.m. train back to London."

"And I have to be back at the surgery this afternoon," Faye added.

"We were just remarking how well the service went," Brother Austin said. "Especially the hymns and the address. You can always rely on the Church of England for good music."

"Very ecumenical of you to take such an active role," George Mason said, appreciatively.

"Relations between our two denominations are much closer than they used to be," the other said, sampling his pint of Guinness. "I can remember that only a few decades ago, when I joined the Aurelian Brothers as a young novice, they were at daggers drawn, metaphorically speaking of course."

The dental hygienist and the detective smiled to each other at his candid assessment.

"Do you think they will ever get back in bed together?" Mason asked, rather provocatively.

The celibate frowned slightly at the detective's choice of words.

"Rather an odd way of putting it, Inspector," he remarked. "And, quite frankly, I do not think reunion is on the immediate agenda. There are still important issues that divide us, and the Anglican ordination of women hasn't helped."

"Time heals all wounds," Faye Walford diplomatically observed, while privately endorsing equality of the sexes in all professions.

"Amen to that!" the cleric remarked.

Their attention now focused on the appetizing dishes placed in front of them. The cold weather and the church service had whetted their appetites. They were more than half way through the meal before Brother Austin raised the delicate question of the missing school funds. But not before he had taken a good swig of his stout, causing the detective to conclude that abstinence was not among the standard religious vows.

"I have been meaning to ask you, Inspector," he began, "if there is any prospect of recovering our building fund, or at least some part of it. My reason for asking is that we have, in fact, been obliged to take out a short-term loan with the diocese. The Visitor, Brother Aelred, wanted to ensure that the new dormitory block would be ready in time for the increased pupil intake next year. Boyce Contractors require a down payment in respect of building materials already purchased. "

George Mason in his turn took a long quaff of Theakston's Bitter, while keenly appraising the fairly rotund cleric, who always reminded him of Friar Tuck. Faye Walford glanced from one to the other, with an obvious personal interest in the flow of conversation.

"There have been significant developments in that regard," he replied, matter-of-factly.

"You mean you have located the culprit?" an agreeably surprised Austin asked.

"We are now fairly sure where your missing funds are," Mason replied, without wishing to go into the complicated details of a double theft.

Brother Austin's jawed dropped, as he nudged the remainder of his meal aside.

"And you didn't inform us of this at once?" he challenged.

"The trial of a party named Ralph Markland is scheduled to begin at the Old Bailey on January 24," George Mason explained. "That name probably means nothing to you - and why should it? - but after the guilty verdict is returned by the jury, and I can see no reason why it would not be, the judge will almost certainly order him to restore to your good selves the sum of fifty thousand pounds."

"This is excellent news, Inspector," Austin said. "I shall inform Brother Aelred the minute I get back to St. Dunstan's. He will be over the moon."

"That might be a little bit premature," the

detective cautioned. "To allay your anxieties about the money, I have run a little ahead of actual events. We are just waiting for the final piece of the puzzle to fit into place, to be absolutely certain the funds we have identified belong to your order. At the moment, we are only ninety per cent sure of our ground. So what I am telling you now is strictly off the record."

The school principal's euphoria subsided somewhat on hearing the detective's caveat. He consulted his watch, quickly drained his glass and got up to leave.

"Must be back in time for vespers," he explained. "I have every confidence in you, Inspector Mason, and I shall not breathe a word to anyone, not to Brother Aelred or to Brother Clement, until I hear definitively from you, one way or the other."

"I assure you I shall contact you immediately after the trial, hopefully with good news," Mason said, watching him pick his way between the crowded tables before turning to wave as he quit the premises.

"You seem to be getting closer to your objective, Inspector," Faye remarked, hoping to draw him out on the subject.

George Mason sipped his beer thoughtfully for a few moments before saying:

"Let me put it this way. I am more optimistic than I was when I last spoke to you."

"You are on to something, I can tell," came the quick response.

"There is no harm in telling you, Faye," the detective said, after a pause, "as someone with a close involvement in this case. But let me warn you in advance that nothing is final at this stage, and I would not want you mentioning anything you hear from me now to your nephew Marcus over dinner this evening."

"Mum's the word," Faye replied, placing a finger to her lips.

"You may or may not believe this," he continued, more expansively, "but I am fairly sure I entertained Maxine's killer to dinner just before Christmas."

"You are pulling my leg, Inspector!" the astonished hygienist replied.

"I am deadly serious," the detective assured her.

"How ever did you come to do something like that?" she asked, as concerned as she was puzzled.

George Mason leaned back in his chair, the better to catch the warmth from the fire, and smiled his most enigmatic smile.

"To obtain evidence," he said.

"And exactly where did this meeting take place?"

"At Chichester," he informed her, without naming the hotel.

"That is a long way from here," Faye remarked. "Aren't you going to tell me her name?"

"It would not be appropriate to do so at the. present time," he replied. "Everything will become much clearer to you as our investigations proceed."

"So how did you catch up with this mysterious individual?" she asked, trying a different tack.

"Modern technology," he replied, airily. "Your half-sister's dinner guest at Les Palmiers on that fateful evening placed two calls from Nice using a phone card. The telecommunications company could trace the destination of the calls by means of a unique code number embedded in it. The first led to a florist at Chester, the second to a night club in Sauerland."

"Sauerland?' the hygienist queried, with a puzzled look.

"A heavily-forested area in north-east Germany," he explained. "Wetzlar, on the River Lahn, is one of the main centers."

"You have been doing your homework, Inspector," Faye complimented.

"Just routine work, Faye," the detective matter-of-factly replied, draining his glass. "Now I really must get a move on if I am going to catch my train."

"I'll give you a lift back to the station," the young woman offered. "Then you will be in good time."

"Finish your drink then," he urged, "and let's go. I have already settled the bill, charging it to field expenses."

Faye Walford smiled her appreciation, drained her glass and slipped on her top coat. She then led the way out to her parked car.

*

It was another two days before George Mason had the opportunity to confer with Chief Inspector Harrington, who had been on a short leave of absence, about developments in the Walford case. Bill Harrington, grumbling aloud about the work that had piled up in his absence, called him into his private office and bade him take a seat.

"Just heard back from the crime lab, Inspector," he began. "And I have good news for you. They have completed their analysis of the DNA sample you managed to obtain from The Windlass Hotel at Chichester. It is a good match for the profile Capitaine Lemaitre sent over from Nice."

"Excellent, Chief Inspector," a buoyant George Mason remarked. "But what took them so long?"

"The forensic specialist had to attend a series of meetings with Interpol over the holiday period, at their base in Lyon, France," his senior explained. "But we should now be in a position to move forward in this case. The superintendent thinks we have spent enough time on it already, to the detriment of other pressing matters. He wants it sewn up as soon as possible."

"Do you want me to go down to Portsmouth to make the arrest?" Mason asked.

"Absolutely," Harrington replied. "She is your pigeon, Inspector. But once the suspect is in police custody, certain matters of protocol will arise."

"What exactly do you mean, Chief Inspector?" his colleague enquired.

Harrington poured himself a tot of the Glenfiddich, to chase his morning coffee.

"In some sense," he said, rather irritably, "we have drawn the short straw. We have done all the legwork, but the only charge we can make against Kramer is one of embezzlement."

"You mean the French have a prior claim?"

"As soon as I inform Capitaine Lemaitre of the DNA match, the French authorities will make a formal request for her extradition, to face a murder charge over what transpired at Les Palmiers last August."

"The Germans will also want her on a blackmail rap," George Mason added. "Do we have any idea who her victim was?"

Bill Harrington quickly consulted his file.

"The day you left for the Knutsford memorial service," he replied, "I received an international call from a certain Oberkommissar Otto Weiss of the Kriminal Polizei at Wetzlar."

"And?" Mason eagerly enquired.

"The blackmail victim's marriage broke up shortly before he was posted back to a military base in North Carolina. He therefore no longer feared that his wife would learn of his extra-marital activities. He named Roslinda Kramer to the German authorities, as the person who had been blackmailing him, in a bid to recover thousands of Deutschmarks he had paid her. The officer in question will shortly be in England on NATO business. Otto Weiss advised him to call here at Scotland Yard and consult with your good self, as the person most informed about the case."

"You still haven't told me his name," George Mason said.

"Major Orin Tuttle," his senior replied, "of U.S. Army Logistics. If he drops by - and I imagine he will, sooner or later – you will have some idea of whom you are dealing with and the relevant background. The Oberkommissar implied that he was a rather truculent character."

"I may well, in fact, be able to assist the major," Mason confidently remarked. "Pull his chestnuts out of the fire, in a manner of speaking."

"And how would that be?" an intrigued Bill Harrington asked.

"Kramer keeps a numbered account with Bank Irmgold in Zurich, where she probably salted away the proceeds of her blackmailing activities. Since she worked at Die Blaue Kugel over a period of years, I imagine Major Tuttle was not her only victim. Otto Weiss knows about her Zurich account already. I sent him a recent interest voucher that turned up by chance at St. Dunstan's School."

"Weiss may just want to get Tuttle off his back," Harrington suggested, "and is passing the buck to you. We are, in any case, streets ahead of the Germans, especially now that these DNA results have come through."

"I shall get down to Portsmouth first thing tomorrow morning," Mason declared.

"Let the Portsmouth Constabulary make the actual arrest," Harrington advised. "You can then confront her with her crimes at the police station. Oh, and you will also need to escort her to Nice, once the extradition papers come through."

George Mason was aghast at the thought of sharing a long plane journey with her, after entertaining her to dinner at The Windlass Hotel. Escorting her up to Scotland Yard was one thing; flying her down to the French Riviera was quite another.

"Couldn't Detective Sergeant Clifford undertake that particular duty?" he requested. "I would feel very uncomfortable doing it, after meeting her at Chichester."

"I thought you would jump at the chance," Harrington rejoined, in some surprise. "Another expenses-paid trip to the Cote d'Azur."

"Rather Owen Clifford than me," the detective emphatically remarked. "The experience will be good for him. I doubt he has been abroad much in the line of police duty."

"I shall give it some consideration," the other replied. "But I am not promising anything. For one thing, Sergeant Clifford doesn't speak French. For another, his wife's expecting their second child any day now. He may even apply for paternity leave, now that the police union has negotiated that benefit on behalf of its members."

"In that case," Mason said, resignedly, "I expect it will have to be me."

"The service comes first, Inspector," Harrington emphasized. "We are professionals, after all. We cannot let personal feelings get involved."

"I expect you are right," Mason conceded.

Back in his own office, he wondered if, in the event, Kramer would maintain a stony silence for the duration of the trip. Or whether she would open up completely as a kind of catharsis, to get everything off her chest. For a former Stasi agent, he mused, the first scenario seemed the more likely. Failing Owen Clifford escorting her to Nice, he might be able to persuade the chief inspector to detail a senior female officer to that particular duty. He would mention it in advance to one or two of his female colleagues, so that any request from above would not come as a complete surprise. He was damned if he was going to accompany a resentful and scornful Roslinda Kramer all the way to the South of France. Would they discuss opera, he wondered? Or yachting? Or Mosel wines?

CHAPTER 14

When Roslinda Kramer returned to her apartment around eleven-thirty following her dinner with George Mason, she was in such an anxious state of mind that she found it impossible to retire, even as she felt quite tired and rather tipsy from the amount of liquor she had consumed. Slipping out of her evening dress, she donned her dressing-gown, fixed herself a hot chocolate and placed a CD on her Sony player. Sinking into an armchair and putting her feet up, it was about half way through a Renata Tebaldi aria that she began to have serious misgivings. Hadn't it all gone a bit too pat, she asked herself? What a remarkable coincidence it now seemed that she had recognized her urbane host as the gentleman in the ticket queue at Paddington Station all those weeks ago! All her training and experience with the Stasi, however, had taught her to beware of coincidence. Genuine coincidences, to her mind, were extremely rare. Contrived ones, on the other hand, were a different matter.

Her host had been entertaining and courteous, a real English gentleman in his herring-bone tweed jacket and bow tie, that she was anxious for the relationship to move forward without any hitches. But were his references to Llandudno and the French Riviera as innocent as they seemed, she wondered, as her cautionary instincts gained the upper hand? Recharging her mug of hot chocolate, she suddenly recalled that Margit Breuer had mentioned an English visitor to the club who had enquired about her. That had struck her as rather odd at the time, since she recalled meeting no one from England, but she had dismissed it from her mind. Right now, it seemed like it could be very relevant. She decided to do something she had not done in a long while, not since her summer trip to Nice: she would ring the club directly. As far as the Kripo were concerned, as confirmed by the local coastguard, she had drowned off the island of Sylt. Would they be in the habit of tapping telephone calls to Die Blaue Kugel, perhaps because American servicemen still frequented it? Placing a call there was a calculated risk, she fully realized, but one she felt obliged to take.

Margit Breuer registered pleasant surprise at hearing directly from her close friend and former associate.

"*Der Englander?*" she enquired, with an air of puzzlement. "Why, that was weeks ago. I do not remember all that much about him, to tell you the truth, Ros."

"Just a general impression will do," Roslinda said. "Approximate age, build, any distinguishing feature, occupation, interests. You know the sort of thing hostesses normally chat about."

"The person who entertained him on that evening will give you a better picture," Margit suggested. "I seem to recall that it was Son Chai, the only hostess we have of genuine Thai nationality. Wait a moment while I check if she is available."

Roslinda hung on the line for a few tense moments.

"*Groetsi,*" Son Chai finally greeted. "Margit tells me you wish to know about our British client. I do remember him, even though we had just a few drinks together. He struck me as the loyal married type, not particularly interested in escort services."

"Could you describe him to me, Son Chai?" Roslinda hastily enquired.

"Around fifty, I imagine," came the reply, "with thinning brown hair and a rather generous build. And he had a rather prominent mole at his left temple."

Mein Gott, Roslinda Kramer thought, with mounting unease. That description could very well fit the person who had just entertained her to dinner.

"Did he also, by any chance, wear glasses?" she asked.

"Only when reading the menu," Son Chai confidently replied, "which took several minutes. He seemed very keen on his food."

That was George Mason too, Roslinda thought, her sense of unease giving way to genuine concern. He had used glasses to study the menu at The Windlass Hotel, then replaced them in his top pocket. He was also something of a gourmet, much like the cad Ralph Markland, of unhappy memory. Allowing that she might be wrong about her dinner host, and that he was not in fact the same person as the one who had visited Wetzlar, she decided not to take any chances. The stakes were too high; the consequences of a misjudgment too appalling.

"Please put Margit back on the line," she requested at once.

"Is everything all right, my dear?" the concerned proprietress wanted to know.

"Pay close attention to me, Margit," Roslinda replied, suddenly realizing the precariousness of her situation. "I need to get out of here as soon as possible. Out of Portsmouth. Out of England altogether. I think the authorities may be on to me."

There was a brief silence at the other end of the line.

"Are you quite sure of this?" Margit Breuer said, skeptically.

"Fairly positive," the other replied. "I suspect that your British visitor of some weeks ago took me to dinner at The Windlass Hotel in Chichester this very evening. The description Son Chai gave me fits him quite closely. I could of course be mistaken, but I am not in a position to take chances."

"Where on earth will you go?"

"I am thinking of coming to Wetzlar," Roslinda replied. "There is nowhere else I can realistically go. I have little ready cash. My meagre earnings have nearly all gone towards living expenses."

There was another pause at the German end of the line.

"You could always stay here at the club, but only for a short while," Margit offered. "It will give me time to find you something more permanent, through our network of former agents. Somewhere off the beaten track, such as Binz, on the island of Ruegen. We have useful contacts there."

"The coastal resort up on the Baltic?" Roslinda replied, perking up a little.

"Pack your things and leave at once," Margit advised. "You could live quietly up there under an assumed name. Perhaps even take up yachting again, in due course. And with your varied experience in the hospitality industry you could probably soon obtain well-paid employment."

"Now you are talking," Roslinda Kramer

replied, more buoyantly. "Listen, Margit, there is no immediate hurry. George Mason, the devil take him, has business up north for a few days. It will give me time to make the necessary travel arrangements."

"*Aufwiedersehen*," Margit Breuer said, rather hesitantly. "And good luck."

Her caller replaced the receiver, crossed the room and sank back into her armchair. How on earth had that confounded Mason traced her to the nightclub, she wondered? And what exactly did he know of her activities since August last? Hadn't she been extremely careful to cover her tracks, changing her address and her appearance, avoiding traceable credit cards and the like? She poured herself a stiff brandy, drank it and fell fast asleep in the armchair, her last conscious thought being of the bogus Commander Ralph Markland. It was he, more than likely, who had betrayed her by giving details of their brief liaison to the police. No flatfoot would have caught up with her unaided, she was convinced of that.

*

George Mason registered disbelief when, on returning to Scotland Yard after his trip north, he received a call from the police superintendent at Portsmouth informing him that no arrest had been made at an address which had been traced from the telephone number Roslinda Kramer had provided following dinner at The Windlass Hotel. The occupant of the relevant apartment had apparently left quite suddenly, without giving notice to the landlord, who claimed that she was in arrears of rent. He poured himself a strong coffee, put his thinking cap on in an attempt to figure out exactly what had gone wrong. There was surely no way she could have guessed his true calling. In fact, the longer the meal had progressed, the more sure he had felt of his quarry. After a few moments' reflection, he sat up in his chair, drained his coffee and smiled wryly to himself. Oberkommissar Otto Weiss had hit the nail on the head in describing her as a cunning and resourceful former agent, who in the German officer's view, was practically guaranteed to come out on top in any duel of wits with Scotland Yard. If that was what Otto Weiss thought, he had better think again.

What would someone like Kramer do, he asked himself, in her unique set of circumstances, if she suspected that the C.I.D. were on her tail and that the game was up, especially if she now had scant means of financial support? Make for the exit, he decided, and by the quickest route possible. That posed a quandary. There had been heavy snow recently, causing flight cancellations. He doubted that she would have risked delays at airports and would more likely have opted for surface travel. The shortest route from Portsmouth to the Continent was the ferry from neighboring Southampton to Cherbourg; the speediest route would be by Eurostar rail service under the English Channel. With those possibilities in mind, he rang the ferry terminal at Southampton, aware that Kramer would need ID to complete a booking. They had no record of a Roslinda Kramer. He then tried St. Pancras International, the London terminus of the Eurostar services to Paris or Brussels. His luck was in. After a few minutes, they were able to confirm from computer records that a Roslinda Kramer had booked a one-way ticket to Paris the previous day, paying in cash. A buoyant George Mason placed a call to Wetzlar.

"Oberkommissar Weiss," came the deep baritone across the line.

"Good morning, Oberkommissar," George Mason began.

"*Guten Morgen*, Herr Mason," the German replied, recognizing his voice immediately. "What can I do for you today?"

"I am calling about our mutual friend, Ms. Kramer," the detective explained.

"Still giving you the slip?" returned the faintly ironic voice. "I had the feeling all along that she would outsmart you. Those Stasi people were exceptionally well-trained. I doubt I can be of any further help."

257

"On the contrary, Herr Weiss," Mason replied, evenly. "You can now give me critical support."

"In what way?" the German enquired, rather skeptically.

"You can arrest her."

"How can I possibly do that, Inspector?" His tone conveyed a degree of annoyance, as well as astonishment, as if the Briton was trying to put one over on him.

"It may interest you to know, Oberkommissar, that our mutual friend left her last-known address in England in some haste yesterday, without settling her rent."

"And you imagine she is headed here?" an incredulous Otto Weiss enquired.

"As I figure it, there is hardly anywhere else she *can* go," the detective reasoned. "For one thing, she must be practically broke by now, without any means of support in this country. For another, the people at Die Blaue Kugel are most likely the only ones who know of her faked death in a yachting accident. In fact, they may have been parties to the deception all along."

There was an awkward silence at the other end of the line.

"All this is most interesting and unexpected, Inspector," Otto Weiss said, eventually. "That is, if you are quite sure of your ground?"

"About ninety per cent sure," George Mason replied. "The suspect has altered her appearance. She now wears her hair bobbed and dyed blond. She may also use heavy eye shadow."

"And if we should draw a blank over here in the Sauerland?" the German objected. "What then?"

"I would stake half my pension," Mason replied, "that is exactly where she will turn up. When you apprehend her, you must contact Capitaine Jules Lemaitre of the Nice gendarmerie immediately and inform him of the fact. The French will then make a formal request for her extradition, on a murder charge."

"A murder charge!" the German officer exclaimed. "At what point did you upgrade things to that level?"

"By matching DNA profiles obtained at a restaurant on the Sussex coast and at a timeshare at Nice. Roslinda Kramer is now chief suspect in the murder of an Englishwoman named Maxine Walford, whom she met on the Riviera last summer."

"You are way ahead of me here," the oberkommissar remarked, with grudging respect. "I thought we were dealing with blackmail."

"You still are, as a secondary charge," Mason explained. "And following that, there is another small matter of embezzlement from a private school in England."

"You really have been doing your homework, Inspector," Otto Weiss grudgingly acknowledged. "And I shall do my best to support you at this end. In fact, I shall order an immediate check on the premises of Die Blaue Kugel and report back to you."

George Mason replaced the receiver in a contented frame of mind, just as Bill Harrington breezed into his office.

"How are things going?" the senior man encouragingly asked, squatting on the edge of the cluttered desk.

"It seems that the bird has flown," Mason wryly replied. "Again."

"You can't be serious," Harrington exclaimed, a puzzled frown spreading across his features. "I have been assuring the superintendent all this week that the Walford case was practically in the bag."

"I strongly suspect," his colleague added, with a sly smile, "that this particular bird will prove to be a homing pigeon."

"Nicely put, Inspector," Harrington replied. "You have an interesting way with words. Ever tried your hand at writing fiction?"

George Mason smilingly shook his head.

"*The Times* crossword is about my limit," he replied. "Usually a combined effort by Adele and myself."

*

Two days later, George Mason, while

waiting to hear back from Wetzlar, rang the dental surgery at Knutsford where Faye Walford worked, catching her just as she was beginning her lunch break.

"At last," he said, "we should have some good news, Faye. My guess is that the suspect has returned to Wetzlar."

"Wetzlar, Inspector?" the hygienist asked. "Where on earth is that?"

"A town some distance east of the Rhine," the detective explained, "in a forested region known as Sauerland. The suspect has strong ties to that area and will probably be looking to friends to help her."

"Assuming that she is arrested," a relieved Faye Walford said, "where will the trial take place?"

"At Nice," Mason explained. "There is sufficient DNA evidence, from traces of saliva found on wineglasses at both Les Palmiers and at The Windlass Hotel, Chichester, to make a convincing case against her."

"What about motive?" Faye prompted.

"That should emerge during the trial. My own view, off the record, is that it was part opportunistic, to enable her get established in England, since she was being sought by the German police for blackmail of a U.S. Army officer; and in part related to Maxine's undercover work for M.I.5."

"What makes you suspect the latter, Inspector Mason?"

The German police informed me that Kramer's partner, a certain Wolf Breitman, was also an agent of the East German secret police, known as the Stasi. He was based in Paris during the time Maxine lived there and was involved in a currency counterfeiting operation aimed at disrupting European economies."

"It truly amazes me, Inspector," Faye remarked, admiringly, "how you could have found all this out, and in such a short time. But what possible connection could there be between this Wolf Breitman and my half-sister?"

"From conversations I had recently with an old contact of mine at M.I.5," George Mason replied, "I was left with the distinct impression, though nothing was said directly, that Maxine may have been involved in exposing Breitman to the French authorities, who were working very closely with the C.I.A."

"But how did the Americans become seriously involved in European currency matters?"

"Because any large-scale manipulation of currency, which was then the ecu, by the way, would affect international exchange rates, to the detriment of the American economy."

"By making American exports that much dearer," Faye said, finally getting the point.

"Exactly," George Mason agreed. "In the

end, the French police, following a tip-off, traced Breitman to a suburb of Marseilles favored by migrants from North Africa. He resisted arrest, there was an exchange of gunfire and he was fatally wounded as a result."

"This Roslinda Kramer you have traced," the hygienist said, "would on your theory have held Maxine responsible for her partner's death? In plain words, the murder was an act of revenge."

"What we would call a grudge killing," Mason remarked. "Mind you, this is completely off the record. The full facts will emerge when the case come to trial."

"I expect you are right, Inspector."

"My deepest regrets that things had to turn out this way," her caller then said, sympathetically.

"Mine too," Faye replied, with feeling. "Please do keep me posted on future developments."

"Absolutely," the detective promised, ringing off.

He then place a call to St. Dunstan's School.

"Inspector George Mason, of Scotland Yard," he said, introducing himself.

"You have reached administration," the woman said, warily. "Where can I direct your call?"

"You must be the new bursar?" Mason tentatively enquired.

"Very new, I am afraid," came the reply. "I am just starting to get the hang of things."

"And are you enjoying your new environment?" he asked. "It is a lovely part of the country to live in. In some ways, I envy you."

"The Aurelian Brothers are very considerate and encouraging," she replied. "And I enjoy involvement with the boys, especially on day-trips to the coast and to the Lake District."

"Now I really am green with envy," Mason said.

"I expect you wish to speak with the principal," the new bursar then politely remarked. "If this is a convenient time."

"Brother Clement has just stepped into the office. I shall hand you over to him."

"Why, Inspector Mason," came the cordial voice of the assistant principal. "Wonderful to hear from you again. How are things proceeding?"

"I have good news for Brother Austin," the detective said, "if it is convenient to speak with him."

"Please hold the line, Inspector. The principal is taking a Latin class with the junior boys. But he won't want to miss your call. I shall fetch him straight away."

"That is very kind of you, Brother Clement."

Moments later, the animated voice of the

school principal came over the line.

"Good day, Inspector Mason," he said. "Clement tells me you have some news to convey."

"You recall," the detective said, "that at our last meeting at The Wheatsheaf in Knutsford, following the memorial service for Maxine Walford, I told you that the case was practically solved."

"I do indeed so recall, Inspector," Austin said, "And I was most gratified to hear it."

"The last piece of the puzzle should fall into place very soon," Mason said. "I anticipate that the German authorities will any day now be apprehending your bogus bursar, Roslinda Kramer."

"What about reimbursement of the stolen funds?" the principal asked, "so that we can repay the loan from the diocese?"

"They will be released immediately after the imminent trial of Ralph Markland," the detective informed him.

"And who might that personage be?" a curious Brother Austin asked.

"A professional conman," Mason explained. "He entered into a liaison with Kramer over the summer and stole the sum of fifty thousand pounds from a joint bank account they had opened at Dartmouth."

"Precisely the amount stolen from our building fund, Inspector."

"I suspect," his caller continued, "that she was aiming to take him to the cleaners. But he turned tables on her and left her high-and-dry."

"Poetic irony, in fact," the principal remarked, with grim satisfaction, "and excellent work on your part, if I may say so. I shall inform our Visitor, Brother Aelred, of developments as soon as he returns from Rome, where he is currently on retreat. He will be very relieved. He still blames himself for all this mess, even after I have told him many times that he acted in good faith and with the best of intentions."

"He should now be able to grant himself a full pardon," the detective quipped.

"Absolution is the word we would more likely use," Austin said. "It is what we receive after confessing our sins."

"We all have our little peccadillos, Reverend Sir," George Mason philosophically remarked.

"That may be so, Inspector, but the Visitor is unusually hard on himself. He is a very ascetic gentleman."

"Give him my good wishes," the detective said, "when you are next in touch with him."

"I shall gladly do that," the other assured him. "Now I must hurry back to my Latin class or the boys will be getting restless."

"Do not let me interrupt the good work," Mason said.

"Whenever you are in the area," Austin added, "perhaps visiting your mother again at Skipton, be sure to drop by. You will always be welcome at our table, modest as it is."

"Nothing would please me more," the detective said, replacing the receiver and calling to mind a certain Sunday in October, when he had dined on thin tomato soup and roast chicken with garden vegetables.

As he rose from his desk to refresh his cup of coffee, he espied a handsome figure dressed in the uniform of the U.S. military standing by his office door. The man had evidently been there waiting patiently for a few moments, while the telephone conversation was in progress. George Mason, a little taken aback, looked questioningly towards him, before suddenly recalling the forewarning Otto Weiss had given him.

"Major Orin B. Tuttle, U.S. Army Logistics," the visitor said, stepping forward with his palm outstretched.

George Mason rose to his feet and shook the officer's firm grip.

"I have been in London on NATO business," the visitor said. "Thought I'd drop by to see you, since I was in the vicinity. I have an hour or so before catching the Eurostar to Brussels."

"More NATO matters, Major?"

"Er...no, Inspector. It will be the first leg of a trip to Dresden on family business. My wife's widowed grandmother lives there. I promised to pay her a visit while on this side of the ocean."

"So what can I do for you?" the detective asked, inviting him to sit.

"The German authorities informed me that you were investigating a certain hostess from a nightclub near Wetzlar."

"Die Blaue Kugel, to be precise?"

The officer nodded curtly, cleared his throat, and said:

"I was stationed in Sauerland at one period, Inspector. My fellow officers and I used the club regularly for off-base entertainment."

"As a result of which," Mason put it, as delicately as he could, "you were compromised."

Orin Tuttle returned a look of considerable surprise.

"You already know about it, Inspector…the blackmail angle, I mean?"

"Oberkommissar Weiss happened to mention that they had a warrant out for the arrest of a hostess based at the club," the detective explained. "They were under the impression that she had drowned in a yachting accident, so their investigation lapsed. It was only when I approached them about a different matter entirely that they realized she was very much alive."

The major gave a broad smile.

"A different incident involving the same woman?" he asked.

"Exactly," Mason replied. "Without going

into details, Major, I can tell you that the suspect should eventually stand trial at Wetzlar for a series of blackmail offenses, including the one involving your good self. But I cannot say when this might take place. It may not be for some quite considerable time."

"Because she is wanted on a different rap?" the major asked, with an ironic smile.

"Exactly," the detective replied. "And it is a much more serious charge."

The officer pursed his lips and weighed up the situation, but did not ask for further details.

"So I am not likely to get recompense any time soon?" he said

George Mason regretfully shook his head and said:

"I can tell you, off the record, that the suspect has funds on deposit at a private Swiss bank, presumably the proceeds of blackmail activities over a period of years. You will be repaid in full, I have no doubt, once all legal proceedings are completed."

The major rose to his feet and smoothed down his tunic.

"I am very glad to hear that, Inspector," he said, offering his hand again. "There is no real urgency in the matter, since I never expected to see the color of that money again. I just wanted to know the current state of the game, and I thank you for the constructive role you have played. It seems that, without your input, the Kripo might never have caught up with her."

"It was a clever ruse she employed, Major," the detective said. "And a very convincing one, since she was a well-known yachtswoman who competed in major regattas."

"She is a woman of many attributes, Inspector. I can attest to that."

Did George Mason detect a certain wistfulness in that remark, he wondered?

"Including some criminal ones, unfortunately, Major Tuttle," he rejoined.

CHAPTER 15

Roslinda Kramer left Portsmouth three days before Christmas, taking the train to Paddington Station. From there, she took the Underground to St. Pancras International, to catch the afternoon Eurostar service to Paris. On arrival at Gare du Nord, she checked her two medium-sized suitcases into the left-luggage depository and crossed to the information desk to enquire the time of the overnight service to Zurich. She learned that it would depart at 10.09 p.m. from Gare de l'Est, involving a short taxi ride to a neighboring part of the city. She then booked a ticket in a first-class sleeping car, knowing from previous experience of European trains how trying were the second-class compartments, with six passengers crowded onto three-tier bunks, often with fretful youngsters in tow. She then strolled outside in light snow, to find a bar where she could pass the interval between trains and get a bite to eat.

Uppermost in her mind, as she tackled a Spanish omelet with a half-carafe of Beaujolais, was George Mason. He would be figuring, she felt reasonably sure, that she would return to Wetzlar, the Sauerland town he evidently associated her with. He might even have made contact with the local Kripo, in the person of Oberkommissar Otto Weiss who, Margit had informed her, now commanded the local force. She would disappoint Mason and head indirectly to the coastal resort of Binz, on the Baltic island of Ruegen, with which she was fairly familiar from her yachting trips from Sylt in earlier days. It was an elegant town with an interesting history. From being a humble fishing village in the Middle Ages, it had grown over the years into one of Germany's classic resorts, noted for its sandy beaches and fine architecture. The Nazis had commandeered it in the thirties for their 'Strength Through Joy' programs; while the Communists had requisitioned all the privately-owned hotels and placed them under trade union management, to make them more populist. That was what socialism had been all about, she ruefully reflected: arranging things for the benefit of the general public, instead of for the wealthy few.

On arrival in Zurich the following

morning, she stored her suitcases in the bank of coin-operated lockers near the boutiques in the lower-level shopping area. She then left the Hauptbahnhof and headed down Bahnhofstrasse, which she had heard described as Europe's most expensive street. Admiring the seasonal decorations in the store windows, she could see why. Goldsmiths, silversmiths, furriers, couturiers, fine art galleries and other outlets aimed at a wealthy clientele vied with each other for the most attention-drawing window displays. Part-way down the broad thoroughfare accommodating traffic lanes and double tram-lines, the aroma of freshly-brewed coffee drew her into Restaurant Graf, where she occupied a window seat and ordered eggs Benedict and a French dark roast with cream. The place was about half-full with Zurchers taking breakfast on their way to work.

With no sense of hurry, she took time over her simple repast, skimmed through the complimentary newspaper, the *Zurcher Zeitung*, paid the bill, quit the restaurant and continued along Bahhofstrasse to the premises of Bank Irmgold. It was a classical-style building set well back from the road and partly screened by unusually bushy conifers. On entering, she was greeted by an elderly official standing behind a polished teak counter.

"What can I assist you, Madame?" he

politely enquired, over half-lenses.

The visitor gave her name and account number.

"I wish to withdraw half my investment," she said.

The banker consulted his computer records.

"Your deposit, Madame, does not mature for another three years," he said. "If you withdraw funds today, there will be an early surrender charge of five per cent for each of the three remaining years."

Roslinda Kramer made a quick mental calculation. She had certainly not wished to touch this money, but to keep it in reserve it for her retirement. But she felt she had no option, in her current circumstances.

"On 50,000 Swiss francs, I would lose 7500," she said.

"I am afraid so, Madame. Do you still wish to proceed with the transaction?"

The visitor brusquely nodded, waiting until the official prepared the withdrawal slip. Her eye took in details of the room, lighting momentarily on a large painting of the lake at Luzern, with the famous wooden bridge in the foreground. She then signed the document and watched the official count out the bills, in a mixture of denominations. As she left the premises, she reflected that, after all, she was only forfeiting the interest the amount would have earned over the full term. The balance of the deposit would help make up for it over time.

Feeling reasonably satisfied with the deal, she retraced her steps along Bahnhofstrasse, calling at Grieder's department store to buy a new winter coat, thinking that the weather would now be quite cold on the north coast of Germany. Something fur-lined would do the trick, she figured, not having felt the need for very warm clothing in the milder climate of southern England. The anorak she had traveled in from Portsmouth would come in useful in the spring, especially if she took up yachting again, which she fully expected to do.

On leaving Grieder's, proudly wearing her stylish new coat while placing her anorak in a carrier-bag, she enquired of a passer-by the way to the city's art gallery, the Kunsthaus. Following the man's directions, she proceeded along Bahnhofstrasse as far as the lake, took a left turn to Belle Vue, a major traffic intersection, and walked up steep Ramistrasse towards a square named Pfauen. She spent a couple of hours in the art gallery there, situated practically opposite a theatre playing Shakespeare. She was particularly interested in the special exhibition of pencil drawings by Picasso, as well as sculptures by Auguste Rodin and captivating alpine scenes by both Swiss and German artists.

Leaving the gallery, she retraced her steps along Ramistrasse, as the city trams sped past on the long downhill run to Belle Vue.

Part-way down, she turned right into Niederdorf, a narrow street leading to the main entrance of the twin-spired Romanesque cathedral. She stepped inside the almost deserted interior for a while and occupied a front pew listening to the organist playing a Bach toccata and admiring the stunning stained-glass windows. Twenty minutes later, her feet well-rested, she continued past the cathedral and browsed through the second-hand bookstores, mainly as a way of avoiding the cold. Hoping to find something to read on the train, she eventually lit upon a copy of Heinrich Boll's *Group Portrait with Lady*, a novel about ordinary civilian life during World War 11.

She immediately bought it, knowing Boll as one of the most prominent modern German authors. She had long been curious about life in the war years, the privations of ordinary citizens, including shortage of rations, restrictions on travel, the secret police and the ban on listening to radio broadcasts in case people picked up the BBC. But there had been nobody to explain things to her. Her parents had both perished during an Allied air-raid, and at the orphanage where she was raised the people in charge wanted to forget the war years and the train of suffering they caused, to look forward to recovery and better times ahead. Placing the novel in her carrier-bag, she left the store and continued along Niederdorf until she came across a small art cinema. The French comedy featuring Gerard Depardieu, one of her favorite film actors, would help pass the remainder of the afternoon in a warm environment.

On eventually leaving the cinema, she walked back down to the embankment and crossed the river by the Water Bridge, reaching Munsterhof, an elegant square bordered by the Liebfrauenkirche on one side and a medieval guildhall on the other. She took time to admire the distinguished architecture, before seeking out a suitable eatery. Zeughaus Keller, a restaurant occupying the former site of the city arsenal, seemed to fit the bill. It specialized in typical Zurich dishes. Having skipped lunch, she was ready for a good meal, opting for bratwurst with roesti and a stein of Hurlimann's, a local brew. Outside the tourist season, the place was barely half-full with what she took to be local people, so service was quick. Lingering over her appetizing meal, she ordered another beer and occupied herself for an hour afterwards reading the evening newspaper, *Zuri Leu*. It was then time for her to retrace her steps along Bahnhofstrasse to the railway station.

Once there, she retrieved her luggage from the locker and went to the booking office to buy a ticket to Hamburg in a first-class sleeping car. On arrival in that northern port early the following morning, she would take the ferry to Ruegen, arriving at Binz on Christmas Eve. She would book into a seafront hotel, she decided, and quietly enjoy the seasonal festivities, the food, the musical evenings and other amenities, while keeping herself mainly to herself. Before boarding the train, now waiting at Platform 9, she bought a copy of the London *Times* and quickly scanned the police report, in case there were any developments in the Maxine Walford case. The newspaper, however, contained nothing more than typical traffic violations and a mugging near Piccadilly Circus. She gave a sigh of relief. So far, so good.

*

George Mason grew concerned by mid-January that he had not heard back from Otto Weiss regarding the anticipated arrest of Roslinda Kramer. On arrival at Scotland Yard at the start of a new week, his first priority was to ring the German officer.

"*Guten Tag, Inspektor,*" the German officer said. "Good to hear from you again."

"*Guten Morgen, Oberkommissar,*" Mason rejoined. "I trust you are keeping well?"

"Never better," came the upbeat reply, "especially after a weekend's skiing in the Harz Mountains."

"Lucky you, Herr Weiss," the detective

said, with a touch of envy. "I am calling about the Kramer case. I have been expecting to hear from you any day in the matter."

"You assured me, Inspector Mason," the other remarked, "that Roslinda Kramer was on her way to Wetzlar. Sorry to inform you that our enquiries here have drawn a blank."

George Mason gasped.

"You have checked Die Blaue Kugel?' he asked, much surprised.

"No trace of her there," Weiss replied, "unless she is hiding behind the wainscoting, like Catholic priests did in the reign of Elizabeth the First."

"You are referring to so-called priest-holes, Oberkommissar," his caller said, "in country houses owned by recusants."

"Recusants, Inspector?" a puzzled Otto Weiss enquired.

"Catholics who refused to attend Church of England services," the detective explained. "They had the Catholic mass said in secret in their own homes, risking fines or arrest if priests were discovered there."

"English history is a fascinating subject," the other said. "Especially the Tudor period. Henry the Eighth, for example."

"You bet, Oberkommissar. More to the point, where actually is Kramer, if not at the night club? I felt reasonably sure she would return there, to tap into a ready source of income."

"It would seem like she has given you the slip again, Herr Mason," Otto Weiss replied, with heavy irony. "I warned you that she is a very resourceful woman."

"And you were backing her, I imagine, in any game of wits with Scotland Yard," Mason pointedly remarked.

"Only because I am more familiar with the Stasi, their training and their methods than you are, Inspector Mason. The question now is how to proceed, if we are back to square one."

Mason thought about that for a few moments.

"I shall send you a copy of our Wanted poster," he said. "It has been modified following information received from a man who had a brief liaison with her at Dartmouth. You could circulate it to police stations throughout Germany."

"I can certainly do that for you," the German officer agreed. "Let us hope it produces useful leads."

"I shall attend to it straight away," the detective promised, ringing off.

He now had to convey the downbeat news to Bill Harrington. He fixed himself a strong coffee before the chief inspector arrived and caught up with the paperwork on his desk, musing all the while on possible scenarios for the ex-Stasi agent. He was loath to admit defeat, yet his only lead on her was Wetzlar, and that seemed to have drawn a blank.

"It is up to the German authorities now," Harrington said, when Mason approached him a short while later. "The ball is in their court."

"I am afraid so, Chief Inspector," Mason conceded.

"Don't be too downcast, Inspector," the senior man added. "You have given it your best shot. The superintendent does not want you to devote any more resources to it, for the time being at least. A new case came in late last week. A series of robberies at antique stores in Belgravia, which we believe are connected. He wants you to assist Owen Clifford in the investigation."

George Mason was pleased in a way to be working on home ground; it allowed him more time for home life. Towards the end of the month, Ralph Markland's trial took place at Westminster Crown Court. Mason did not personally attend the proceedings, owing to other commitments. He read a report of it in the newspaper. The jury found him guilty on all counts. The judge, Chief Justice Aidan McCullough, sentenced him to eight years in prison, while directing that his assets be seized so that financial restitution could be made to Constance Fleet and to the Aurelian Brothers. Markland was contrite, expressing his remorse to Fleet, who attended the trial. His career as a conman was effectively over. On laying his newspaper aside and finishing his breakfast, he placed a call to St. Dunstan's School. The principal answered the phone.

"Did you read the outcome of the trial, Brother Austin?" his caller asked.

"I have not yet had the opportunity to read *The Yorkshire Post*, our daily newspaper," Austin replied, "but Brother Aelred advised me that Ralph Markland was due in court yesterday."

"Good news, Brother Austin," Mason said. "Markland was found guilty – a cut-and-dried case, really – so the stolen monies will soon be restored to your building fund."

"I am very gratified to hear that, Inspector Mason," the cleric said. "And we Brothers are very grateful for the role you have played in achieving this successful outcome."

"Only a partial success, I am afraid," the detective said. "The main culprit, Roslinda Kramer, remains very much at large. The trail has gone cold."

"I am truly sorry to hear that, Inspector," came the reply, "especially for Faye Walford's sake."

"I have yet to break the news to her," the detective said. "We firmly believe Kramer went back to Germany. The authorities there are looking into it."

"Let us hope they achieve results, Inspector," the principal remarked. "On a different tack, Brother Clement and I would like to show our appreciation of your sterling work by inviting you and your wife to a performance of our school play next month."

"Indeed?" George Mason said, a little taken aback by the unexpected offer.

"The senior boys are staging Shakespeare's *Richard 111.*"

"About the king whose remains were recently found under a parking lot near the city of Leicester?"

"The very same," came the reply. "Richard was killed at the Battle of Bosworth Field in 1485 A.D. and buried nearby in the grounds of what was then probably a nunnery."

"The victor, Henry Tudor, became Henry the Seventh?"

"Quite so, Inspector. You know your English history well."

"Just a passing acquaintance, Reverend Brother," his caller diffidently replied.

"Then how about the play?" Austin then said. "It will, of course, be preceded by dinner in our guest room."

An image of thin soup and boiled cabbage, typical boarding school fare, passed through the detective's mind. But that would be in the refectory, he mused. The guest room sounded much more promising.

"Adele and I would be delighted to accept your kind invitation," he said.

"Then please enter June 25 in your diary.

We shall expect you both here around six o'clock."

Replacing the receiver, Mason went to tell Adele, who was rather late rising.

"That is one of Shakespeare's greatest plays," she said. "His first big hit, in fact, at the Globe Theatre. And we can combine the event with a visit to your mother at Skipton."

*

On arrival at Binz on Christmas Eve, Roslinda Kramer booked into Strand Hotel for a few days, under the name Gertrude Winter, using one of the fake passports the Stasi had issued to her. It gave her time to find her own place, while enjoying the seasonal dishes and the evening chamber concerts given by local musicians. It being low season, she did not take long to find a small apartment in a leafy street running parallel to the promenade. By the middle of January, she had obtained a job as a bar tender through an employment agency specializing in hospitality services. The compensation was modest, but she counted on supplementing it with generous tips, once the tourist season got back into full swing. Colleagues at Kurhaus Hotel, an imposing Victorian edifice looking out to sea, promised that trade would begin to pick up late-March, when retirees would arrive ahead of family groups in the summer.

The storied resort suited her well. As the weather improved over the course of a rather mild winter, she took long walks across the beach and along the pier, feeding the circling gulls with table scraps. As Easter approached, she visited nearby Jasmund National Park, the smallest such amenity in Germany, noted for its steep chalk cliffs, sea eagles and extensive woodland, part of the vast ancient beech forests stretching to the Carpathian Mountains in Romania, over one thousand miles to the east. She tended to keep to herself, declining invitations from fellow-workers, as from persistent and elderly lone males frequenting the Kurhaus. Her recent experiences with Markland and Mason had cured her for the time being of romantic-cum-financial liaisons.

On Easter Day, which fell mid-April, Margit Breuer paid her a visit, inviting her to dinner at La Pergola, a well-regarded Italian restaurant specializing in dishes from Sicily. Her guest arranged for a colleague to cover her bar shift, leaving her free in the evening. The two friends walked in fine weather from Kramer's apartment to the far end of the strand, occupying a table in a window alcove, giving a good view across the bay.

"So far, so good, Ros," Margit Breuer said, as they scanned the menu.

"Binz suits me fine," her friend remarked.

"I have a nice apartment and secure employment. I am also living under an assumed name. As far as people here are concerned, I am Gertrude Winter."

"With a fake Stasi passport?" Margit ironically enquired.

Kramer nodded.

"The old firm is proving useful," she said, "in ways I would never have anticipated."

"The main thing is that you are now safe, Ros," her host said. "I suspect that the Kripo have lost interest in you. Oberkommissar Weiss with two junior officers called at Die Blaue Kugel. They asked if I had news of you, which I of course denied. They then did a search of the place with a fine toothcomb. It took them quite a while, too, in view of all the nooks and crannies in the century-old building."

"Did they seem satisfied with the result of their search?" Kramer cautiously enquired.

"They have not been back since January," Margit said. "I would say that you are in the clear."

"That is good to know and very reassuring, my dear friend."

As the waiter approached, they ordered St. Joseph's Day pasta, a traditional Sicilian dish featured as an Easter special. To help it down, they ordered a bottle of Barolo.

"You look good, Ros," Margit commented. "Your hair is thick and beautiful as ever."

"It must be all the sea air," Roslinda said. "I have grown my hair longer over the past few months. I had it bobbed and dyed in England, to fool the police."

"I wish I could have seen you then!" her friend said, with an amused smile.

"I doubt you would have recognized me, Margit. It was a disguise I adopted after seeing a Wanted poster of myself in a police station window! Can you believe that? I cannot imagine for the life of me how they got hold of my likeness. I have often racked my brain over it."

"But you are as smart and resourceful as ever, I am pleased to note," Margit said, filling their glasses with the Italian red. "You will pull through, Ros. Tell me, is there anything I can do for you, holed up as you are in this relative backwater?"

Her guest sipped the wine pensively, with a wry smile at the last remark. After a pause, she said:

"We are a bit off the beaten track here, I must admit. Which is probably a good thing. What you could do for me is send a bunch of white peonies to my mother at Valley Care Home, Llandudno. If I send them from here, there is always the chance, slim though it may be, that they could be traced back to me."

"Good thinking, Ros," came the reply. "I can certainly do that much for you. Is your mother keeping well?"

"Declining fast, I am afraid," her guest said, with a heavy sigh. "I had the opportunity to visit the care home last year, just before moving to Portsmouth. She did not recognize me. I expected that, but at least I had the assurance that she is being well looked-after."

"The Brits are good at that sort of thing," Margit opined. "It's the welfare state, well-funded by the taxpayer."

"Absolutely, Margit," her friend agreed. "I suggest you send the flowers anonymously via Inter-flora, from Hartmann's store at Wetzlar. Pay in cash. That will give my mother a big lift."

"Very thoughtful of you, my dear Ros. You have been a wonderful daughter to her. And don't forget. If you ever suspect the authorities may be on to you, there are safe houses set up by former Stasi operatives for the benefit of any former agents in difficulty."

"I shall remember that," the other said. "By the way, this pasta tastes wonderful."

"It is the freshly-caught sardines that really make it," her friend said.

"With just a hint of saffron?"

After the appetizing meal, rounded off with apple strudel and coffee, they strolled along the beach in gustier weather, as the wind had picked up meanwhile. They stood for a while watching the breakers crash against the pier and the gulls circling overhead, before it was time to head back to the ferry terminal so that Margit Breuer could catch the last boat back to Hamburg.

"Do you intend to take up yachting again, Ros?" her friend asked, before boarding.

"I expect so," came the reply. "I can rent a boat from Binz Marina, to use on Thursdays, weather permitting. That is my day off."

"You could always visit Sylt," Margit said. "I know you loved it there in the early days."

"I expect I shall, fairly often," came the reply.

CHAPTER 16

By the end of May, George Mason had completed his joint investigation with Owen Clifford into the series of daylight robberies at Belgravia. Most of the stolen items were recovered. Faye Walford had contacted him several times over the past few months about progress regarding Roslinda Kramer. Bill Harrington reluctantly now allowed him to devote a bit more time to the case, pending another high profile case coming up in London. Without a very clear idea of how to proceed, having heard nothing from Oberkommissar Weiss in several weeks, he placed a call to Green Fingers at Chester, to enquire if further orders for white peonies had been made. Drawing a blank there, he telephoned Valley Care Home, Llandudno, the only connection he had to Kramer apart from the night club at Wetzlar. The matron promptly answered.

"George Mason of the Metropolitan Police here," he began. "Can you tell me, Matron, if Gertrude Kramer received any visitors in recent weeks?"

It seemed a long shot, but he reasoned that, if the former Stasi agent had not been located in the Sauerland, she may somehow have doubled back to England. His luck was in!

"Nobody has visited Gertrude so far this year," the matron informed him. "But she did receive a bunch of white peonies during Easter Week."

"*Eureka!*" the detective exclaimed half-aloud. "Do you happen to know the origin of the gift and the name of the sender?"

"I noted the name at the time," the matron replied, "because it was so out-of-the-ordinary. The peonies were sent through Inter-flora by Hartmann's florists, Wetzlar, wherever that is."

"It is a town in north-east Germany," the elated detective explained. "That is very helpful information, Matron. Many thanks."

"Only too pleased to be of help, Inspector," the woman replied. "Best of luck with your enquiries."

On replacing the receiver, Mason crossed to the general office and fixed himself fresh coffee. A breakthrough, at last! Had the Kripo at Wetzlar fallen down on the job, if the suspect was right there under their noses, shipping flowers to Wales? He placed a quick call to Germany.

"*Guten Tag, Inspektor,*" came the upbeat voice of the oberkommissar. "What can I do for you today?"

"I have some interesting information, Herr Weiss," Mason confidently announced. "A bunch of white peonies was recently sent from a firm called Hartmann's in your home town to Roslinda Kramer's mother living in a care home at Llandudno."

"Llandudno, Inspector?" came the puzzled query.

"A resort town on the Welsh coast," his caller explained.

"The significance of this?" the German officer enquired.

"It must mean that Kramer is active in your area," Mason said, wondering if Otto Weiss wasn't being deliberately obtuse. "She has occasionally sent flowers to her mother. I discovered that much last year from a florist at Chester."

There was a pause at the end of the line, as the import of the Scotland Yard agent's remarks sank in.

"What you say is most interesting, Inspector," Weiss eventually said. "But I cannot believe that our suspect has been living here in Wetzlar all this while. We have your Wanted poster on display in this and neighboring towns. Someone would surely have recognized her by now and contacted the authorities."

"One would certainly have thought so," Mason agreed. "What do you propose to do now, Oberkommissar, since the ball is back in your court?"

"I shall pay a call to Hartmann's this very day," Weiss assured him, "to substantiate your claim and follow up with further enquiries. I shall also authorize another search of Die Blaue Kugel."

"I look forward to hearing from you about the result," his caller said, ringing off and crossing to the chief inspector's office to inform him of this new development.

Oberkommissar Weiss, for his part, promptly left his office and drove across the River Lahn to the southern fringes of the town. He parked outside Hartmann's and entered the premises, pausing momentarily to admire the spring blooms on display outside. The proprietor, Kurt Hartmann, greeted him in some surprise, accustomed to seeing the officer at his store only about twice a year, at Christmastide and on the occasion of his wedding anniversary, which occurred in July.

"*Guten Morgen, Oberkommissar,*" he cordially greeted.

"*Guten Tag, Herr Hartmann,*" the officer replied.

"We have some lovely new hybrids in store," the florist said, hoping to make a good sale.

"I am here about a rather different matter,

today," his visitor said. "I need to trace a consignment of white peonies sent from this store during Easter Week."

Hartmann, surprised at the unusual request, carefully consulted his sales records.

"It was made on April 18, Oberkommissar," he informed him.

"Do you have the name of the customer, Herr Hartmann?"

"It is recorded as a cash sale and an anonymous gift," the other replied.

Otto Weiss scowled.

"Could you at least give me a description of the purchaser?" he asked.

"Afraid not," the florist said. "I was over in Holland during Easter Week, touring the tulip fields. My young assistant, Fraulein Hummel, would have dealt with that."

He called to the girl, who was trimming daffodil stems in a back room. She stepped briskly into the store front.

"Oberkommissar Weiss needs a description of the person who ordered white peonies on April 18," he said.

The assistant thought for a few moments, trying to recall a sale she had made about two weeks ago. Eventually, she said:

"I do vaguely remember the client. It was a woman of medium height, with shoulder-length brown hair tinged with gray."

"Approximate age?" the visitor prompted.

"Mid-to-late fifties, I should estimate," the

girl replied. "And she wore a pale-beige three-quarter-length coat."

That description could fit any number of women in Wetzlar, Otto Weiss reflected. It could also fit Margit Breuer, but certainly not Roslinda Kramer, who had chin-length blond hair and heavy eye shadow, according to the Wanted poster George Mason had forwarded.

"You did not recognize the woman?" the officer asked.

Fraulein Hummel shook her head.

"I moved here from Giessen just a few weeks ago," she said. "I do not know very many people here yet."

"Ilsa recently graduated in horticulture from Giessen Polytechnic," the proprietor proudly added.

"My sincere congratulations, Ilsa," the police officer said. "And the best of luck in your rewarding new career."

"Thank you very much, Oberkommissar," the girl said, with a broad smile, before retreating to the back room to resume her task.

"And how is Gudrun keeping?" Kurt Hartmann enquired.

"My dear wife is recovering from a bout of flu," Weiss replied, with a sigh. "She should be back at the high school in a couple of days."

"Give her my best wishes for a speedy recovery," the florist said, as the officer turned to leave.

Back at his desk, Otto Weiss figured that George Mason could be on the right track. It seemed likely that Kramer had got somebody to send the flowers on her behalf. Did that mean the suspect was in hiding right here in Wetzlar, under his very nose? Not necessarily, he concluded: she could be anywhere in Sauerland, or in any other part of Germany. She could even be abroad, perhaps in Austria or Switzerland. She was as crafty and resourceful as ever, he had no doubt, and would carefully cover her tracks. He would await the result of his underlings' renewed search of Die Blaue Kugel before ringing London. He spent the rest of the morning catching up on paperwork, before leaving for lunch at Hoeffler's, a local Weinstube specializing in various types of schnitzel.

*

Roslinda Kramer, alias Gertrude Winter, had taken advantage of the fine spring weather to go sailing on her days off. Renting a yacht called *Der Schwann* from the local marina, she made some day-trips to Sylt, of which she had fond memories from her years with the East German secret police. Having noted in the press the date of the annual regatta, she headed out towards the island again during the first week in

June. A few years ago, she had performed commendably in competitions along the north coast, without winning a major prize, and had even been considered for her country's Olympic sailing squad. Feeling fit and relaxed, she was of a mind to try her luck again, figuring that nobody on Sylt would recognize her now, after a long interval. Tacking past the nudist beach, while also noting the windsurfers the island was famous for, she made for Westerland, one of the main communities. Mooring her yacht, she left the harbor and proceeded along the promenade to register at the address of the organizing committee she had obtained from *Binzer Abendblatt,* her local evening newspaper. She would use the vacation time she had earned over the past few months to compete in the two-day event.

Feeling well-pleased with herself, she had a salad lunch at an ocean-front cafe, noting that the resort was already quite full of visitors this early in the season. From table conversations around her, she identified some of them as Danish, recalling that the Frisian Islands, of which Sylt was part, had in earlier times belonged to the province of Jutland. Other nationals she noted, among a predominance of German retirees, were Dutch and Belgian, speaking Flemish or French. On continuing an hour later along the promenade to reach the main shopping center, she kept half an eye open for any stray Englishmen, diverting herself with the thought that George Mason must be kicking himself for the way she had eluded him. At the same time, he seemed uncannily aware of her movements and she was not able fully to discount the possibility of him turning up even here, or at Binz. At a sports outfitters on Lindenstrasse, she chose a stylish new outfit for the regatta, visited the bookshops and returned late-afternoon to her yacht for the long sail home.

On arrival late-evening, she found a letter from Margit Breuer waiting for her. Fixing herself a mug of cocoa, she opened it expecting to find nothing more than the usual pleasantries and accounts of her friend's doings since she saw her at Eastertide. What she read caused her to rise from her armchair and pace the room in agitation. After a while, she calmed down, poured herself a stiff brandy and read the letter again. Her friend had written that the Kripo had visited Die Blaue Kugel yet again, going through the labyrinthine old warren of a building very thoroughly! They obviously expected to find, if not herself in person, at least traces of a recent visit. They had also asked Margit if she had shipped flowers to her mother. Margit had denied all recent knowledge of her, of flowers or of any residents at a certain care home at Llandudno.

Roslinda Kramer bit her lip in puzzlement. How could the police possibly have known about the peonies? George Mason must have been behind it, she decided. Had he somehow got wind of Valley Care Home and the fact that she sent flowers there at fairly regular intervals? She did not see how that was possible, yet what other explanation could there be? And what else did the Scotland Yard agent know about her, that he had also passed on to the German authorities? It was a disturbing scenario, but at least she should be safe enough here at Binz for the time being. Margit would never betray her and the Wanted poster displayed at the local Polizei Dienst was not a good likeness. It showed her with short blond hair and eye shadow, a description that could only have been provided by Ralph Markland from their time at Dartmouth. The British police must have caught up with him, she mused with an ironic smile, and interrogated him about monies withdrawn from Wessex Bank. He was most likely now in jail, where he most certainly belonged.

Margit was recommending that she enter a safe house, an idea she had first brought up over dinner on Easter Day. She would need to give it serious thought, realizing that the agreeable life she had made for herself at this storied resort must come to an end, if the police were still actively pursuing her.

George Mason evidently had more acumen than she had credited him with; it could not be ruled out that her presence at Binz would not somehow be discovered. She could not telephone Margit, since calls could be traced. Neither could she e-mail her, because she could not afford a computer and it would be risky to use the facilities at Kurhaus Hotel, where she worked. She would need to await her friend's next letter, which would be sent after Margit had made contact with the safe house, wherever that was. Meanwhile, she would continue training for the regatta she had set her heart on entering. Finishing her drinks and suffering from physical and nervous exhaustion, she fell fast asleep in the armchair.

Two days later, a second letter from Margit arrived, announcing that she had contacted a commune near Dresden, in the state of Saxony. It was self-supporting, her friend wrote, with a large farm, dairy, bakery, brewery and workshops for carpentry and general maintenance work. It also had cultural amenities, including a well-stocked library, art-rooms and a small chamber orchestra. There were also sports and keep-fit facilities. Margit assured Roslinda that she would be perfectly safe there, long-term. She would be among friends and fellow-sympathizers, including former Stasi colleagues. There was a degree of nostalgia in the former East Germany for the way of life under the previous regime. The local Kripo, even if they suspected the commune's true purpose, would stay clear, since many of its officers were former Stasi agents themselves.

Roslinda Kramer smiled to herself on reading all that. The commune had evidently been well-thought-out, to provide a fulfilling life to its members. In some ways, she mused, it resembled a kibbutz. Margit had gone out on a limb to help her and she felt very grateful to her. Immediately after the regatta, she would take the ferry from Westerland to Hamburg and catch an express train to Dresden. From there, she would hire a taxi to the address given in the letter and start her life over again. It would almost be like being back in the old firm, with remnants of the Stasi, especially those who had reason to avoid the law. Although most of the former secret police had been successfully absorbed into normal civilian life, there would be some who, like herself, were still actively pursued by the police.

*

Some days before the annual regatta was due to take place, Otto Weiss received an unexpected telephone call from Sylt.

"*Guten Morgen, Oberkommissar,*" his caller began. "Kommissar Jurgen Brandt here, of the Sylt Kripo."

"Guten Tag, Kommissar," the Wetzlar officer returned. "To what do I owe the pleasure of your call?"

"The harbor master at Westerland has come forward with some information that I think will interest you," the local officer explained. "He is here in my office just now. I shall pass you over to him directly."

"Danke, Kommissar," Weiss said, wondering what was afoot.

"Let me introduce myself, Oberkommissar," the second caller said. "My name is Wolfgang Schmidt. I am harbor master at Westerland. The reason for my call is that I have been observing over the past few weeks a certain yachtswoman hereabouts, with the growing feeling that I had seen her before, some years back."

"What makes you think that, Herr Schmidt?" an immediately alert Otto Weiss asked.

"Each sailor has a certain style," the other replied. "It may be the order in which they do things, such as lowering the mainsail first, or the jib. How they dress the rigging. How they handle the boat at sea. Their favorite berth. Simple things like that give each one a distinctive profile over a period of time."

"Very observant of you, harbor master," the impressed oberkommissar remarked. "Why are you telling me this?"

"Because I have seen the Wanted poster

featuring Roslinda Kramer on display outside the local police station. After a while, the penny dropped. The yachtswoman I have been observing with much interest recently is, I feel almost certain, the same person as the fugitive you are seeking."

"You knew Roslinda Kramer in former times," Weiss asked, in some surprise, "before she was presumed drowned in a boating accident?"

"I did not know her personally, Oberkommissar, but I knew of her," came the reply. "She used to be a regular visitor to Westerland and was often spoken of in yachting circles during the Communist regime. Aware of her keen interest in sailing, I went the other day to the headquarters of the organizing committee, to see if she had registered for the regatta. My hunch was correct. Her yacht, *Der Schwann,* is entered in the main event, under the name Gertrude Winter!"

"This is most interesting, Herr Schmidt," the oberkommissar said, anticipating a breakthrough in the long-drawn-out case. "But how did you conclude that Gertrude Winter and Roslinda Kramer are one and the same person?"

"Based on the growing feeling that I had seen the woman before, I paid close attention when she sailed into Westerland, usually on a Thursday. I trained my telescope on her to get a clearer view.

Although her likeness on the police poster is somewhat different - mainly the hair-style, in fact - certain features are unmistakable."

"Can you enlarge on that, harbor master?"

"The rather prominent forehead and the square line of the jaw convinced me it is the same person. Her hair now looks as it did back in the old days – thick, with good color, no trace of gray."

"The regatta takes place…?"

"This weekend, Oberkommissar."

"Many thanks, Herr Schmidt. I commend you for your public-spiritedness."

"My pleasure," the other replied, ringing off.

Otto Weiss sat back in his swivel-chair to weigh the implications of this stunning and unforeseen development. Minutes later, he rose from his desk and crossed to the dispenser on the far wall, to pour himself a glass of water drawn from mineral springs at Baden Baden, the noted Black Forest spa. On regaining his seat, he placed a call to London, hoping to catch George Mason at his office. He was in luck.

"Good to hear from you again, Herr Weiss," the detective said, in some surprise at not having heard from that quarter days ago.

"I have some interesting news for you, Inspector," the German officer said.

"Relating to the Walford case?" Mason optimistically enquired.

"Get a handle on this, Inspector," Weiss continued, using idiomatic English he had acquired from conversations with the American military. "If my sources are correct – and I have no good reason to doubt them – Roslinda Kramer is now well, active and residing at Binz."

"Binz?" asked the puzzled detective.

"It is a resort on Ruegen," his caller explained, "an island in the Baltic Sea. She is going by the name Gertrude Winter."

"You don't say so!" Mason exclaimed. "That sounds like her, all right. The suspect used that name when I met her for dinner at The Windlass Hotel."

"Probably one of several false identities provided by the Stasi," Otto Weiss observed, "backed up, most likely, by a fake passport."

"How did you catch up with her?" the intrigued detective then asked.

"She has always been a keen yachtswoman," his caller said. "You may remember that she was at one time presumed drowned in a yachting incident."

"I do recall you telling me something along those lines," Mason remarked.

"Kramer has apparently taken up yachting again, Inspector. Wolfgang Schmidt, the harbor master at Westerland, slowly began to recognize her as a result of weekly visits she has made there since Easter. He at first thought he was mistaken, since he was fully aware of the publicity surrounding her supposed death, but closer observation over a period of time convinced him that Gertrude Winter was in fact none other than Roslinda Kramer."

"How reliable is this informant?" the detective wanted to know.

"Wolfgang Schmidt has a long and distinguished record of service at Westerland. He claims that each sailor has an unmistakable style. He figured that a keen sportswoman like Kramer would be drawn to the annual regatta at Sylt, so he checked with the organizers. He discovered that she has, in fact, registered for the main event, giving an address and telephone number at Binz, for contact purposes."

"What prompted him to notify the police?" George Mason asked.

"He noticed your Wanted poster, Inspector," Weiss explained, "which was displayed outside Westerland Polizei Dienst. The suspect has since reverted to her original hairstyle and does not use eye shadow, but Schmidt was still able to make out characteristic facial features."

"That is one observant guy!" his impressed hearer remarked.

"Isn't he so?" Otto Weiss replied.

"Your next move, Oberkommissar?" George Mason enquired.

"The regatta will take place this weekend, Inspector. You have time to get over here, to take part in the formal arrest, if you so wish."

"*If* I so wish, Herr Weiss?" came the upbeat reply. "Would I pass up an opportunity like this?"

"I did not imagine you would, Inspector Mason," came the jocular reply. "Make your way to Sauerland, an area you are already familiar with, the best way you can. I shall meet up with you at Wetzlar. We could then drive up to Hamburg together and catch the ferry to Ruegen."

"Sounds good," Mason said, thinking he would need to leave London the very next day to make it in time.

*

Roslinda Kramer, alias Gertrude Winter, drew her small savings out of her bank account and took a cab to Binz Marina, placing her two suitcases below deck before hoisting sail and heading off towards Westerland. She arrived there late Thursday afternoon, two days before the regatta was scheduled to take place. She had taken the small amount of vacation time due to her, intending to make good use of it. Her colleagues at Kurhaus Hotel wished her the best of luck on Sylt, without suspecting in the least that they would not see her again. The harbor master, Wolfgang Schmidt, who had been keeping a weather eye open following his conversation with

Oberkommissar Weiss, greeted her quite cordially as she stepped ashore and secured her boat.

"Here for the regatta, Fraulein...?" he asked.

"Winter," she replied. "Gertrude Winter."

"Pleased to meet you, Fraulein Winter," he said. "I have, as a matter of fact, noticed you on several occasions over the past few weeks."

"I have visited Sylt fairly often since Easter," she curtly replied. "Yachting is in my blood. And, yes, I shall be taking part in the regatta."

"I wish you the best of luck," the other said. "But I should warn you that the weather forecast is not all that good. You could be in for some very choppy conditions this weekend."

Roslinda Kramer returned an indulgent smile, shrugging off his concern.

"All the more challenging," she jauntily replied. "I shall take things in my stride."

"I have no doubt you shall," the harbor master cryptically replied, following her with his gaze as she left the quay and strolled confidently along the promenade.

As she continued on her way, Roslinda Kramer felt satisfied that the harbor master had not recognized her. Otherwise, he would surely have approached her long before this, on one of her previous visits. She, on the other hand, had recognized him almost at once. He was Wolfgang Schmidt, who had been deputy harbor master under the Communist regime, a person with whom she had never had many dealings. He had aged little, she thought, in the intervening years, succeeding to the top job no doubt on retirement of the previous master, whose name for the moment eluded her. A white-haired older man, she seemed to recall, who had seen service as a submariner in World War 11. He also had a Doberman constantly by his side.

Good luck to Schmidt, she thought, as she booked into a modest family hotel on the sea-front. Leaving her shoulder-bag and a large carrier-bag in her room, she went directly to the bar for a quick snack and a glass of chilled Riesling. Feeling refreshed, she repaired to the hotel lounge to study navigation charts for the main competitive event, the hundred-mile grand circuit off the southern coast of Sweden, calling at Malmo and Visby. Tomorrow morning, she decided, she would do a practice run, avoiding the ports. Returning the charts to her room and unpacking her few belongings, she laid out on the bed an elegant new outfit and stood back to admire it. Well-pleased with herself, she took a long walk along the sea-front to ease the tension that had been building up, partly ahead of the regatta, partly as a result of Margit's letters. She would have a late dinner and afterwards watch television in the residents' lounge, where she might meet other competitors who had registered for the same, or for a different, event. It invariably interested her to swop nautical yarns with fellow-mariners; they could often be quite hair-raising, given how unpredictable the ocean was.

*

George Mason had originally intended to arrive at Westerland late on the day before the regatta. He had driven up with his German colleague early Friday morning, having reached Wetzlar by rail on the Thursday evening. They had reached Hamburg in good time to catch the 6 p.m. ferry to Sylt, but severe weather conditions had caused the service to be cancelled. There was nothing for it but to book hotel accommodation in the old Hansa port.

"Can you imagine a regatta taking place in these conditions, Oberkommissar?" he skeptically asked, as they sat down to dinner in the restaurant of a harbor-front hotel.

"An interesting point, Inspector," Otto Weiss remarked. "I imagine the organizers will do their utmost to stage it. For one thing, the Baltic is more sheltered than the North Sea. And for another, the worst of the storm may well blow out overnight."

"If it heads west, towards the British Isles," his colleague agreed, "that should give the competitors reasonably good conditions."

"This is the remnant of a major tropical storm originating in the Caribbean," the German officer remarked. "It will affect a wide area of northern Europe for most of the weekend, I expect."

"You mean, Oberkommissar," Mason wryly observed, "that we may have more fake drownings?"

Otto Weiss returned a broad smile at that remark.

"I appreciate your point, Inspector," he said. "If Kramer had the merest hint that we two would be arriving at Westerland tomorrow – weather permitting – she might well be inclined to pull another stunt like that."

"Abandon her yacht among the skerries and make good her escape a second, a third, or even a fourth time?"

"You have a fine sense of humor, Herr Mason," the other said. "And you take things as they come. An excellent temperament for a police officer."

"*Danke, Herr Weiss,*" the visitor said, thinking that his opposite number would no longer be expecting Kramer to outwit him. He had at last earned the respect of the Wetzlar Kripo.

"Now what should we have for dinner?" Weiss said, as they scanned the menu.

"I will rely on you for a typically local

dish," his visitor said.

"Then I would suggest the rouladen," came the considered reply. "That would be bacon and onions wrapped in thin slices of beef. *Blumenkohl,* or cauliflower in plain English, with sauteed potatoes, would go well with it."

To help it down, they ordered steins of Czech pilsner and spent a pleasant hour or so swopping details of interesting cases they had helped solve. After the meal, they took a stroll through parkland bordering the Elbe, a river that had featured prominently, Weiss explained, in Hamburg's turbulent history, including a raid of hundreds of Viking ships whose warrior crews had ransacked the city in the seventh century. They then returned to their hotel for a good night's sleep.

The next day, after a light breakfast of yoghurt and muesli, they drove to the ferry terminal. The storm had abated somewhat and the 10.15 a.m. service made steady progress through the moderate swell, to arrive just a few minutes behind schedule at Westerland. Kommissar Jurgen Brandt and the harbor master, Wolfgang Schmidt, were there to greet them. Otto Weiss introduced his British visitor to them; they in turn welcomed him to Sylt.

"Did our friend, Ms. Kramer, alias Gertrude Winter, duly arrive?'" the oberkommissar enquired.

"She checked into a hotel here two days

ago," Kommissar Brandt informed him.

"And she is currently taking part in the main event, the grand circuit off the coast of Sweden," Wolfgang Schmidt explained. "The yachts are just rounding the headland now."

The two visitors peered out to sea.

"The yacht with the red jib is Kramer's," Schmidt pointed out.

It was barely a hundred yards out, Mason noted; its skipper plainly visible on the aft deck, waving towards onlookers on the quay.

"At what hour do you expect them back?" he enquired.

"By 6.00 p.m. at the earliest," the harbor master said, "depending on weather conditions, which are apparently turbulent."

Otto Weiss left his BMW on the quayside parking lot and accompanied his associates to the marina at the far end of the shingle beach. There was a festive atmosphere. Flags representing the various nationalities of the competitors fluttered in the stiff breeze. Stallholders sold everything from souvenirs to grilled bratwurst and chilled drinks. Officials were setting out trophies on a long table. The Mayor of Westerland, in official regalia, stood among a group of civic dignitaries. George Mason was interested to spot the Union Jack on display, indicating the presence of at least one British competitor. Groups of spectators, some with field-glasses, were following some of the minor events taking place in local waters, just off-shore.

"Quite an occasion," George Mason remarked, as the quartet approached the marina.

"The annual regatta is the major sporting and social event on Sylt," Jurgen Brandt explained. "There will be a civic reception for the winners, followed by a dinner-dance for all competitors, local officials and organizers. You will be most welcome to attend, Inspector Mason."

The English visitor exchanged ironic looks with Otto Weiss, before saying:

"Much as I would like to take part in the festivities, Kommissar Brandt, I can hardly look on this as a social occasion."

"Don't be too hasty, Inspector," the oberkommissar mildly chided. "Let us see how things develop later today. I, for one, would be keen to take part in the dinner-dance."

"They put on an excellent spread," Wolfgang Schmidt said, "prepared by a team of top chefs."

The visiting detective did not see how he could object, given the others' enthusiasm. After mingling with the crowd, admiring the trophies and watching off-shore activities, Kommissar Brandt proposed a snack lunch. He led the way to a café just off the beach, where they ordered open sandwiches and soft drinks, to help pass the time agreeably until the main event was concluded. They lingered there until contestants in the grand circuit were finally sighted on the horizon. They then quit the restaurant and headed for the quay, fifteen minutes before the leading competitor neared the dock. It sported the Belgian flag, followed minutes later by a trim vessel flying the Union Jack.

"Looks like our man is the runner-up," Mason said, with satisfaction. "But where is Roslinda Kramer?"

The harbor master trained his telescope on the leading boats, which began to arrive in fairly quick succession. None of them, however, sported a red jib. George Mason and Otto Weiss exchanged ominous glances and stood for a while gazing out to sea. Wolfgang Schmidt, noting their concern, said:

"There is time yet, gentlemen. There are always a few stragglers in the main event. I suggest we go along to the presentations and afterwards attend the dinner-dance. Your countryman, Inspector Mason, is up for a prize, I believe. You may wish to introduce yourself."

"I will certainly congratulate a fellow-Briton," the visitor said. "I may even buy him a drink."

Just over an hour later, in the interval between the award ceremonies and the evening festivities, the quartet retraced their steps to the quay, where a regatta official was posted to record arrivals.

"Are all the boats back in now?" Otto Weiss asked him.

"All except *Der Schwann*," the man replied. "I have been keeping a look-out for it."

"Have any of the skippers reported seeing a vessel in distress?" Kommissar Brandt asked.

"No, sir," came the assured reply.

"An interesting situation, Inspector Mason," Oberkommissar Weiss remarked, turning to his visitor. "Another drowning do you think?"

"Fake or real?" Mason grimly responded, aware that his German counterpart would be thinking his quarry may have outwitted them yet again.

"Contact the coastguard, Herr Schmidt," Jurgen Brandt then said, "and ask them to send a search boat out. Have them also alert their colleagues at Malmo and Visby."

"They had some rough weather out on the Baltic late this afternoon," the recording official said. "A fresh squall came in from the north. That may account for the delay. We can do little now but await the coastguards' findings."

George Mason and Otto Weiss reluctantly left the quay and made their way to the dinner-dance, after booking overnight accommodation. After the four-course meal, an orchestra played for ballroom dancing. Mason's reluctance to shake a leg was soon overcome by a young member of the organizing committee, who took him in hand for the greater part of an entertaining evening.

At breakfast the following day, Kommissar Brandt called at their hotel with the following news:

"*Der Schwann* was located in the marina at Malmo, gentlemen. There is no sign of its skipper, who apparently did not check in with the regatta officials there."

Otto Weiss, with raised eyebrows, gave George Mason one of his signature ironic looks.

"It would seem that Kramer has stolen a march on us again, Inspector," he said.

"But at least it does not appear to be another staged drowning," Mason replied, unwilling to accept defeat. "That woman has to be somewhere, Oberkommissar. It is our job to find out where."

"Amen to that," the other said. "But I doubt she is still at Malmo."

With that, they thanked the local kommissar for his assistance, finished their meal of ham and poached eggs and drove down to the harbor in good time for the morning ferry to Hamburg. By early evening, they were back in Wetzlar. Otto Weiss cordially invited Mason to spend the next couple of days as his guest, introducing him to his wife, Gudrun, a homely woman who made the visitor most welcome. She prepared a dinner of lamb cutlets with rice and Brussels sprouts, while the oberkommissar invited his guest to share a sauna bath with him. To that end, he went ahead to the bottom of his rambling garden to light the wood stove in the sauna hut. On his return, fifteen minutes later, the two men undressed in a bedroom, slipped towels round their waists and headed down the garden path. It was not George Mason's first experience of the Finnish bath. He had used the public sauna in Helsinki some years ago, while working on the John Ormond case. Major Viljo Forsenius, of the Helsinki Police, had also once invited him to his private sauna at his home in Kotka, on Finland's south coast.

"I see you are not a novice at this, Inspector," Otto Weiss remarked, impressed at how his visitor expertly ladled water onto the top of the stove, causing steam to hiss up to the low ceiling and settle back, tingling, on their shoulders.

CHAPTER 17

Roslinda Kramer, on docking at Malmo, took the next ferry to Hamburg, where she entrained for Berlin. After spending the night in a cheap hotel near the railway station, she took the connection from Berliner Hauptbahnhof to Dresden. Gazing out of the carriage window, as the high-speed train crossed the north German plains, she reflected on events of the previous day. On leaving Westerland quay at the start of the grand circuit, she had noticed while waving to spectators two men dressed in police uniforms, accompanied by two others in civilian dress, one of whom she recognized as the harbor master. They could merely have been spectators, she reasoned. Or they could have been there on routine business, to check that the regatta had got off to a good start. Their presence, however, had nagged at her as she ventured out into the North Sea.

She was fully aware that Wolfgang Schmidt had sometimes trained his telescope on her when she moored her yacht at Westerland. Was that merely voyeurism, she wondered, from her habit of sunbathing topless on the foredeck? Or had he been spying on her? His presence on the quay with two Kripo agents inclined her not to take chances. Could that confounded George Mason have somehow tipped off the police as to her current whereabouts? Was the fourth man on the quay even the detective himself? She could not make out his features clearly at a distance, but he had the same height and build as the person she recalled meeting at The Windlass Hotel, Chichester. Survival became more important than finishing first in the main event. She saw no other option but to abandon her yacht and reach the commune in Saxony Margit Breuer had recommended as soon as possible. It was called Lindenhof, just outside the city of Dresden.

On reaching her destination, she checked the times of local bus services. She then made for the station restaurant, since she had not eaten a square meal since a full breakfast at the Westerland hotel she had stayed at before setting out on the grand circuit. The quick-service counter offered a selection of pasta dishes. She chose spaghetti carbonara with side salad and a bottle of Perrier, which she took to a corner table, selecting a newspaper from the rack on her way. Partway through her satisfying meal, she happened to glance over to the far side of the restaurant, mainly occupied by commuters waiting for suburban trains. She noticed a tall gentleman in a U.S. military uniform staring hard at her. He seemed vaguely familiar. Quickly reverting her gaze to her newspaper, it struck her that she might have met him at Wetzlar, where she had known a number of American servicemen. She soon dismissed the notion, however, as being too improbable after the passage of years.

Glancing up again, after scanning the headlines, she realized that the man was still looking her way. It made her uneasy. She checked her watch. The bus was due to leave in five minutes' time. Nudging her plate aside, she rose from her table and quit the restaurant, aware that the man had also hurriedly left his place. On quickly boarding the bus, she noticed that he had walked right up to it, but would not be able to see her clearly because of the tinted windows. As the bus pulled slowly away from the station forecourt, it suddenly struck her who the man was. It was Orin Tuttle, an officer at the American base near Wetzlar, whom she had blackmailed years ago!

*

On the morning following his arrival at Wetzlar, George Mason placed a call to Scotland Yard from the Weiss residence, in order to bring Bill Harrington up-to-date on developments in the Walford case. He was aware that his senior would not be too pleased with what he was about to say, but in the circumstances that could not be helped. On getting through, he was pleasantly surprised to find his senior in an upbeat mood.

"What have you been up to, Inspector," Harrington asked, "in the last few days, apart from sunning yourself on the coast?"

"Oberkommissar Weiss and I have been following a strong lead to the island of Sylt," his colleague explained. "We got a tip-off from the local police that Kramer had entered for the annual regatta."

"And, of course, she gave you the slip again," the chief inspector taunted.

"How would you know something like that, Chief Inspector?" a puzzled George Mason enquired.

"Because I received a phone-call late yesterday afternoon from a Major Orin Tuttle, of U.S. Army Logistics. He claimed to have paid you a visit a short time ago regarding a former hostess at Die Blaue Kugel."

"Roslinda Kramer!" Mason exclaimed.

"Get this, Mason," Harrington continued.

"Tuttle claimed to have recognized her in the restaurant at Dresden Hauptbahnhof. He then observed her boarding a bus on the station forecourt."

"The major indicated to me that he would be in that city, visiting a relative of his wife," George Mason said. "This could be the breakthrough we need, after her abandoned yacht was found at Malmo."

"I suggest you get down to Dresden as soon as possible," his senior said, "before she eludes you yet again. This is becoming something of a routine, Inspector, and it does not reflect well on the Metropolitan Police."

There was no mistaking the irritation in the chief inspector's voice, as George Mason replaced the receiver. He went directly to the dining-room, where the oberkommissar and his wife were finishing breakfast, and told them the news.

"We shall drive down there straight away," Otto Weiss said, draining his coffee and rising from table. Leaving the dining-room, he returned minutes later dressed in uniform, kissed Gudrun good-bye and led his visitor outside to his parked BMW.

Hours later, after a drive through some very scenic parts of Germany, much of which was new to the English visitor, they pulled up outside Kripo headquarters in Dresden, a modern building fronting the River Elbe. Oberkommissar Gunther Graf received them in his office.

"You have had a long trip, gentlemen," he said. "I trust it is not a fool's errand."

"We have it on good authority," Otto Weiss explained, "that a former member of the Stasi named Roslinda Kramer, who may be going by the name Gertrude Winter, and who is wanted by the authorities in several countries for a spate of crimes, was sighted yesterday evening boarding a bus outside the Hauptbahnhof."

"Indeed, Oberkommissar Weiss?" the local officer said, carefully weighing that surprising piece of information.

The two visitors hung patiently on his words. Eventually, Oberkommissar Graf, clearing his throat, said:

"The Lindenhof commune, out in the country a short distance from here, is a favored destination of former Stasi agents. We in the police generally leave them to themselves and choose not to interfere."

"To let bygones be bygones?" Otto Weiss pointedly asked.

"Exactly," came the reply, "unless criminality is suspected."

"Inspector Mason and I are here to make an arrest, Herr Graf."

"On what grounds, Oberkommissar?"

"Initially on a charge of blackmail," his Sauerland counterpart explained. "Other charges will follow."

"Quite a Pandora's Box, it would seem,"

Graf replied, rising from his desk. "I shall drive you both out there now. Would you be able to recognize the individual in question?"

"Absolutely," George Mason replied. "I had the dubious honor of taking her to dinner not very long ago."

With that, they left the police station and drove out into countryside bordering the Elbe. Twenty minutes later, they were on the approach road to the commune. Mason noted with interest that it was a large farming complex, with crops growing in the fields, barns and what appeared to be a dairy. Farm animals, including Friesian cattle, sheep and free-range chickens, were in evidence. The driver drew up at the main entrance, parked his Audi and led the way indoors. An affable elderly man with white hair and a trimmed beard, clad in light-green overalls, greeted them in some surprise.

"The purpose of your visit, *meine Herren*?"

"We wish to ascertain if a certain Roslinda Kramer, who may also use the name Gertrude Winter, arrived here yesterday evening," Otto Weiss said.

The man's eyes opened wide in surprise, tinged with alarm.

"She did indeed," he said. "Roslinda, whom I knew quite well in earlier days, arrived yesterday and expressed a wish to join our community. I saw no reason to deny her request. As a gifted and resourceful woman, she will fit in well with both new and former colleagues."

Resourceful is an understatement, Mason thought, but did not say as much. He waited in keen anticipation as the commune head went deeper into the building to locate her. Minutes later, she was standing in front of them.

"You!" she exclaimed, recognizing the English detective.

"It has been a long saga, Fraulein Kramer," Mason said. "But at last we have caught up with you."

"I am arresting you on a charge of blackmail," Oberkommissar Weiss said, "initially in respect of a Major Orin B. Tuttle, of the United States Army."

The suspect's jaw dropped, her face darkened. What a curious twist of fate, she thought as she was led outside to the waiting squad car, that she should run into one of her victims just as she was beginning to feel home and dry. On the drive back to the city, she turned with grim resignation to George Mason and said:

"I am curious to know how you managed to track me, Inspector, just to set my mind at rest on that score at least."

"It would be small comfort to you to learn the full facts," he cagily replied, not wishing to reveal her devotion to her mother as her Achilles heel. "But I can tell you about one significant lead."

"Which was?" she impatiently asked.

"The Wanted poster, Fraulein Kramer. Someone on Sylt recognized you from it."

"I can imagine who that someone might have been," she said, thinking of the harbor master. "But how on earth did you manage to obtain my likeness in the first place? I have been racking my brains over that for a long time."

"By a purely fortuitous circumstance," Mason replied. "As the commercial photographer hired by St. Dunstan's took pictures of the front of the school for publicity purposes, you happened to glance out the window of the ground-floor bursar's office. A good image was captured, which we mocked up into a poster."

The woman looked crestfallen on hearing that and shrank into herself, saying little for the duration of the trip. It was evident to her that she had unwittingly contributed to her own downfall.

"On my return to London," Mason said to Otto Weiss, as they reached police headquarters, "I shall contact Capitaine Jules Lemaitre at Nice and advise him to apply for extradition."

"The blackmail rap, in the circumstances," the oberkommissar said, "will have to remain a secondary charge."

"As will the theft of money from St. Dunstan's," Mason added, "which at least has been recovered."

Gunther Graf formally entered the charge of blackmail in the records and led the suspect to a holding cell, pending further procedures. The two visitors thanked him for his assistance, bade him good-bye and drove swiftly through the night to Sauerland.

*

A few days after his return from Germany, George Mason and Adele, accompanied by Faye Walford, arrived at Dovestones village late Saturday afternoon. The principal, Brother Austin, met them at the railway station and drove them to the school. On arrival, he had the kitchen staff provide a pot of tea in his office, before giving then a brief tour of the site of the new dormitory block, now slowly rising from its foundations.

"We are back on schedule," he announced, "to have all in readiness for the start of the new school year in September."

"I am so pleased, Reverend Sir," George Mason said, "that recent regrettable events have not caused too much delay in the project."

"Thanks to you, Inspector," the cleric remarked, "they did not."

"Your handling of the case was masterful, Inspector," Faye Walford enthused. "I was beginning to have my doubts as the months passed, I must confess, that you would ever catch up with Maxine's killer. But I never really gave up hope."

"It was a difficult case, Faye," the detective said. "Kramer is a very cunning and resourceful woman, well-trained by the Stasi."

"What was the key factor in your success, Inspector?" Brother Austin wanted to know.

His visitor thought about that for a few moments, as their guide led the group through the extensive gardens at the rear, before redirecting their steps towards the main building.

"Kramer's Achilles heel," he said, at length, "was, interestingly enough, her devotion to her mother. "Gertrude Kramer resides at a care home in Llandudno, which I had occasion to visit last year. Her health is failing and her daughter was in the habit of sending her white peonies from time to time. That filial gesture eventually proved to be her undoing."

"How sad is that, in a way!" Faye Walford remarked. "Apparently, Kramer was apprehended after taking part in a regatta off Sylt." The dental hygienist had been brought up-to-date by George Mason on the drive from Knutsford.

"Wherever is that?" a bemused Brother Austin enquired.

"It is an island in the North Sea," Adele Mason enlightened him.

"Quite amazing," Austin said. "Wait until I tell the Visitor, Brother Aelred. He will be bowled over by that news. He did some sailing himself, in his younger days, off the Isle of Wight."

With that, he led the way into the guest room, where the visitors were treated to roast pheasant with baked potatoes and asparagus tips. Two bottles of premier cru Burgundy were fetched from the school cellars to help it down. Brother Clement expertly decanted them before carving the bird.

"The play is scheduled to begin promptly at seven," the assistant principal said, serving generous portions. "Enough time for a relaxed meal and for you, Inspector Mason, to regale us with more details of your successful investigation."

"I can certainly do that, Brother Clement," the detective assured him. "At least about aspects that are not sub judice. You yourself played a significant part in the outcome."

"Indeed, Inspector Mason?" the intrigued cleric replied. "How was that?"

"The commercial photograph you produced very early on in the investigation proved very useful. The Wanted poster we mocked up from it was a key factor in her arrest. The harbor master at Westerland, who had known the suspect as a keen yachtswoman during the Communist regime, recognized her from it and alerted the German authorities. We managed to pick up her trail again at Dresden, after she eluded us at Sylt. Oberkommissar Weiss and I made the arrest at a farming commune in the area."

"We are very glad to have played a small role in your solving of the case," Clement said, with evident satisfaction.

"Amen to that," Brother Austin said.

"My husband told me you are putting on *Richard III* this evening," Adele remarked, suddenly changing the subject. "It seems rather heavy fare for boy actors."

The principal returned an artful smile, while sampling his wine.

"It is a simplified version, Mrs. Mason," he explained, "prepared by our senior English master, Brother Benet, to give them a taste of Shakespeare. The complete play would take far too long for a school performance."

"We concentrate on the princes in the Tower and events leading up to the Battle of Bosworth Field," Clement added.

"Where Richard met his nemesis, I believe," Faye Walford said.

"In the shape of Henry Tudor," the knowledgeable Adele added, "who ascended the throne as Henry the Seventh."

"Who begat Henry the Eighth," her husband added, "and all that that led to."

"The English Reformation, among other

things," Brother Austin wryly remarked.

.

Made in the USA
San Bernardino, CA
26 March 2017